The Unexpected Ally

A Gareth and Gwen Medieval Mystery

THE
UNEXPECTED
ALLY

by

SARAH WOODBURY

The Unexpected Ally
Copyright © 2016 by Sarah Woodbury

This is a work of fiction.

www.sarahwoodbury.com

To Anna
for being there

Cast of Characters

Owain Gwynedd – King of Gwynedd (North Wales)
Cadwaladr – Owain's younger brother, former Lord of Ceredigion
Cadwallon – Owain's older brother (deceased)
Madog—King of Powys
Susanna—Queen of Powys, sister to Owain Gwynedd
Llywelyn—Prince of Powys

Rhun – Prince of Gwynedd (deceased)
Hywel – Prince of Gwynedd (illegitimate)
Cynan – Prince of Gwynedd (illegitimate)
Madoc – Prince of Gwynedd (illegitimate)
Iorwerth – Prince of Gwynedd (legitimate)
Cadifor—Hywel's foster father

Gwen – Gareth's wife, a spy for Hywel
Gareth – Gwen's husband, captain of Hywel's guard
Tangwen – daughter of Gareth and Gwen
Meilyr – Gwen's father
Gwalchmai – Gwen's brother

Evan – Gareth's friend
Gruffydd – Rhun's former captain
Conall — agent of the King of Leinster
Rhys— Abbot of St. Kentigern's Monastery
Lwc – Abbot Rhys's secretary
Anselm – Prior of St. Kentigern's Monastery

1

St. Kentigern's Monastery, St. Asaph

March 1147

Gwen

Abbot Rhys, formerly the prior of St. Kentigern's monastery but recently elected to abbot, was dressed for the weather in heavy robes, cloak, and black boots. Before becoming a monk, Rhys had been a soldier and a spy for King Henry and Empress Maud. He had also been associated with several investigations Gareth and Gwen had been involved in over the years.

When Rhys had greeted them last night, Gwen had noted the way the gray had taken over what a few years before had been predominantly brown hair, and that his beard was almost completely white. His brown eyes were just as thoughtful and kind as ever, however. Rhys had been leaning against the top rail of a paddock, adjacent to one of the monastery barns, but at the sight of Gareth and Gwen coming towards him in the predawn rain, he threw back his hood, and his face lit with genuine affection.

"I'm glad you're here, though I regret the need."

Gareth lifted his (good) shoulder in a half-shrug and pushed back his hood too. "We're staying in your guesthouse. We might as well be of service."

The thin man standing next to Rhys wasn't nearly as welcoming. As Rhys and Gareth gripped forearms, the man tugged on the abbot's sleeve, a motion Rhys ignored at first, but then as the man did it again, he turned to listen. "Abbot Rhys, surely it isn't proper for a woman to be here under these circumstances."

"It's all right." Gwen gestured to the young monk in his early twenties whom Abbot Rhys had sent to collect them. "As Brother Lwc can attest, I was already awake."

When the man made to protest again, Rhys put a hand on his upper arm. "All is well, Anselm. Lady Gwen has my countenance."

Now that Rhys had named the man, Gwen knew who he was: this was Prior Anselm, the man who'd replaced Rhys when he'd been elected abbot. Because Anselm had not risen from his bed last night to greet them when they'd arrived, Rhys now hastily introduced them to each other. Anselm was hardly taller than Gwen herself and had a nose too long for his face.

Gwen tried not to take offense at Anselm's objections. It wasn't as if she hadn't encountered men like him before, and she was here only because Rhys himself had asked for her. At Rhys's calming words, Anselm subsided, though his expression remained skeptical, and he looked at Gwen through narrowed eyes. But since Gwen had earned the right to stand at Gareth's side, she decided she could be charitable. Nobody liked having their strongly held opinions ignored.

"Where's the dead man?" Gareth spoke matter-of-factly.

"Over here. I'm sorry, but this isn't going to be pleasant." Rhys pulled open the gate to the paddock. The ground was mucky under their feet, churned by hooves and made worse by the rain. They'd had fine weather in Shrewsbury a week ago, but they had known that it couldn't last.

A water trough, eight feet long, three feet wide, and two feet deep, big enough to allow several cows to drink at once, was positioned on the western side of the enclosure. Lwc raised his torch, and Gwen put the back of her hand to her mouth at the sight of what the torch illumined: a man lay at the bottom of the trough. He was fully submerged in the water and very dead.

The thick piece of buttered bread Gwen had purloined from the guesthouse kitchen earlier that morning lurched in her stomach. It was only a quarter of an hour ago that she'd been returning to her room when Lwc had halted at the top of the stairs, gawping at the sight of her, and asked her to wake Gareth and come with him. Fortunately, Gwen had dressed completely upon rising, not wanting to disturb the sensibilities of any stray monk who might be wandering the guesthouse at that hour. All the monks should have been asleep in their dormitory, taking advantage of whatever time they had left before they were obligated to rise for Lauds, the monastery's dawn prayers.

At the time, Gwen had recognized Lwc because he had brought the travelers bread and wine the previous night, before showing them to their rooms.

"God be praised that you're already awake." Lwc had halted in front of her. "Abbot Rhys sent me to find you and your husband."

"Someone is dead?"

The young monk's eyes widened. "How did you know?"

Gwen chose not to explain that there seemed to be no end to the variety of ways she and Gareth could be informed of a murder. And yet, every time was exactly the same, which was how she'd known the reason for the summons before Lwc had even opened his mouth. "Is it a monk?"

Lwc had shaken his head. "A stranger."

Gwen had fully expected to be shown a body in yet another new and awkwardly gruesome position—one perhaps she and Gareth hadn't encountered before. In a way, that would have been normal. What was far more surprising was not only how tidy and unfussy the scene appeared—if the man hadn't been underwater, he could have been sleeping—but that Gwen knew him. More than that, she and Gareth had suspected him of murder last summer. As she stared down at Erik, a half-Welsh/half-Danish soldier-spy, who'd mostly recently been spying for Prince Hywel, Gwen had to wonder who could possibly have sneaked up on such a large man and killed him.

Even though Lwc had seen the dead man earlier, before Abbot Rhys had sent him to fetch Gareth and Gwen, he gave a low groan of discomfort and ran a hand through his hair, making it stand on end. The torchlight hardly cut through the murk and the rain, but its light was enough to show that Lwc's face was paler than it had been. Two weeks ago, before Gwen and Gareth had ridden to Shrewsbury and become embroiled in an investigation there, Gwen would have reminded herself that a dead man wasn't a sight to get used to. Now she knew that for her own protection, the more quickly she was able to treat the dead with detachment, the better.

King Owain's company had arrived at the monastery only a few hours before, having suffered through a torrential downpour for the whole journey from Caerhun, where'd they'd spent the previous night. St. Asaph was some fifteen miles as the crow flies short of Denbigh Castle, King Owain's ultimate destination and his stronghold in eastern Gwynedd. It was from there that the king had launched his assault on Mold Castle last winter, and it was from there that he intended to counter the might of Dinas Bran, the seat of King Madog of Powys.

Or rather, that had been the plan until Abbot Rhys had insisted that he had a say in the matter. Not surprisingly, given his former profession as a spy, Rhys had learned of the events surrounding the current hostility between Gwynedd and Powys and felt it was his duty to intervene. He'd asked for both Madog, King of Powys, and Owain, King of Gwynedd, to meet at St. Asaph to discuss their differences before resorting to violence. The two kings were brothers-in-law, after all, and Rhys was concerned about his flock, the people of this region, across whose lands the war would be fought.

When Gareth and Gwen arrived after midnight with King Owain's party, they were wet, cold, and exhausted, but pleased to have a comfortable place to stay after so many days on the road. They had changed into dry clothes before falling asleep on pallets the monks had spread across the floor for them. Thus, when Gwen had gone to wake Gareth at Lwc's request, albeit reluctantly, all he'd had to do was scoop up his sword, boots, and cloak, which had dried before the fire during the night, and leave the room with her.

As he'd entered the corridor in front of her, however, Gwen had noted the pinpoint of blood seeping through his shirt. He'd been stabbed in the left shoulder a week ago in Shrewsbury when he and Gwen had been captured by a band of slavers and held captive in an old mill. The blood was a healthy color, and so far the wound hadn't festered. She was almost daring to hope that it would heal well—if he was able to rest it. To investigate a murder was the last thing he needed right now.

But Abbot Rhys probably didn't know about Gareth's injury—she certainly hadn't told him of it in their brief meeting last night—and Gareth would never do so if someone didn't press him. She also knew that Rhys wouldn't have summoned Gareth if he wasn't truly needed. The sight of Erik dead in the trough verified Rhys's need.

"Suicide, clearly."

Gwen's head came up at Anselm's words, and she quickly rearranged her expression so the surprise—and the completely inappropriate laughter that bubbled up in her throat—didn't show.

"Excuse me?" Gareth said.

Anselm gestured towards Erik's body, his expression a mix of condescension and satisfaction at his own intelligence. "That's the only plausible explanation. Few men could be strong enough to hold down such a large man, and nobody drowns accidently in a trough only three feet deep. He has to have killed himself."

Gwen's eyes went to Abbot Rhys's face before she quickly looked away lest either openly show their disbelief.

Gareth was the first to attempt a counter suggestion. "Perhaps he was simply drunk, fell in the trough, and didn't have the wherewithal to rise."

Anselm canted his head. "I commend you on your charity, Sir Gareth, and thank you for your suggestion. It is always better to think the best of everyone and not jump to the worst conclusion." He bowed grandly in Gareth's direction.

Gwen blinked again, still at a loss for words. She'd already been thinking that Anselm looked a bit like a shrew, and now his supercilious expression was firmly entrenched in her mind, and she feared she would never dislodge it.

Abbot Rhys raised a hand, cutting through the companions' stark incredulity and Anselm's self-satisfaction. "Thank you, Prior Anselm, for your thoughts. If you would do me a personal favor and return to the monastery to see to your brothers,

I would be most grateful." He glanced to the sky for a moment, checking the condition of the light.

In the short time Gareth and Gwen had been talking to Rhys and Anselm, some of the darkness had lifted, though with the heavy cloud cover and rain, it was hard to tell exactly how far off dawn really was. Sometimes when Gwen was up early tending to Tangwen, her daughter, or taking a few moments to herself before the rest of her family woke, she liked to go outside as the sun rose. Even when clouds covered the sky as they did this morning, she would close her eyes and breathe—and it was almost as if she could feel the moment the sun lifted above the horizon.

There wasn't time for that today, even if Gwen could have benefited from the peacefulness of such a moment. The needs of the dead took precedence, as they always did. Or rather—it wasn't the needs of the dead that required seeing to, but those of the people left behind, who might suffer because of what the living had done. The dead suffered no more.

"In particular," Abbot Rhys continued, "I will need you to ease the minds of many of the younger novices, since it will be impossible to keep what has happened here from them. It would also serve me well if you would lead our dawn prayers. I suspect that the loss of this young man will occupy much of my attention this morning."

"As you wish, Father." Anselm might have spoken his conclusions about suicide with assurance, but at least he didn't insist on standing outside in the rain any longer than necessary, and he definitely looked pleased to have been asked to lead the service in the abbot's absence. He canted his head again in what Gwen assumed he meant to be an accommodating manner, turned away without complaint, and started back down the path to the monastery proper.

Then Rhys turned to Lwc. "Perhaps you could arrange for a cart to move this poor soul. We'll need at least two men to lift him." He glanced towards Erik again. "Maybe three."

"Of course, Father." Lwc handed his torch to Gareth before following Anselm at something of a faster pace. He would be heading towards the dormitory where the monks slept. That left Rhys alone with Gareth and Gwen.

They watched Lwc go until he was out of earshot, and then Rhys smiled apologetically and pointed with his chin in the direction his brothers had gone. "Prior Anselm is newly appointed to his post at the request of the bishop. Up until now, I have found him less than reliable under pressure, so I am pleased with how well he comported himself this morning."

Gwen managed to suppress an unladylike snort of laughter at Rhys's words. The intervention of the bishop explained a great deal, since Gwen couldn't imagine that Rhys would have chosen Anselm as his second-in-command if he'd had a true say in the matter. She looked down at the ground to hide her amusement. The hard rain of the night had left puddles everywhere, and Gwen's fresh dress was soaked to mid-calf. She sighed and hoped that yesterday's dress would be dry by the time she returned to the guesthouse.

Gareth was still talking to Abbot Rhys. "The variety of God's creation is boundless, Father. I'm sure the bishop saw in Anselm some redeeming characteristics that are less clear to the rest of us mortals."

Rhys's eyes brightened, and he reached out to Gareth's left shoulder, meaning to show affection as one old soldier to another, but Gareth took a quick step back before Rhys could touch him. Rhys arrested his hand in midair, the unasked question of why Gareth didn't want to be touched plain on his face.

Gareth gave the abbot a rueful look. "I was stabbed last week, and I cannot deny that my shoulder hurts when anyone touches it."

"Gareth!" Rhys turned to Gwen. "My dear, you should have said!"

"I would have said something when we arrived, but Gareth doesn't want me talking about it, even though I know how much his injuries are hurting him."

Gareth looked daggers at Gwen, but she smiled beatifically up at him, and added, "He was hit hard on the head too."

Rolling his eyes, Gareth turned back to Rhys. "I'm healing well. The knife hardly penetrated."

"Not for lack of trying, Father," Gwen said, not willing to let Gareth underplay his pain. "Gareth's left shoulder blade stopped the knife, but the blade cut through the muscle, and the wound bleeds easily if he moves too much."

"What, then, are you doing in St. Asaph with King Owain's army?" Rhys looked from Gwen to Gareth and back again.

Gwen spread her hands wide. "There's so much to tell you, and this probably isn't the place." She tipped her head in a motion not dissimilar to Anselm's. "For now, suffice to say that it is better to be here than at Aber."

Rhys huffed a laugh. "Aber must truly be a dangerous place."

"You don't know the half of it," Gwen said.

2

Gareth

As females, Gwen and Tangwen, Gareth and Gwen's daughter, had no business riding with the king and his men to St. Asaph, especially since Gwen was pregnant. If Gareth had known in advance about King Owain's transformation from bedridden mourner to vibrant monarch, he would have left Gwen behind at Dolwyddelan Castle with Mari, Hywel's wife, where they'd spent the last night of their journey from Shrewsbury before reaching Aber. But they'd discovered that the king was well only at the moment of their return to Aber. King Owain had been leaving the castle, supplied for a journey, with an army of men around him. Though Abbot Rhys had invited him for a peace conference, the king was prepared for war.

Their surprise at Owain's resurrection had driven out any other thought, and when the king had beckoned to everyone in Hywel's party to follow him out the gate and onto the high road heading east, they'd complied. By the time the company had ridden to Caerhun, some ten miles from Aber, it would have been more of a burden to send Gwen away than to let her stay.

In retrospect, Gareth wouldn't have left Gwen at Aber anyway. Though King Owain hadn't openly stated that he and his wife, Cristina, were estranged, he'd implied it, and the coldness between them was plain for all to see, even just from the couple's brief exchange in Aber's courtyard. King Owain's wife was difficult to live with under normal circumstances, but Gareth would have been jeopardizing his own marriage if he'd left Gwen with Cristina when the queen was feeling slighted and unhappy.

Now, with another murder investigation before them, Gareth wasn't sorry to have Gwen by his side. In Shrewsbury, they'd considered telling Hywel that these murders were taking too great a toll on them and their family and that they couldn't pursue them anymore. In the aftermath of their captivity and the investigation's resolution, however, they'd decided that they couldn't turn their backs on the necessity of having *someone* do what they did. Until such a person appeared, they would instead strive to be more careful to protect their family—and their own hearts.

With another dead body at their feet, and a man they knew at that, that was going to be easier said than done. Gareth indicated Erik with a tip of his head. "I should probably have a look before the others return."

"Yes, yes, of course," Rhys said. "I wouldn't have woken you if I didn't think this was murder."

"I know." Gareth raised the torch higher so it would shine directly into the trough and on Erik's face, clearly visible beneath the water. The rain had all but stopped, so there were fewer raindrops leaving ripples in their wake to mar the surface. "I don't have to tell you, Father, that we've done this before, and you can leave the investigation to us."

"It's why I had Lwc wake you, of course." Rhys sighed. "I gather from the way you reacted when you saw this man's face that you knew him personally?"

"Both of us do—did—and you did too, after a fashion." Gwen leaned over the trough, frowning. "He was in Aberystwyth."

"I don't think the good father ever met him, Gwen," Gareth said.

Gwen looked up at Gareth. "Oh, well—" she glanced at Rhys before returning her attention to Erik's face, "—his name is Erik, and he has served quite a few lords over the years, including Prince Godfrid of Dublin and Prince Cadwaladr. After Aberystwyth, he became Hywel's spy, after a fashion, having been cast off and abandoned by Cadwaladr."

"That is quite a list of masters." Rhys pursed his lips as he studied Erik's body. As a former soldier, he would have seen fallen men before, and for a murder scene, this was cleaner than most. "Given that he served Cadwaladr, am I to understand that he didn't much care whom he served as long as he was paid?"

"You can assume it." Gareth lifted one shoulder to shrug. It was becoming a habit lately to raise just his right shoulder, since the left was injured—though, in point of fact, his left shoulder had bothered him on and off for years, so he wasn't even sure if the habit was new. He was intensely grateful that it had been the left side that the bandits had injured, rather than the right, lest he end up completely crippled. "I had no idea he had returned from Ireland."

Rhys glanced at Gareth. "Why would he have gone to Ireland?"

Gareth paused for a moment, gathering his thoughts and debating how much he could tell Rhys without violating Prince Hywel's confidence.

Gwen had no such reservations. "After Rhun died, Prince Hywel sent Erik to Ireland to look for Cadwaladr, who has allies and family members within many Irish kingdoms, as well as in Dublin. As a former Dublin Dane, Erik speaks—I'm sorry, spoke—both Danish and Gaelic, so he really was the best man to send."

"I see."

Gareth focused on Rhys's face. "Do you?"

"Prince Cadwaladr's duplicity and treachery are familiar territory for me, and I am also aware of his role in Prince Rhun's death."

"How did you hear of it?" Gwen said.

"Father Alun of St. Mary's Church in Cilcain travels to St. Kentigern's from time to time seeking advice. He was particularly shaken by the events of last autumn, and he gave me a full accounting of what happened that week from his understanding."

Gareth nodded. "I am hoping to speak to you about what happened from mine."

Rhys looked at him gravely, understanding Gareth's need for counsel and solace without him having to articulate further. Gareth and Gwen had spoken of their grief at length to each other, of course, but as a former warrior, a priest, and a friend, Rhys was a man upon whom Gareth could not only depend but to whom he could pass his burdens for a while.

"Who found him, Father?" Gareth said.

"The brother in charge of the milking, a man named Mathonwy. He sent one of his lads to Anselm, who woke me. Once I saw the body, unlike Prior Anselm, I knew that it was murder, so I sent Lwc to find you. I let Brother Mathonwy attend to his duties elsewhere until he was needed here."

"Who is Lwc, exactly?" Gareth wasn't asking the young man's origins so much as why he had been the one to accompany Rhys to the murder scene.

"He is my secretary, also newly appointed. He refuses to allow me to leave my chambers without him." Rhys smiled half-apologetically. "The bishop determined that in my advancing years my workload was too heavy and sought to lighten it by sending me an assistant. He arrived with Anselm last week, and already I find him indispensable."

"Ha!" Gareth laughed under his breath. "Advancing years ... the bishop doesn't know you very well, does he?"

"You are an irreverent young man." Rhys shook his head, though he was smiling. "I suspect that you, like me, are far older than when we first met." It was a sobering reminder of all that had happened—and all that had been gained and lost—in the last three and a half years. "I will make the milkman available for you to question."

"Thank you, Father," Gareth said. "He can give us an idea of the earliest Erik could have died, since I imagine the body wasn't here yesterday evening when the cows were milked."

"Presumably not," Rhys said—and then, his eyes bright, he put out a hand before either Gwen or Gareth could say anything. "I know. Never presume."

Gwen had gone back to surveying the body. "It's odd that Prior Anselm's thoughts went first to suicide. Do you know why that might be?"

"I do not. We received him as our prior as a transfer from a brother house far to the south, and I know little of his origins beyond what the bishop told me and what Anselm himself has chosen to reveal." Rhys tapped a finger to his lips. "Perhaps it was a mistake not to learn more."

Rhys's mind had already made a leap Gareth hadn't yet considered—namely that Anselm might have had something to do with Erik's death and was attempting to pass it off as suicide rather than murder.

"Was Anselm where he was supposed to be all night?" Gwen said.

"He wasn't present at Matins, our night office, but that's because he's been feeling poorly for several days and has been sleeping in the infirmary. I wouldn't have asked him to come out this morning, but he was the one who woke me." Then Rhys shook his head. "Anselm is far too small a man to have held down Erik."

Gareth waved a hand. "We will question everyone. While on the whole I agree with your assessment of Anselm, it is too early to draw conclusions, especially since we haven't yet removed the body from the trough."

"Unless Erik was killed elsewhere and the body moved, the man who strangled him would have had to be right in the trough with him," Gwen said.

There was a pause as both men looked at her, and then they bent forward to see what she was seeing. "You think he was strangled?" Rhys said.

"Even from here I can see the bruising on his neck," Gwen said.

Rhys released a sharp puff of air. "So it is murder."

Gareth had noted some discoloration around Erik's neck, but bending over hurt a little more than he wanted to admit, so he'd resolved to wait to decide what he was seeing until they got Erik out of the trough. Now that Gwen had pointed out the marks, however, they were unmistakable, even through the water, as she'd said.

Rhys rubbed his forehead with the back of his hand. "Why did he die here?"

"That is one of a dozen questions we can't yet answer." Gareth's lips twisted in a rueful smile in case his words had come across as more dismissive than he intended.

Gwen's boots squished in the mud as she took a few careful steps back from the trough. "The earth is so churned up, Gareth, that I'm afraid we aren't going to learn anything from footprints, but maybe daylight will bring us a better perspective." She frowned. "I hate seeing him there. I wish we could take him out of the trough now."

Gareth gingerly straightened his back. "We have no place to lay him, Gwen. Another few minutes to wait for the cart won't hurt him worse than he already is."

Almost as if wishing made it true, the moment Gareth stopped speaking he heard the sound of hooves clopping.

Rhys turned to look towards the road that lay to the west of the barn. "Ah. There they are." Then he glanced back to Gwen and Gareth and explained, "The track that leads from here straight back to the monastery is too narrow for a horse-drawn cart. Lwc would have arranged for a driver and cart to leave the monastery by the front gate and take the long way around. The cart will have to travel a short distance past the barn on the road before he reaches a gate, which will give him access to the track we see in front of us. Everyone should be here soon."

When Lwc had led Gareth and Gwen from the guesthouse, he'd taken them through the monastery's protected gardens and out the back gate to reach the extensive pasture and farmlands owned by the monastery and worked by the monks who lived in it. The paddock in which they found themselves was attached to a barn that was part of a farmstead directly managed by the monks and one which supplied the monastery with milk and eggs. To the left of the barn was a fence and then the road Rhys had mentioned. Beyond it lay the monastery's mill and mill race on the Elwy River.

Sure enough, a few moments later, men could be heard through the mist talking softly to one another, coming towards them from the monastery grounds. It was Lwc with three assistants. Shortly thereafter, a cart pulled by a single horse arrived from the opposite direction, having reached the barn from the north. The monk driving it maneuvered the cart until the bed was as close to the entrance to the paddock as he could get it. Then two of the men who'd accompanied Lwc pulled a thick, six-foot board from the bed and carried it between them towards the trough.

The third man hastily laid down four stones in the muck to keep the board from getting dirty, and the others set the board down on them. Gareth could have told them it was a lost cause, since the moment they lifted Erik from the trough and set him on the board, it would sink six inches farther into the mud, but he didn't say anything. Without the stones, the board definitely would become mired, and he had enough on his trencher without telling other men how to do their job.

Gareth gently pulled Gwen back to give the men room to work, and with a heave, they got Erik's body out of the trough and onto the board (which sank as predicted). Then, grunting with the effort, and with Erik's body streaming water, the three assistants and Lwc lifted the board and carried it to the back of the cart. Gareth didn't even attempt to assist them. He was more of a hindrance than a help in any circumstance that required the use of his left arm. While he hated feeling useless, he didn't need a glare from Gwen to know that his limited strength should be reserved for the coming days and the discovery of Erik's killer, not expended in lifting the dead man himself.

Rhys had been watching the activity with his arms folded across his chest and a finger to his lips. As the monks settled the body in the bed of the cart, he turned to Gareth. "We have a room along the cloister set aside specifically for the washing of the dead. If we take Erik there, is that an acceptable place for you to examine him?"

"That will be fine. You know well our requirements."

"Sadly, yes." With a flick of his hand to two of the monks who'd come with Lwc, he sent them running back to the monastery, presumably to prepare the room for Erik's arrival. Then he held out his elbow to Gwen. "May I escort you back to the guesthouse, my dear? We may have stood together over several dead bodies in the past, but we can let Gareth shepherd this one home without us, can't we?"

Gwen frowned but took his arm. "I'm perfectly capable of helping Gareth with whatever needs doing, Father."

"I am well aware of that, but you are looking a little pale to me." He glanced at Lwc and the last monk who'd helped lift Erik. "Come, my sons. We've all had enough excitement for one night. Sir Gareth and Brother Ben will ensure that Erik is delivered safely."

For a moment, Lwc's chin stuck out as if he was going to dig in his heels and not go with Rhys. The trip to get the cart had enlivened him somewhat, and he wasn't looking nearly as pale as before. Gareth suspected that he'd experienced more excitement in the past hour than in his whole career as a monk. A flash of insight told him also that Rhys was taking Gwen away not so much for her sake, but because he didn't care for Lwc to spend any more time with the body than strictly necessary.

But then Lwc's expression cleared. He bent his neck in an accepting bow and hustled off with the others with only one regretful glance back.

That left Gareth alone with the last remaining monk, the aforementioned Ben, who was the driver of the cart. He nodded at Gareth before climbing into the driver's seat and taking the reins. Rather than sit beside the monk, even if that would have been more comfortable, Gareth opted to ride in the cart bed, since someone had to sit with the body to ensure that the board Erik was on didn't slide off the back end of the cart.

Gareth slotted his torch into the holder beside the cart seat and banged each boot in turn into the wheel of the cart to knock off the worst of the mud. Then he grasped the rail of the bed with his right hand and swung himself over it to land with a thud in the bed of the cart. It wasn't a terribly graceful move, but it was more than he could have done even two days ago. With a feeling of satisfaction, Gareth lowered himself into a sitting position beside Erik's head.

It was still dark enough that they needed the torch in order to see. Eventually the sun would rise, and Gareth looked east with some anticipation. The clouds were showing signs of thinning, such that the darkness that congealed under the trees around the barn was slightly less gloomy.

Ben snapped the reins to get the horse moving. In an attempt to minimize the distance Erik's body had to be carried from the paddock, the cart had been parked so the horse faced north. Thus, as they lurched forward, Ben apologized for how out of the way their trip was going to be: "The only way to reach the monastery from here is to follow that road." He tipped his head to indicate the road to the west that ran between the barn and the river. "But there's a fence between us and it, so we have to head down here a way to reach a gate that's wide enough for the cart to go through. We use handcarts around here mostly."

"That's fine, Ben." Gareth braced himself as the cart rocked and jostled along the narrow track. Then as it steadied, he focused his attention on Erik.

A quick inspection revealed that the dead spy had no purse on him, nor a weapon, indicating that his murderer had taken them away with him. Robbery was as good a motive for murder as any at this point, though given Erik's profession as a spy, simple theft seemed the least probable. More likely, the killer took his possessions because he had something valuable or important on him, or to keep him from being easily identified. Possibly, they were somewhere to be found in the trees and bushes around the enclosure—or perhaps in the river. Gareth would come back when the sun was fully up and bring a larger complement of men to search.

The rocking of the cart smoothed out enough that Gareth was able to let go of his fierce grip on the side rail. He moved to a half kneeling crouch and started patting Erik down, going through his clothing in advance of his more thorough examination later. Unsurprisingly, Erik had hidden pockets in his clothing—to hold weapons if nothing else—but Gareth found no secret knives, darts, coins, rings, or valuables of any kind in them. He did find a jagged slash in Erik's shirt, along with a matching wound in his belly beneath it. The existence of the wound went a long way to explaining how someone could have strangled Erik in the trough, if that was indeed what had happened. The wound was another thing Gareth would need to examine more closely once Erik was brought inside.

"What did you get yourself involved in that got you killed?" Gareth spoke the words out loud, prompting Ben to turn around and look at him. Gareth raised a hand in pardon. "I knew him in life. He wasn't a friend, but he would want me to find his killer."

"Yes, my lord." Ben turned back to face front. "I can't say I have ever encountered a murdered man before."

"Then you are fortunate ... for I have encountered far too many." Gareth said the last words under his breath, not for Ben's ears. The monk didn't need to be burdened with Gareth's cares.

Silent now, Gareth gazed down at the body with pursed lips. He felt a trickle of rain on the back of his neck, and he pulled up his hood, regretting that he had no sheet or blanket with which to shield Erik from the elements—not that he could get any wetter than he already was. While Gareth hadn't liked or trusted Erik, ever since the big half-Dane had accepted Hywel's offer of a position, he had done nothing to warrant Gareth's suspicion.

Gareth bent to the body again and put his hand to Erik's neck, matching the size of his hand and fingers to the bruises on Erik's throat. They appeared to have been made by someone with larger hands than Gareth had. When a dead man bore marks such as these, more often than not the killer had sat on the victim's chest, holding him down with both hands—one above the other—gripping his neck. This left finger imprints on the victim's neck that followed a predictable pattern. If the killer's right hand was above his left, the killer's right thumb would have pressed hard on the right side of Erik's neck and the marks of four fingers would appear on the left side. The killer's left hand would have marred Erik's skin in a reverse pattern.

In this case, however, while both thumb imprints were where they should be, the right side of Erik's neck had only three finger marks, while the left side had four. It appeared to Gareth that the fifth and smallest finger on the killer's left hand had put no pressure on Erik's neck—or at least not enough to leave a mark. Gareth turned Erik's head this way and that, wanting to make sure of what he was seeing. He had just reached out a hand to the torch, thinking the light would enable him to see the bruises better when—

"Who goes there?" Ben slowed the cart, which hadn't been going very fast to begin with.

Abandoning his inspection for now, Gareth rose to his feet and stood in the bed of the cart just behind Ben's seat. He placed his hand on the hilt of his sword, and his eyes searched both sides of the narrow track. "Did you see something?"

"I-I-I thought so, my lord." The wind chose that moment to pick up, blowing by them from the southwest, and then the clouds above their heads unleashed another deluge. The men ignored the rain as best they could, squinting forward into the murk. "I thought I saw something up ahead, near the gate I told you about."

Pushing back his hood again in order to expand his field of vision, Gareth jumped off the back of the cart, a little more gingerly than he'd climbed into it, and walked to the front. With a glance and a nod at Ben to stay where he was, Gareth paced forward, his eyes searching both sides of the track. The familiar creak of a water wheel sounded off to the left. Never mind that it was barely six in the morning—the miller was working. Gareth made a mental note to question him as to whether he'd seen or heard anything this night. The mill was monastery property, but that didn't mean the miller himself was a monk who slept in the dormitory. Experience told Gareth that either a miller or his apprentice often stayed overnight on the premises, and if that was the case here, one of them might have heard something.

Ben was standing on the cart seat. "Anything?"

"Not that I can see—"

Both sides of the cart way erupted with men, three of whom launched themselves at Gareth at the same instant: the one from the front came at him with a long knife, one that Gareth easily blocked with an upsweep of his right forearm. But then two more men cannoned into him from behind, the first of them catching him around his waist and falling with him to the ground to land on top of him. Gareth's stupid left arm was useless to hold them off, and before he knew it, he'd been kicked in the stomach several times to subdue him, he had a sack over his head, and his arms were pinioned behind his back.

Regardless of the abuse he was taking, he continued to struggle and scream, desperate to get away. In Shrewsbury, men had made him captive for a time—and had almost killed him in the process. That was more than enough helplessness for a lifetime, but Gareth's attempts to fight off these men came to nothing. However, instead of carrying him away—or killing him—the men rolled him into a little stream that ran to the right of the path.

The recent rains had raised the water level from what might in the summer be next to nothing to a running torrent a foot and a half deep, and as Gareth's face went under the water, his anger and fear turned to utter panic. The weight on his back prevented him from rising. He knew he should preserve his strength and his air, but inside his head he was screaming that he was not going to die as Erik had. He was as desperate as he'd ever been in his life.

But within a few heartbeats, the weight on his back lifted. He couldn't see or hear anything underwater and inside the sack, but he got his knees under him and surged upwards out of the stream. The sacking pressed on his face but he shook his head to loosen the cloth and took in his first gasping breath that was more akin to a sob. A few more breaths and he was able to start working at the rope that bound his hands behind his back. It seemed that the men had sought to contain him only temporarily, because the bonds weren't tight, even if they were stiff from being submerged in cold water. After a few moments of effort, he was able to pull his hands loose.

He ripped the sacking off of his head and threw it aside. He remained on his knees at the edge of the path, the panic fading—though as his breaths came more easily, the pain in his wounded ribs and his left shoulder rose, and he didn't have to look at his wound to know that it was bleeding again.

He spat on the ground to rid himself of the last of the stream water and pushed to his feet. Ben lay in the middle of the path, curled up in a ball with his hands to his head. He was moaning in pain and bleeding from a gash in his forehead. The right side of his face was red and puffy.

And while the horse and cart were where Ben had halted them before the attack—Erik's body was gone.

3

Hywel

Hywel stopped two steps outside of the gatehouse, his mouth falling open at the sight of Gareth and a young monk leaning drunkenly against one another as they struggled to walk. Gareth wouldn't be drunk at this hour of the day, or any day for that matter—Hywel knew that like he knew himself—and a second look had Hywel hastening forward. The monk was bleeding from a gash along the line of his scalp, and Gareth was holding his left arm bent and pressed to his belly. He was shivering and every item of clothing he was wearing—from shirt and breeches to cloak and boots—was soaked.

"What happened to you? I mean ... I can see what happened to you, but why are you out here at this hour, wounded again and sopping wet? It's raining, but—"

The gatekeeper must have been watching too because he was only a step behind Hywel. Sputtering his protests at the state of Gareth and the young monk with him, he hastened past Hywel and ducked under the monk's arm to support his other side. Once beneath the gatehouse, the gatekeeper waved an arm to signal to other monks in the courtyard that he needed help.

Now that the sun was up and Lauds was over, the monastery was alive with activity, and two monks responded, hurrying forward with the hems of their robes raised so they wouldn't trip in their haste to help. Hywel caught a glimpse of the sandals they wore beneath their robes as a sign of poverty and affinity with Jesus Christ. Hywel would have liked to point out to them that the Lord Christ had lived in the Holy Land, where Crusaders reported that it was hot most of the time. Nobody had asked him, of course, so it was just as well he'd never had a vocation for the Church. He had little patience with impracticality and, regardless, didn't approve of men having cold feet. But then, he had cold hands and feet no matter how careful he was to keep them warm.

Once the two monks took their brother from Gareth, Hywel ducked under Gareth's good arm to support him and followed after them. St. Kentigern's monastery consisted of a cluster of a dozen buildings surrounded by a ten-foot-high stone wall. Named several hundred years ago for its founder, the monastery lay on the eastern bank of the River Elwy, not far from the bridge they'd crossed in the middle of the night to reach St. Asaph. Other than the wall and the church itself, the monastery buildings were constructed in wood, a far less expensive option for a relatively poor parish.

With its location in eastern Wales, St. Asaph was the intersection of more than just a river and many roads. For six hundred years it had sat at the crossroads between countries: first between Welsh and Saxon lands, later between Welsh and Norman ones, and now between Gwynedd and Powys. The current conflict was merely one episode of a much larger, long-running war.

St. Kentigern's had suffered because of it. Hywel didn't know if the stone wall that surrounded the property had been built since Rhys had become prior a few years ago, but it was newer than the rest of the monastery—and had been added for good reason. The church had burned to the ground in war at least twice, and it was only since King Owain had risen to power in the last ten years and more or less stabilized relations with Chester and Powys that the monastery had achieved a degree of prosperity.

With war looming again between Gwynedd and Powys, that peace might be at an end. It was little wonder that Rhys was endeavoring to do everything within his power to stop the fighting before it started.

As he helped Gareth hobble along towards the guesthouse, Hywel said in an undertone, "Tell me what happened."

"Did you hear about the murder?" Gareth said.

Hywel nodded gravely. "Erik. Gwen told me." He shook his head. "My father knows too, and we are both worried. If someone killed Erik, it was for a reason that doesn't bode well for us."

"You're assuming he was doing your work?" Gareth said.

"I would have thought so."

"Did you know he had left Ireland?"

"No—only that he'd found no sign of Cadwaladr there. But of course, we know now that Cadwaladr never went to Ireland."

"When did you last hear from Erik?" Gareth said.

Hywel gave Gareth a sharp look. "Do you suspect me?"

Gareth huffed a laugh. "No, my lord. I genuinely want to know what he could have been doing in the village of St. Asaph."

"I have no idea." Hywel glanced at his friend's profile. Gareth was in obvious pain, but as they crossed the monastery courtyard, he got his feet under him better and was able to walk a little straighter. "So, are you going to tell me what happened to the horse and cart that was hauling the body to the church?"

As with every church or monastery Hywel had ever been to, St. Kentigern's church was oriented on an east to west axis, so that the sun rising in the east on the spring equinox would shine through the high windows behind the altar. Because the monastery lay to the north of the road that ran from east to west through St. Asaph, when one came through the southern gatehouse from the road as they just had and entered the central courtyard, the church occupied the entirety of the courtyard's north side, while the guesthouse was to the left and the stable to the right.

The monks' cloister and all its associated buildings were on the other side of the church, accessed by a narrow passage on the east side past the stables and by a broader path to the west that took parishioners to the main door of the church.

"We still have the horse and cart, which we left where it was. It seemed like too much effort to drive when it was empty anyway—" Gareth cleared his throat, "—but unfortunately we have been robbed of the body."

Hywel gaped at Gareth for a heartbeat and then released yet another involuntary laugh. "What is it with you and missing bodies?"

Gareth shook his head, laughing under his breath himself. "As you may recall, my lord, that one time the loss was *your* doing."

"So you say." Hywel stayed smiling. "But you still haven't explained why you are so wet. It looks like you climbed right into the trough with Erik."

"Not quite. When the body was taken, three men came at me. More attacked Ben, and that means there had to be still more to steal Erik's body and get away successfully. My attackers held me face down in a stream with my arms tied behind my back and sacking over my head. They let me go before I drowned, obviously, but by the time I got free of my bonds, they and the body were gone."

Hywel was aghast. "Where did this happen?"

"On the path leading north from the barn. There was no entrance onto the road for a good hundred yards or more, and they were waiting for us in the bushes on either side of the gate."

"So they could be anywhere by now." Hywel made a disgusted sound at the back of his throat.

"I can tell you only what I saw, which wasn't much. They left the cart behind and took the body."

"Erik isn't exactly a lightweight either," Hywel said.

"That's one reason they needed so many men. Just lifting him requires at least three people."

"That means they had horses close by, though I suppose with the river just across the road, they could have put him in a boat."

Gareth cleared his throat. "At this point, we're better off not assuming anything."

They'd reached the guesthouse door, and rather than go through it, Gareth reached with his right hand for the frame of the door for support and settled himself into a sitting position on the top step leading up to it. He let out a sigh and leaned back against the door.

"Gwen said Erik was strangled and drowned," Hywel said.

"Stabbed, strangled, and drowned, actually." Gareth's eyes stayed closed.

"Always important to be thorough."

Gareth opened his eyes and gave Hywel a wry look. "I wasn't expecting a brush with death quite this soon after my last one. I did promise Gwen I'd do better."

"Some things can't be helped."

"Apparently not." Gareth shook his head. "I would have been dead if the men who attacked us had wanted to kill me. Why didn't they? They're already into this for one murder. What's two more?" He leaned forward slightly so his weight was no longer on the door. It wasn't intuition—merely that he'd heard, as Hywel had, the thudding of footsteps on the floor of the room behind him. Then the door opened to reveal Gwen standing on the threshold.

She looked down at the top of Gareth's head. Even from that angle she would be able to see that he was soaked to the skin. "You're bleeding! Why? What happened? You were just supposed to bring the body to the church!" She dropped to her knees beside her husband.

Gareth leaned his head against the frame of the door, exhausted. "It turned out to be a harder task than anticipated. I'm really glad you weren't there." He reached out and took Gwen's hand, stopping her from patting him down in a quest for more wounds. "I'm all right, *cariad*."

"I'll be the one who determines that!" Gwen pried her fingers out of Gareth's hand and moved them to his left shoulder. She gingerly peeled back his shirt to inspect the damage. "Do I dare ask if Erik's body made it to the church?"

"It didn't," Hywel said, deciding it was his duty as Gareth's lord to deflect her ire.

Gwen stopped what she was doing and looked up at him. "Really?"

He nodded. "A group of men stole it. It's too early to say who they were or why they did it. Your husband is wet because the perpetrators threw him into a stream beside the road while they absconded with the body."

"Sweet Mary." Gwen rested her forehead on the side of Gareth's head for a moment, and he reached out again to grasp her hand as it rested gently on his chest.

SARAH WOODBURY

"I really am all right," Gareth said. "I took a hard fall, but I didn't hit my head."

She sighed and went back to her ministrations. "Did you see which way they went?"

Gareth had closed his eyes again. After a pause, when no response seemed forthcoming, Hywel answered for him, "He didn't."

"This is all very strange." Gwen had Gareth's shirt off by now and was studying his wound. It might seem an odd location to tend to him, but the light was better outside now that it was daylight than it would be in the guesthouse common room, which even on a bright day had only the one window and the fireplace or candles to light it. "It doesn't make sense that they would steal the body now. Why didn't they take it after he was murdered? If they had done so in the first place, we never would have known that Erik was dead or that a crime had been committed."

Hywel moved under the eaves of the guesthouse to get out of the rain, which had begun to fall with some intensity again. "I'm afraid we don't have enough information to answer that question." He eyed his captain. "Will he live?"

"I suppose so." Gwen looked up at Hywel. "Would you mind helping me get him inside? He's starting to shiver."

They got Gareth to his feet, through the doorway, and over to a low stool by the fire. As Gareth sat, seemingly exhausted by even that short walk, his wet clothes dripped water onto the floor, forming a puddle at his feet. The fire was blazing in the hearth, however, and Hywel was glad to go to it too with his hands out to warm them. Gwen disappeared up the stairs in the direction of their room on a quest for bandages and dry clothes for her husband.

Proving that he was awake after all, Gareth said, once Gwen was out of earshot, "Erik was doing more for you in Ireland than simply looking for Cadwaladr, wasn't he?"

Hywel made a noncommittal noise. "Why do you say that?"

"Because he sent word that Cadwaladr wasn't in Ireland. If his tasks were done, he would have come himself."

"True."

When Hywel didn't embellish his answer, Gareth prodded him. "What was he doing?"

Hywel sighed. "Politics."

Gareth's face was towards the fire, and he spoke softly so his voice didn't carry on the off chance there was anyone else but Hywel to hear. "You are looking for allies."

It was a guess, but a good one. Hywel chewed on his lower lip, not so much stalling for time as gathering his thoughts. He hadn't been deliberately keeping this information from Gareth so much as simply not discussing it. "Since Rhun's death, I have felt that my position in my father's household is more precarious than I would like. Cristina is ambitious, and with two sons already, she has a right to be. My father's current state of mind implies there might not be any more sons with her, but I didn't know that when I sent Erik to Ireland ... and you know my father."

"Yes," Gareth said. "He can be very forgiving."

"The priests would say that isn't a fault, but—"

"But you realize more than ever that you have to make your own way and develop your own allies."

"Yes." Hywel looked down at Gareth. "Hopefully my father will live another twenty years or more, but war is everywhere, and life is uncertain. I must be ready to take the throne on my own terms when the time comes, and that means I need men. I will have Welshmen, for certain, but a pledge of support from Irishmen and Danishmen would not go amiss."

"Your brothers will support you," Gareth said. "Cynan and Madoc, for two."

"Will they? I'd like to think so, but we have a long tradition in Wales of parceling out land to all sons in equal measure, regardless of the fact that the kingdom is weakened, if not destroyed, as a result. Cynan knew Rhun hardly at all, and while he knows me better, how long before he realizes that he is now next in line for the throne?"

"When Rhun was alive, the idea of you becoming King of Gwynedd was a distant future." Gareth chewed on his lower lip as he thought. "Now it's a real possibility. Men die for all sorts of reasons."

"My father has many sons, and each one will want something. I will have to appease them for their support."

"Or fight them."

"And maybe kill them," Hywel said.

4

Hywel

"We will pray that it never comes to that." Gwen stepped back into the common room, a bundle of clothing in her arms.

Hywel looked down at his feet and spoke in an undertone. "It will come to that." He was with friends, so he could be completely honest.

And it wasn't only his father's sons that Hywel would have to fight. Fifteen years ago, Cadwallon, who was Hywel's uncle and his father's older brother, had died in fighting near Dinas Bran, but he'd spent years systematically attacking each of his uncles in turn to eliminate them and their claim to the throne of Gwynedd. He'd done it for his father, Gruffydd, and for himself, knowing that he would one day be king. Unfortunately for him, it had turned out badly in the end, and it was Owain who'd reaped the rewards of Cadwallon's sacrifice.

Gareth knew as well as Hywel that he was right, and he grimaced. "It is your assumption then that Erik was working for you still?"

"Yes, though I have no idea what he was doing here."

The sound of boots scraping on wood came from the opposite side of the room through the doorway that led to the dining room. Then Conall, the agent of Diarmait mac Murchada, King of Leinster, appeared. He'd ridden with them from Aber at King Owain's invitation, one that at the time had seemed impossible for anyone to refuse. With bright red hair still tousled from sleep and so many freckles it would be impossible to count them all, he was the very vision of what an Irishman should look like. The bruises he'd received when he'd been captured by the same band of slavers in Shrewsbury who'd hurt Gareth were finally fading. And it was clear from his stance that while his cracked ribs still pained him, they were healing too, maybe more quickly than Gareth's wounds, especially after today's assault.

Conall waved the piece of bread in his hand. "I couldn't help overhearing some of your conversation and thought I ought to make my presence known."

Hywel grunted, not liking the idea of Conall being a party to the majority of what he and Gareth had talked about. Conall couldn't unhear it, however, and Hywel motioned that he should enter the room. "You heard that Erik is dead?"

"Yes, and that Gareth has done himself another injury."

"Merely renewed the old one," Gareth said. "I was starting to feel a little better too."

Conall stepped behind Gareth to peer at his bare back. "Ah."

Hywel snorted. He liked this Irish spy. He had an air about him that implied constant amusement, though what had happened to him in Shrewsbury had been far from amusing. Like Gareth, Conall appeared to have a good mind, though he was more willing than Gareth was to compromise his honor in the service of his lord. Hywel suspected that it made him both better and worse at his job than Gareth, and Gareth's honor hadn't been something Hywel had regretted for a single moment since he hired him—not even when Gareth was on the trail to catching Hywel himself in wrongdoing. Gareth's sense of honor was the reason that Hywel had brought him into his retinue in the first place.

"If you two would give me a moment, I'll get Gareth out of these wet clothes and bandaged." Gwen gestured with her head that Hywel and Conall should leave them for the dining room. "Perhaps you could ask the cook to prepare breakfast for two more?"

Gwen had essentially given Hywel, her lord, an order, but Hywel had known her since he was a boy, and with a hint of a smile at the way she mothered him, her husband, and everyone else, he led Conall from the room. He wouldn't have been embarrassed to see Gareth stripped naked, and he would have been surprised if Gareth would have felt discomfited either. Upon reflection, however, Gwen was probably less concerned about Gareth's modesty than his reaction to being bandaged. She didn't want him to feel the need to hide his weakness and pain because he didn't want to show it in front of other men more than he already had.

Hywel settled himself at the long table in the dining room in the seat closest to the fire. The monks lived a frugal existence, with the only fire for their personal use in the warming room underneath the dormitory, but they didn't expect such sacrifice from guests, something for which Hywel was very grateful. Hywel didn't think he'd learned much from Rhun's death—other than how full of grief and anger he could be and still walk—but he knew one thing: life was too short to spend cold.

Conall went to the fire too and put out his hands to warm them.

Hywel studied the Irishman for a moment and then said. "If you know anything about Erik's death, tell me now."

Instantly, Conall turned to him, both hands up in a gesture of appeasement. "I know nothing. I saw nothing. I have never been to St. Asaph before. I have never met a half-Dane named Erik. I was fast asleep from the moment my head hit the pallet after I was shown to my room until the bell rang for Lauds. The monk who served me breakfast told me about Erik's death, but I knew nothing else about it until I overheard you speaking to Gareth and Gwen."

That was about as comprehensive a denial as it was possible to give, and Conall had done it with his eyes on Hywel's and a completely straight face. Hywel let out a low laugh. "Erik is half-Welsh too. He used to serve Prince Godfrid of Dublin—and after that, my uncle Cadwaladr."

Conall's eyes lit. "A man flexible in his allegiances. Men like that are good to know as long as you never turn your back on them."

Conall was a spy, so he knew well the vagaries of men's loyalties. But he might have been specifically referring to the shifting nature of allegiances in Ireland, such that Leinster had at times been allied with Dublin Danes like Godfrid, sometimes ruled them, and at other times fought alongside the Irish clans who opposed them. King Diarmait had even entreated the Normans in south Wales to come to the aid of Leinster against the Danes, perhaps not knowing that the Danes had asked those self-same Normans for help against the Irish.

For Hywel's part, he had Welsh, Irish, and Danish blood, but he specifically owed his friend Godfrid, the son of a former king of Dublin, a debt that he suspected he would be working off in the next year or two as Godfrid and his brother finally acted against the usurper of their throne, a fellow Dane named Ottar. How involved the Irish lords of Ireland would be in the fight for the throne of Dublin remained an open question. That was one reason Hywel had been so amiable to Conall: it never hurt to be on the right side of a king of Leinster.

"And then Erik spied for you," Conall said, not as a question.

"It was a recent arrangement, and possibly not one that weighed too heavily on him as I didn't know he'd returned to Wales. I have no notion as to what he might have been doing in St. Asaph."

"Most likely he was coming to speak to you." Conall went to the narrow window to gaze out at the courtyard. He held his left arm somewhat gingerly across his lower rib cage in an attitude Hywel had seen him in quite often. Never having met Conall before he was injured, Hywel didn't know if the stance was normal to him or because he was nursing aching ribs. "If he'd arrived at Aber not long after we left, he could have ridden here hard on our heels to arrive within an hour of us. It might be just like a spy to attempt to enter the monastery by the back way rather than go through the front door after midnight."

Hywel let out a breath of air that was almost a laugh. Leave it to Conall, the outsider, to see things differently from anyone else. "I hadn't thought of that. If it turns out you're right, I will beg forgiveness when I pray for him. Since Erik's last message we've been a little busy—" Hywel laughed for real now, "—but you remind me that I did leave word with Aber's gatekeeper, in the moments before we left, that if Erik appeared he was to tell him where I'd gone."

Conall turned to look at him, his eyes assessing. "Likely he was killed to prevent him from speaking to you."

"What could he have had to tell me?" Hywel clenched his hand into a fist and banged it on the table, frustrated that he honestly had no idea. His mind went immediately to what new and terrible plot his Uncle Cadwaladr might have set in motion, but without Erik alive or access to his belongings that might tell them something, Hywel was at a total loss.

"If someone followed him from Aber, or he was recognized once he arrived, they could have surprised him." Conall tapped a finger of his right hand to his lower lip as he thought. "Though I must admit, all of this had to have happened in a very short amount of time, and if that's the case, his death might have been a matter of a chance encounter rather than premeditated."

"Perhaps it isn't that he followed us from Aber but that he was already here, waiting for me, knowing that I would eventually come through here on my way to Mold." Hywel sighed, acknowledging again, as he seemed to be doing more and more of late, that the price for serving him was often very high. If Erik's death wasn't enough to prove it, Gareth's wounds were a daily reminder.

"In that case, wouldn't he have made himself known to some of the men already here?" Conall said. "Prince Cynan's encampment lies less than a mile from the monastery. Doesn't your brother oversee this region for your father?"

"He does, but I doubt Erik would have sought him out," Hywel said. "Erik's and my arrangement was known to only a few—or rather, to only one other person."

"Gareth." Conall grinned. "Then it was known to two because Gwen knew as well."

Hywel laughed. "Indeed. Regardless, I have yet to speak to Cynan, so perhaps I'm wrong and Erik did go to him. At the very least, one of his men or a monk here at St. Kentigern's might have seen Erik and be able to tell us about his movements. Such questioning is a task that Gareth and Gwen usually take charge of."

"I offer you my service as well in this matter." Conall spoke formally, and there was no doubting that he felt he could be of use.

Hywel eyed the Irishman, not sure he was entirely ready to trust Conall with an investigation, though the events in Shrewsbury implied that he could, at least in regard to something over which the King of Leinster had no stake. He canted his head, deciding for the moment that he'd include him. "I accept. Our first task, since we can't know Erik's mind and are deprived of all evidence of his death, is to find out if anyone in the village, the encampment, or the monastery saw him. Even more, we should simultaneously be searching for the people who took his body. Hopefully questions about one will lead to answers about the other."

Gareth appeared in the doorway. "This is a small community. Someone had to have seen something. And Erik was an easy man to remember."

"Have you ever investigated a murder before, Conall?" Hywel said.

Conall contemplated Hywel for a moment before answering in a completely even tone. "No."

Hywel hadn't meant his question as a criticism. He genuinely wanted to know because it would help Gareth to figure out how much direction to give Conall as the day progressed.

Gareth tipped his head. "I would be grateful for your help. Between the two of us, we might have one working body." He snorted laughter.

"You need more than just Conall, Gareth, if not to help with the questioning then to watch your backs." Hywel glowered at his captain. "You surely need it."

"You have me." Gwen slipped through the doorway, which Gareth was mostly blocking, and came forward to the table.

Hywel had forgotten to call for breakfast, and he sent an apologetic look in her direction as he reached for the bell above the mantle. "I will find other men to help, Gareth. You will stay here, Gwen. I won't risk you. It doesn't bear thinking about what would have happened if you'd ridden in the cart with Gareth—or instead of Gareth."

In a lowered voice, Gareth added, "What I really need you to do, Gwen, is question the monks working within the monastery walls."

Gwen expression turned more than a little mutinous, but she didn't argue out loud, just gave both men a brief nod. Then a monk bustled through the kitchen door, carrying a tray of food and drink for breakfast. He began setting out the dishes on the table. The smell was heavenly. Given the fire, it came as no surprise to Hywel to learn that Abbot Rhys didn't skimp on other important things either.

Eyeing the monk, Hywel spoke his next words carefully, not wanting to talk of anything important in an outsider's presence. "As for you, Conall, if you help Gareth, it might delay even longer your return journey home."

Conall shrugged. "Another day or two of absence from Leinster will hardly matter one way or the other. My king knows where I am and when I tell him of what I have learned he will not begrudge time spent in the royal court of Gwynedd. Besides, I'm in no condition for a sea voyage."

The monk bowed to them and departed, at which point Gwen began pouring breakfast mead into cups for each of them, and Hywel reached for a serving spoon to ladle porridge into his bowl.

Gareth turned to Conall. "You should know by now, but it's only fair to remind you again, that our investigations have a tendency to be far worse than any sea journey." Gareth accepted a cup from Gwen and looked at her over the rim. "In fact, sometimes they include them."

Gwen smiled, though Hywel knew that the memory of her journey to and from Dublin as Cadwaladr's captive was one of the worst periods of her life. "I will do as you ask and speak to the monks." She gave a low laugh. "Heaven knows I've done it before when you didn't want me wandering about by myself. I'll need a sketch to show them, Gareth."

"I'll make several." Gareth nodded his head to Hywel. "If we discover anything that pertains to the king or to you, my lord, I'll let you know immediately. But until then—"

"Until then, I am the *edling*." Hywel spoke matter-of-factly, surprised to find himself completely unresentful of the fact that he was leaving the investigation of Erik's death to others. "My duty is to my father and to address the treachery of my Uncle Madog."

Gareth snorted into his cup. "You do seem to have your share of treasonous uncles, my lord."

Hywel looked up from his wooden bowl, taking in Gareth, Gwen, and Conall in a single glance. Despite another murder, a healing shoulder wound, and a brush with death, his friend was laughing again. Hywel was glad to see it. He wasn't sure where Gareth's amusement and the general banter around the table was coming from, but it was a welcome change from the heaviness of heart they'd all felt over the last few months in the wake of Rhun's death. "It may be that our interests will coincide before we're through."

5

Gwen

Gwen wasn't pleased to be relegated to questioning the monks as she had at Aberystwyth and Shrewsbury, but she understood why Hywel had given her this task and Gareth had backed him up: they were genuinely afraid of losing her.

She understood too why the men felt that way and couldn't add to their burden by knowingly putting herself in danger again. Staying behind at the monastery did mean that she could check in with Tangwen and Gwalchmai (who were still asleep) every so often. Above all, she was a mother, so she couldn't be sorry that she would remain safe—for her own sake, for Tangwen's sake, and for that of her unborn child.

She also wasn't sorry that staying behind gave her a chance to speak to Abbot Rhys again. He'd been a monk for only ten years, but that Rhys would become the abbot of his monastery had been a foregone conclusion from the moment he'd chosen the Church as his vocation. Gareth had trusted him almost from the moment the two had met, and Rhys had become a friend to both Gwen and

Gareth in the subsequent years. Although Rhys had initially balked at Gwen's participation in the investigations that came their way, he had grown to accept her presence, learned from her, and now treated her in the fashion of a proud and beloved uncle. As a rule, priests and monks didn't get to have children, and she was pleased to have adopted him in some measure into her own family.

Thus, after she'd eaten and checked on Tangwen again—and resisted the temptation to lie down on the pallet beside her daughter—she went in search of Rhys, finding him in the abbot's quarters. These were a suite of rooms in the west range of the cloister. As she arrived, he was finishing breakfast.

At the sight of her entering the room, Rhys pushed away his bowl with its remains of porridge and rose to his feet to greet her. "Did you find something?"

His expression was so hopeful, Gwen hated to disappoint him, but she shook her head sadly. "Not yet, but I did want to congratulate you on your rise to abbot."

Rhys made a *huh* sound in the back of his throat and gestured that she should sit in the chair on the other side of his desk. Then he sat too and clasped his hands in front of him. "I don't know if congratulations are really in order, my dear. Some would say that my job and that of a sheepdog are much the same."

"But you are so good at it," Gwen said. "It's always nice when someone outside your immediate friends or family acknowledges your particular skills. Just because you were a warrior once doesn't mean you didn't have a head for managing money and men."

Rhys smiled. "You are as sweet as ever. Now—it was kind of you to congratulate me, but that isn't really why you're here, is it? Tell me what you need from me."

"I think you already know the routine, Father. We need to question everyone in the monastery about Erik. We don't know anything about his movements over the last months, never mind the last few days. We don't even know if he arrived last night, or weeks ago."

"And you don't have a body to examine for clues." He grimaced. "Despite that lack, did Gareth get enough time with it to estimate when he died?"

"No, except that the condition of the body tells him that Erik wasn't in the water for more than a few hours. That could mean he died shortly after midnight and was put in the trough directly, or if he died longer ago, that the body was moved."

"How does he know that?"

"It has to do with the way the blood pooled, discoloring Erik's back, and the extent to which the skin wrinkled and loosened on his fingers—" Gwen broke off as Rhys raised one hand.

"I understand. No need to explain. I accept Gareth's judgment in this matter."

Gwen smiled gently. "I'm sorry. You've been involved in these deaths before, and sometimes I get carried away with my explanations."

"I must be growing squeamish in my old age. Don't mind me."

Gwen moved a hand dismissively. "It's fine. For now, we're working on the premise that Erik died during the night between sunset and when your milkman found the body this morning. We're hoping that among all the people in St. Asaph last night, someone will have noticed something amiss."

"Men can be restless during those hours, myself included, though I saw and heard nothing that could be useful." Rhys eyed her. "While you question my brethren, what will Gareth be doing?"

"He and Conall—that's the Irishman we've befriended—are going to survey the murder site, speak to the monk who found Erik, and try to find some sign of the men who took the body and where they might have taken it. Why they might have taken it will have to wait."

"I can tell you the answer to that: they took it to cover up wrongdoing," Rhys said, speaking like the churchman he was. "I've just come from talking to Brother Ben, the monk who was driving the cart. Ben says he never saw the faces of the men who attacked him. They wore their hoods pulled down over their foreheads. He was not subdued quite as forcefully as Gareth, however, and he was able to count five of them.

"Gareth couldn't even tell us that much. Three attacked him at once. He almost drowned." She shuddered.

"Your husband does have a knack for finding trouble, doesn't he?" Rhys reached a hand across the desk, and she took it, squeezing once.

Despite her worries about Gareth's wellbeing, Gwen managed a smile, though inside, her heart quailed again at how badly injured he was. Since Shrewsbury, with the long journey on horseback home to Aber, the two-day ride to St. Asaph, and then this new attack, Gareth was pushing the edge of what his body was capable of recovering from without real rest. He needed to be in bed.

She and Gareth had resolved to take the investigations they encountered in the path of service to Prince Hywel with a lighter heart, if at all possible, and also to strive to avoid entangling her family members in them more than could be helped. That they were faced with another murder so soon after the last one was troubling, and it was even more troubling that they not only knew the dead man, but that his profession was akin to theirs: there was no getting around the fact that Erik had been a spy, and he may well have been killed for it.

"It's going to be all right, Gwen. Will you tell me what happened in Shrewsbury?"

It was as if Rhys could read her mind, and to have him so solicitous had tears pricking at the corners of Gwen's eyes. She closed them for a moment, forcing her shoulders to relax and the lines that had formed on her forehead without her realizing it to smooth.

And then she told him all about the couple who'd impersonated her and Gareth; the quest to discover the impersonaters' identities; how it had led her whole family to Shrewsbury where they'd become embroiled in another investigation; and how the end result implicated Cadwaladr and Madog in nefarious activities.

When she finished and met Rhys's eyes, she found him studying her, more concern in his expression than she'd ever seen.

Gwen lifted one shoulder in imitation of Gareth. "Gareth and Hywel want to keep me out of danger. We came close to dying in Shrewsbury, and they don't want to risk me again."

"We men can't help feeling protective of you, Gwen. You know that." Rhys frowned. "I too am concerned about what happened in Shrewsbury and particularly about the wounds you and your husband sustained."

Gwen opened her mouth to say that she herself hadn't been injured, but Rhys had already thought of that and forestalled her. "I'm not talking about just physical wounds, Gwen. You cannot survive what you endured and remain unchanged." But then he sighed. "Unfortunately, right now I have duties to attend to or I would be the one to take you around the monastery. I assume Prince Hywel has thought far enough ahead that he has assigned a guard to you?"

"That he has. Gareth's friend, Evan, has consented to come along. I think he's angry at Gareth for leaving him behind as much as he has in recent weeks. Otherwise, the number of fighting men you have in the region means they'll be tripping over themselves this week, seeing danger in every shadow. Wait until you meet Hywel's foster father. He isn't a large man, but he's ferociously protective of Hywel."

"As well he should be." Rhys slapped both thighs sharply and stood. "They rode east expecting a war and got a peace conference and a murder instead."

Gwen tipped up her chin to look at him. "Only the youngest among them could be sorry about peace." Then she hesitated, biting her lip. She hadn't risen to her feet yet, even though Rhys was implying that their meeting was over by rising himself.

"What is it, Gwen?"

"King Owain is very angry. It is hard to see how Madog could be in the right in any way. He tried to kill Hywel."

"I understand that Madog's offense against Hywel cannot go unanswered," Rhys came around his desk and looked down at her, "but Madog's grievances against Owain and Gwynedd run deep and are not limited to what occurred this month. You know that."

Gwen nodded. "I suppose I shouldn't complain about my task today. Solving a murder is easy compared to what's in store for you."

Rhys laughed and held out his hand to help her to her feet. "I am aware that King Owain is here only out of respect for me. I think he *wants* a war."

"He lost a son," Gwen said simply. "But peace or war, I can be grateful that Gareth's injuries will keep him out of the fighting for the foreseeable future."

Rhys smiled broadly. "God works in mysterious ways, doesn't he? A week ago, you would never have said that Gareth taking a blow like he did would be a blessing. And now—"

Gwen's eyes lit. "And now I would! Thank you for reminding me that good can come from any setback. In truth, we rode here with King Owain because we could do nothing else, but if the king had realized how unfit Gareth was, he would have left him behind at Aber."

"Then it is just as well he didn't know, since I have need of Gareth. Again, we can be thankful even when circumstances don't seem to call for it."

6

Gwen

Rhys moved towards the door and opened it. "Lwc! I need—" He cut himself off at the sight of his assistant already standing in the doorway with an eager expression on his face.

"Yes, Father?"

Even though he was quite a few years older than her brother, Lwc reminded Gwen very much of Gwalchmai, and she almost laughed again.

Rhys recovered from his surprise and gestured to Gwen. "Lwc, I would like you to be Gwen's escort around the monastery. She and her guard, Evan, who serves Prince Hywel, are to have full access to all areas of the monastery and to every monk, barring those in the infirmary. We need to find this killer before he strikes again."

Lwc straightened his shoulders to an almost military bearing. "Yes, Father." Then he hesitated. "What about Prior Anselm? He's been feeling poorly of late and sleeping in the infirmary rather than in his cell, but he was about earlier."

"If he's in the infirmary, don't disturb him," Rhys said. "We know already that he didn't recognize the dead man. I will speak to him myself later."

"Why choose me, Father?" Lwc said.

"Because I don't have to explain to you the seriousness of what has occurred, and I know you will be discreet."

The expression on Lwc's face as he looked at Rhys was one of hero-worship. "You can count on me, Father."

Rhys settled a hand on his shoulder. "I know I can. That's why I chose you for this task."

It was still raining as Evan, Gwen, and Lwc set out from Rhys's office. Gareth had made it clear that he would be speaking to the brothers who worked in the fields and gardens, so it was Gwen's job to take on everybody else. The monastery at St. Asaph was Welsh in origin, having been founded by St. Kentigern five hundred years earlier, before there were any Roman monastic orders in Wales at all. It was a poorer monastery than the Abbey of St. Peter and St. Paul in Shrewsbury from which she'd just come and was home to one hundred monks.

In typical more equitable Welsh fashion, St. Kentigern's employed few laymen to work for them. Compared to the abbey in Shrewsbury, Gwen was much more comfortable here, among Welshmen, speaking Welsh and with Welsh customs and norms. It had been odd to be in England, even if only seven miles from the Welsh border, and find that what she thought was normal and made sense perhaps didn't quite. But even a hundred was a great many men to question in a day.

Roughly half the monks in the monastery worked within a stone's throw of the guesthouse, and the rest were scattered far and wide in the fields and pastures which the monastery controlled. With the idea that they might as well start with what was closest, their first stop was the scriptorium. Gwen and Evan waited in the corridor for Lwc to pace importantly ahead of them and prepare the monks for Gwen's arrival. He left the door open, however, and Evan watched with bright eyes as Lwc lectured his fellow monks on discretion. Gwen herself suppressed a smile and looked down at the ground.

As they waited, Evan stretched his back and shoulders, loosening his muscles. "I, for one, am not sorry that I'm not out there in the muck fighting men of Powys today."

"I would that men never went to war again," Gwen said, "but I don't see how the abbot will achieve peace, even if he wants it desperately. At the same time, I can't see what Madog has to gain from fighting."

Evan pursed his lips before speaking. "He has more men than we do."

Gwen frowned. "He does?"

Evan waggled his head. "We all know it. Since Rhun's death, King Owain has been neglecting his kingdom. Not as many lords have rallied around his banner as might have a year ago."

"I didn't know." Gwen bit her lip. "That's bad—bad for all of us."

"It is a bargaining piece for Madog, who is clearly in the wrong at the moment. The key will be getting both sides to back down without losing face."

Then Lwc returned, looking satisfied. "They are ready, but I can tell you already that none of them know anything."

Gwen struggled not to grind her teeth, since she had wanted to be the one to question them without predisposing anyone to conclusions. She should have said something before Lwc went in there. It was fine giving the young monk the satisfaction of leading them, but he knew nothing about investigations. If she allowed him to continue as he had, he would hinder her.

"Thank you, but you know I have to ask." Then she leaned into him and whispered. "You intimidate the others because you are the abbot's secretary. I am grateful for your assistance with the questioning, but it would be better if you let me do the talking from here on out. As a woman, I am less threatening." She raised her eyebrows innocently as she finished her little speech.

Lwc nodded emphatically. "Yes. Yes, of course. I understand."

"Thank you." Gwen looked at Evan. "If you wouldn't mind, I'd prefer it if you stay by the door too."

Evan smirked from behind Lwc's back, having enough experience working with her and Gareth to know full well what Gwen had just accomplished. He nodded, acquiescing so it would be easier for Lwc to do the same.

Gwen entered the room and went to each monk in turn, introduced herself, and explained that Gareth had asked her to show the image of Erik to as many people as possible in hopes that somebody had seen him. Unfortunately, Lwc was right that none of the six monks in the scriptorium claimed to have been awake in the middle of the night other than for the vigil of the night office. None of them had ever seen Erik before, even when Gwen added to their understanding of the black and white image by describing his size and coloring.

As Gwen and Evan progressed through the monastery, they found nobody with useful information. Not in the laundry, among those who worked in the kitchen or the stable or tended to the needs of Abbot Rhys, or among the novices. The guesthouse had been completely taken over by King Owain and his retainers, so there were no guests to question this time. Even the monk who oversaw the gatehouse had been aware of no activity last night or any night that seemed to have a bearing on Erik's death. Everybody looked at the sketch of Erik that Gareth had drawn and shook his head.

This particular monastery was unfamiliar to Gwen—Gareth had been here only briefly several years ago—but she'd spent time in monasteries in the past, most recently in Aberystwyth and Shrewsbury. It was enough to have grown familiar with how things were supposed to be done. Above all, especially in a monastery run by Abbot Rhys, there was dignity, reverence for God's creation, and order. Gwen could see it in the well-trimmed hedges and the carefully edged pathways through the garden. The guesthouse had been sparsely but adequately furnished and immaculately swept and dusted. The bread last night had been a small slice of heaven.

Gwen suspected that every book and paper in the scriptorium was aligned perfectly with every other, and woe betide the novice who spilled his ink.

What's more, Rhys had an entire monastery of innocent monks.

More than a little disheartened, though Gwen knew she shouldn't be since this was part of the job of an investigator, and it was more usual than not to spend a great deal of time asking questions nobody could answer, by mid-afternoon Gwen and Evan found themselves underneath the gatehouse tower, watching the rain cascade off the roof and spatter on the flagstones of the courtyard.

They hadn't deliberately saved the questioning of Brother Pedr, the gatekeeper, for last, but he had been the last monk Lwc had brought them to. Pedr hadn't been any more helpful than anybody else, and Lwc had departed for afternoon prayers with yet another satisfied look of a job well done, if fruitless in the end. Pedr, as gatekeeper, had remained behind, since (as he told them) his duty didn't stop for prayers, and he would say them alone in his little room at the base of the tower. As an older monk, he was no longer suited to manual labor, but his mind remained sharp, even if his knees creaked when he walked.

And as it turned out, the need for him to stay was shown to be true a moment later by the arrival of a lone monk, who appeared out of the rain, head bent and cloak clutched tightly around himself, having come from the east. He was an older man, one who upon first impression appeared to be very much in the vein of Abbot Rhys. Like the abbot, he was dressed sensibly for the journey in boots and cloak, though still in the robes of a monk. He dismounted within the shelter of the gatehouse tower, pushed back his hood, and looked around for someone to speak to. He spied Gwen and Evan at the same moment that Pedr came hurrying from his watch room.

"Welcome, brother!" Pedr said. "You look as if you've come far."

The newcomer had already opened his mouth to speak to Gwen and Evan, but he swung around to Pedr. "I am Brother Deiniol from St. Dunawd's Monastery southeast of Wrexham. I am sent here by my abbot to Abbot Rhys on a matter of utmost urgency."

"We are at prayers at the moment, but you are welcome to join them in the church until we've finished—"

"I have missed the vigils, but this cannot wait." Deiniol shook his head vehemently in case Pedr was going to argue with him about it.

Pedr pursed his lips, clearly unhappy at the thought of interrupting afternoon prayers, but then Evan raised a hand. "I'll speak to the abbot. Don't worry, I'll be as discreet as I can."

Evan's lifted hand had opened his cloak, which he'd been holding closed against the weather, and at the sight of Evan's surcoat, Deiniol drew in a breath. "You're a man of Owain Gwynedd!"

Evan's expression turned to one of puzzlement. "Of course I serve Owain Gwynedd, as does everyone here. Where do you think you are?"

Deiniol's face paled even more. "Powys."

Evan snorted. "St. Asaph hasn't been part of Powys for years."

"But what-what are you doing *here*, at the monastery?" The stutter seemed uncharacteristic for a man of Deiniol's bearing, but his shock was genuine.

Gwen decided she ought to step in, since the two men seemed to be speaking past each other. "We are here for the peace conference that Abbot Rhys has called to reconcile Powys and Gwynedd. If you were looking for room in the guesthouse, it is full."

"That's-that's not why my abbot sent me. Just after St. Dafydd's day, our monastery was robbed and burned by a party of Owain Gwynedd's men. It's the theft of our relics and a safe haven for our brothers that I'm about."

Brother Pedr made a hasty sign of the cross. "That is troubling news indeed. You are sure they were King Owain's men?"

"We have no doubt of it. The yellow and red lion standard was plain on the chests of every one of them." Deiniol's eyes strayed again to Evan's chest, and then he shook his head and averted his eyes as if looking directly at Evan pained him. "To think that men in the service of the king could sink so low."

Gwen had a hand to her mouth. She wanted to protest, to deny that what Deiniol said could be true, but he seemed beyond appeasement. Instead, Brother Pedr put a hand on Deiniol's arm. "The world is a dangerous place. Know that you have come to a safe haven, regardless of who else is here. The Church is neutral ground and provides sanctuary and hospitality to all." As he finished speaking, his eyes went to Evan, who nodded and headed out into the rain to fetch the abbot.

Though Deiniol's eyes never left Evan's back as he loped away from them across the courtyard, he also nodded weakly, taking in a breath and letting it out. Some of his anxiety faded to be replaced by relief that he was no longer in the presence of a soldier from Gwynedd.

Pedr turned his attention to Gwen as if he felt it was now his job to appease her. "The lawlessness along the border between Wales and England is well known."

"It is." Now that she'd had time to absorb Deiniol's news, Gwen's expression turned thoughtful. "In fact, before he joined Prince Hywel's retinue, Gareth learned to read as payment for protecting a convent from exactly this kind of banditry."

"Surely that villainy wasn't perpetrated by the men of the King of Gwynedd too?" Deiniol said.

Gwen let out an exasperated sigh that she immediately swallowed and turned into a smile. "No."

She still wanted to say more, but she decided not to. Deiniol was not to be persuaded, at least not now and not by her, that the men who'd sacked his monastery couldn't have been sent by Owain Gwynedd. Only household knights and men-at-arms in the retinue of a man of the royal house wore the colors of the House of Aberffraw. That meant that if Deiniol was correct in their identity, the men involved belonged either to the king, to Hywel, or to one of Hywel's younger brothers, Cynan or Madoc.

Gwen knew for certain that the men hadn't been sent by Hywel. King Owain had been in mourning on St. Dafydd's Day and in no condition to be sending men anywhere, much less to sack a monastery. That left Madoc and Cynan, except their hands had been completely full—first with the preparations for, and then with the actual taking of, Mold Castle. To think that either of them would have ordered men to Wrexham to sack a monastery on the side was laughable.

Furthermore, what better way for a group of bandits operating in Powys to deceive the populace than to disguise themselves as men of Gwynedd? Everybody would be looking at their surcoats and not their faces, and Gwynedd and Powys had been at odds for long enough—forever almost—that most Powysians distrusted men of Gwynedd as a matter of course.

Pedr met Gwen's eyes, and he made a rueful face. He was a monk and secluded from the world, but he wasn't a fool. It had occurred to him too that Deiniol's assumptions about what had gone on in Wrexham weren't necessarily the real facts.

Because they both continued to smile gently at Deiniol, he knew nothing of their disbelief, and he said, "I am relieved to know that the king has come to the monastery in peace. The

Church can call him to account for what his men have done, rebuild our monastery, and return our wealth to us."

Pedr patted Deiniol on the shoulder. "Meanwhile, we will find a bed in the dormitory for you."

Deiniol managed a genuine smile, and the act transformed his face from a fairly weathered and severe visage to one far more open. "If not, I am not above sleeping in a stable. If it was good enough for our Lord, I can hardly argue."

More as a distraction while they waited for Evan to return with Abbot Rhys than because she thought she might learn something from him, Gwen pulled out the sketch of Erik. "Do you recognize this man?"

Deiniol's brow furrowed as he took the paper from her, looking from Erik's picture to her face. "Does this have anything to do with what happened to my brothers?"

"I didn't learn of the destruction of your monastery until you told us. This is a different matter."

Deiniol returned his attention to the image. Like many men of his age, his eyes troubled him, and he stretched his arm out as far as it would go in order to better see what Gareth had drawn. "My goodness, I think I do recognize him. I saw him on the road a few days ago. I had stopped to rest at a village well in order to slake my thirst, and he came following after. It was only a quarter of an hour before he was heading west again at a rate far faster than my old nag could travel."

"You spoke to him?" Gwen's heart sped up.

"Very briefly. I can't say I know anything about him." He paused, hesitating.

"What is it?" Pedr urged.

Deiniol licked his lips. "I hate to speak ill of any man, but—"

Deiniol hadn't had a problem speaking ill of the men of Gwynedd, but as he was from Powys, that prejudice would have been instilled from birth. Gwen let the gross untruth pass without comment and said instead, "We really do need to know anything you can tell us about your encounter with him."

Deiniol gave a curt nod and handed the paper back to her. "He was very gruff, unpleasant even. He wouldn't look me in the eye when I spoke to him and had no interest in conversing. He left in a hurry, as if someone was chasing him."

Gwen could have said, *or as if he had urgent news to deliver*, but again held her tongue. That was information she didn't need to share with anyone but Gareth, Hywel, and Conall.

Then Evan appeared out of a side door of the church, Brother Anselm rather than Abbot Rhys in tow. She didn't know Anselm at all, he didn't like her, and thus she didn't want to question Deiniol in front of him. So she had time for only one more question. "Where did this sighting take place?"

"In a little village north of Llangollen."

As Deiniol spoke, Evan reached the shelter of the gatehouse. Taking in the sketch of Erik in Gwen's hand and her intent expression, he said, "Llangollen did you say? That is the seat of King Madog's power. My king will want to speak to you of what you saw along the way."

He couldn't have forgotten Deiniol's fear of him, but he was as dismissive of the idea that men of Gwynedd were responsible for the sacking of Wrexham as Gwen was. Deiniol, however, held up his hands in a gesture that implied both ignorance and that he wanted to keep Evan away from him. "I know nothing of this war and want nothing to do with it."

Evan's eyes narrowed, but Gwen sighed. "You forget that Gwynedd is here looking for peace."

"So you say." Deiniol let out a breath. "You cannot blame me for being distrustful."

"Surely any further conversation need not be had in the rain." Anselm shot Evan an irritated look. From what Gwen had gleaned about Anselm so far, it was a common expression for him. To his credit, Anselm was right. It had been rude of her to keep Deiniol outside all this time rather than inviting him inside to warm his hands at Pedr's grate or in the guesthouse common room.

Deiniol turned to Anselm. "I would be most grateful to shed these wet robes and warm myself at a fire—and if someone could care for my horse? He has come a long way."

"I'm surprised you had a horse to ride if these bandits destroyed everything as you say," Evan said.

Deiniol's breath quickened in the face of Evan's renewed skepticism. "He was the only one not taken by the marauders. They saw him for what he was—an old fellow who'd been put out to pasture and was no longer useful even for riding. It has taken me so long to get here because he needed to rest—and truth be told, I fell ill and had to take shelter in a village for over a week. It might have been better to have walked directly here, but once he and I started out, I couldn't abandon him, nor he me, no matter how urgent my task."

The bell in the tower tolled, indicating that afternoon prayers were finally over. As soon as one of the younger monks, who served as a stable boy, left the church, Anselm snapped his fingers at him, and he changed direction to answer Anselm's summons. Then Anselm held out an arm to Deiniol in a welcoming gesture. "This way, brother, if you will."

Deiniol set out into the rain, but then he hesitated in midstride before he'd gone more than three or four paces and turned back. "Oh—another thing—" he retraced his steps, "—that man you asked me about wasn't alone. Another rode with him."

7

Gareth

The near drowning aside, being thrown on the ground had not done Gareth's shoulder any favors, and he was trying very hard not to think about how much pain he was in, which was why he hadn't said anything to Gwen about it. Not that she didn't know, of course, but he felt as if talking about it would only make what he was feeling more real—and force him to address the pain rather than ignore it.

Besides, it was only pain. The wound was bandaged again and not bleeding (much), and while the damage he'd sustained today might have set his progress back a few days, his heart was still beating. As long as he could breathe, he could work. Working was better, in fact, than lying in bed feeling sorry for himself.

Of all the people in St. Asaph, Conall was the one person who understood intimately how he was feeling, so it was with some camaraderie that the two of them walked (rather stiffly) side by side in the rain. Although they didn't have far to go initially, because of the ground they had to cover today and their various ailments, they had saddled their horses and now led them through the monastery gardens.

Once outside the back gate, they mounted and rode towards the barn. They'd spent all morning canvassing the village for anyone who'd seen Erik, and they'd spoken to the miller regarding his whereabouts the previous night. So far nobody had witnessed anything unusual or, if they had, they weren't talking about it. They'd had no luck so far with any witnesses, and now Abbot Rhys—in Gareth's mind he would always be *Prior Rhys*—had arranged for the brother who served as a milkman to meet them at the barn where he'd found Erik's body.

"Are you sure about not returning to Ireland?" Gareth said to Conall. They were keeping their horses to a walk so as not to jar any of their injuries. "Is your king really so sanguine about where you go and what you do?"

Conall laughed and instantly sucked in a breath at the pain. "The king gives me free rein to serve him as I see fit. Given that the issue of the slave ring is resolved, my immediate return home seems less necessary. The king will find that no more women are being taken from Ireland, and that was the point of the entire endeavor."

"And you see nothing wrong with establishing a relationship between Leinster and Gwynedd."

Conall raised his eyebrows. "Would you?"

"Not at all. Owain and Diarmait are cousins, both descended from Brian Boru, but I don't think they've met for many years, and certainly not since Owain took the throne of Gwynedd."

"Men of power can always use a friend though."

"As can less elevated men."

Conall grunted his assent. "Yes, they can."

Gareth was liking this Irish spy more and more, and he truly hoped he could trust him. So far, Conall had given him no reason not to. Gareth had taken a similar risk four years ago in befriending Godfrid, one of the princes of Dublin, and he'd had no cause to regret it. Still, he would be fighting on Godfrid's behalf sometime in the near future, at the behest of both Hywel and Owain. If the relationship with Leinster developed through Conall, he wondered if someday he could expect to do the same for Diarmait.

Ireland had always been a source of strength for Gwynedd's kings. Over the years, many had retreated there when pressed, using it as a place to gather support or even an army with which to return to Gwynedd. Cadwaladr had done exactly as had his father before him—three times. However, while King Gruffydd had put his mercenaries to work overthrowing Norman control of Gwynedd, Cadwaladr had brought an army of Danes to pressure his brother into absolving him of murder.

But Gwynedd had not often returned the favor, for reasons that were not clear to Gareth, unless it was simply that Ireland was a quagmire of shifting political alliances. Despite what Hywel said about needing allies should things go awry in Gwynedd, beyond what was strictly necessary, he should not allow himself to become involved in what went on there. Ruling a kingdom adjacent to

England was bad enough without being caught in the middle among warring Irish clans and Danes.

As had been the case for King Owain, the unexpected death of Diarmait's older brother had raised Diarmait, the second son, to the throne. Unlike King Owain, however, Leinster was subject to a greater lord, Tairrdelbach, the King of Connaught and the high king of Ireland, who did not approve of Diarmait's ascension and who'd sent his armies rampaging through Leinster rather than accept it. Hywel believed Tairrdelbach feared Diarmait and saw him as a rival for the high kingship. Which he probably was.

Further complicating matters for Gwynedd's loyalties, both Tairrdelbach and Diarmait believed themselves to be the rightful rulers of Dublin and its Danish citizens. Ottar had gone on bended knee to Diarmait and paid tribute for his kingship. Once Brodar and Godfrid overthrew Ottar, as they planned to, they would have to bow to Leinster as well.

"Who are you to King Diarmait, really, such that he trusts you so completely?" Gareth said.

"I am his sister's son, which could be a reason *not* to trust me, I admit," Conall laughed under his breath, "but I saved his life once. For all that King Diarmait is—" here Conall paused, searching for the right word, "—thought to be cold, even heartless at times in his dealings with his people, he sees through his own eyes and makes his own judgments."

"Any man who does so deserves respect." Gareth canted his head. "I didn't know you were a nobleman. I apologize for my familiarity."

Conall made a dismissive gesture. "You earned your knighthood on the field of battle. There is no difference between us." He glanced at Gareth. "I am fortunate that Diarmait trusts me enough to give me freedom of action few kings allow. It is something like the freedom you have, it seems, and you are not noble."

"Thank goodness!" Gareth laughed.

Conall nodded. "Even better to be trusted for the man you are. In my experience, it is a rare man who values his own conscience above his lord's."

Gareth tsked through his teeth. "It isn't like that."

"Actually, I think it is."

Gareth hadn't told Conall anything of his wanderings as a younger man, and he wondered where he had heard of them. Evan, perhaps, who was known for having a too loose tongue where Gareth was concerned. Regardless, Gareth made no reply because they had arrived at the barn. As arranged in advance, not only was the monk who'd found Erik's body waiting for them, but two young soldiers as well—and very welcome ones at that. Llelo and Dai, Gareth's adopted sons, grinned at him as he dismounted, and then Dai broke ranks and wrapped his arms around his father's waist.

Gareth rocked backwards as he took Dai's weight and let out a *whuf* of air. "Easy now." He patted Dai's back and distanced himself somewhat gingerly.

"Sorry!" Dai looked his father up and down, glaring at him. "I heard you were injured in Shrewsbury. You should have brought us with you."

"Maybe I should have, but you were needed at Mold, and I didn't anticipate trouble."

"You should know by now, Father, that if you don't find trouble, it finds you," Llelo said.

Gareth smiled as he reached out his good arm to pull Llelo into a hug as well. "I've missed you both."

The boys had been ten and almost twelve when Gareth and Gwen had encountered them stranded in England. Three years on, they were learning to be soldiers under the tutelage of Cynan, Hywel's younger brother, who oversaw these lands from Denbigh. Both had grown a foot since they'd come to him. At nearly fifteen, Llelo could look Gareth in the eye, and even though he was two years younger, Dai wasn't far behind.

Gareth introduced the boys to Conall and then all of them to the milkman. His name was Mathonwy, a fine old name that belonged to the great Welsh god-hero and father of all Gwynedd.

Llelo and Dai pulled the horses into the barn out of the rain. In the daylight, the barn was revealed—surprising to Gareth, given how orderly everything else at the monastery was kept—in a sad state of disrepair. While the floor was swept clean, the tools were tidied away, and the roof was solid, as would be necessary to keep out the weather and prevent the hay in the loft from getting wet, the walls allowed plenty of daylight to enter the interior. They hadn't been filled in with wattle and daub in some time. Maybe since St. Kentigern founded the monastery.

The monk noticed where he was looking and nodded. "Father Abbot says—and I concur—that the rot in the timbers cannot be repaired. We will use the barn until it falls down, but we've just finished a new one a quarter-mile down the road. Only the cows return here now, as they are creatures of habit and are most unsettled by changes in their routine. The pigs and chickens are already in their new homes."

"Good to know." Gareth crossed the floor to reach the rear door, which gave easy access to the enclosure where Mathonwy had found Erik.

Mathonwy gestured helplessly to the trough. "He was just there. I'd come for the cows. As soon as I saw him and realized what I was seeing—and that it wasn't my brain addled from lack of sleep—I ran to wake Prior Anselm."

"Given that he'd been prior for only a week, I'm surprised that you went to him and not Abbot Rhys, who has more—" Gareth paused as he tried to think of how to phrase what he was asking, "—experience in these matters." The question put Mathonwy on the spot, but Gareth had his tricks as an investigator, and he genuinely wanted to know what Mathonwy thought of his new prior, since Gareth's first and second impression hadn't been positive.

Mathonwy wiped the smirk from his face almost the instant it appeared, but Gareth saw it and acknowledged that he'd guessed right about what was behind it. He wouldn't be surprised if Mathonwy wasn't the only longtime member of St. Kentigern's who was less than impressed with the new prior the bishop had foisted on them. "He hasn't been with us long and isn't the type to have steady hands when they're needed. But it was his right to be woken first, so I did so. I've been at the monastery a while now, and until recently it's always been Prior Rhys to whom we went."

Gareth smiled. "In my head too."

"But then Anselm showed that he had some good sense and woke the abbot immediately, so all's well that ends well."

Gareth could understand Mathonwy's satisfaction. He'd followed the rules, done the right thing, and been rewarded for his faith.

"I understand that your previous abbot was elderly?" Conall knew something about investigations too. Now that rapport had been established, it was time for questions before Mathonwy remembered that he had duties elsewhere.

"Yes. Prior Rhys had taken over many of his tasks even before he became abbot."

"When were you last at the barn?" Gareth said.

"I was here for the evening milking. The cows know to come to the barn as the sun is setting. I rarely attend Vespers, though sometimes I manage to slip in at the end."

It was standard practice in any place within hailing distance of a chapel—in other words, all through Wales and England—to keep time by the cycle of prayers and the ringing of church bells. The first prayer of the day was *Matins*, the night office, at midnight. The morning was marked by dawn prayers, called *Lauds*, *Terce* at mid-morning, *Sext* at noon, *Nones* at midafternoon, *Vespers* at sunset, and *Compline* or evening prayers before retiring to bed. These hours were managed by a water clock in the monastery courtyard and a candle clock in the church itself, though the exact moment of the prayers was less important than the keeping of them.

"Did you see anyone or remember anyone in the area yesterday evening?" Gareth said.

"I'm sorry. I noticed nothing. It was raining and cold, and I confess I was looking forward to my dinner after Vespers."

Gareth put up his good hand. "I understand. Had you ever seen Erik before—not necessarily here but anywhere?"

Mathonwy shook his head regretfully.

"Where are the cows now?" Gareth said.

"In one of the pastures." Mathonwy indicated east with a bob of his chin, and his eyes twinkled as he said, "I'm afraid you won't get much out of them."

Gareth coughed a laugh and went to the door of the barn to poke out his head. A stone wall protected the pasture to the east of the barn. A style and gate that allowed access through it lay just across the cart way from where Gareth stood. Gareth had seen enough of St. Asaph in the times he'd come through here to know that the monastery's pasture lands were extensive, and this nearby field was one of dozens within hailing distance of the barn. The sheep and cattle would be moved from field to field to give the grass in each pasture time to grow.

Then Gareth returned to Conall's side. "Do you have any more questions for Mathonwy?"

Conall pursed his lips. "I assume you don't manage the barn by yourself? How many helpers do you have?"

"I have two most days at the new barn and one who helps with the cows. But he was in the infirmary yesterday with a fever," Mathonwy said. "I didn't see him all day and had to do the work myself."

"His name?" Gareth said.

"Roger."

"He's Norman?" Gareth said, surprised to learn of a Norman monk in a Welsh monastery.

"A Norman father who didn't acknowledge him and a mother who died shortly after his birth, though she lived long enough to saddle him with a Norman name," Mathonwy said.

Gareth frowned. "I hear Prior Anselm has been ill on and off too. Did you go to the infirmary to wake him?"

"No, he was in his cell this morning, though now that I think on it, he was in the infirmary at the start of Matins because I went to check on Roger before the prayers to see how he was faring and Anselm was in a nearby bed." He rubbed his chin. "I suppose I went to his cell out of habit after finding the body."

"We'll speak to Roger and Anselm later if they're well enough," Gareth said. "Thank you for your assistance."

Mathonwy bowed and departed, presumably to his other duties. That left Conall and Gareth at the scene of the crime, along with their young guards, who'd spent the conversation patrolling the exterior of the barn, rain or no rain. Dai and Llelo took their responsibilities very seriously. Still, while Gareth wanted his foster sons trained to be knights, he hoped that Cynan wouldn't pound Dai's natural effervescence out of him. The boy had always been a spark of sunshine, no matter how rainy the day, and Gareth would hate to see him lose it.

Gareth went to the door of the barn, reluctant to enter the rain. "A great deal can happen between Vespers and Lauds."

"I never saw the body," Conall reminded Gareth. "Does the timeline Mathonwy report coincide with the condition Erik was in when you examined him?"

"I didn't get enough time with him to call it an examination," Gareth said dryly. "We were waylaid so quickly, but the body was cold and somewhat stiff, which normally would tell me that he'd been dead since yesterday evening, possibly since just after Vespers, but the fact that he'd been submerged in water throws the timeline completely off."

Conall had moved to stand beside Gareth, but now he stepped into the rain and turned to face him in order to look up at the door to the hayloft. Reminding himself that if a man avoided work because it was raining, he would never do any work at all, Gareth moved out of the shelter of the barn's roof to look with Conall. Raindrops pattered on his face to the point that he couldn't just squint against them but had to hold up a hand to block the fall of water from the sky. The hayloft door had been left ajar. "What are you thinking?"

"Nothing definitive, but I was wondering again what Erik was doing here. He had to have come to the barn for a reason that made sense to him, and not because he was planning on being murdered."

Gareth barked a laugh. "I would assume not."

"Which means he came to the barn to meet someone or to rest. He could have preferred not to pay for a room for the night—"

"Or he decided to sleep in the barn because he didn't want anyone to know he was in St. Asaph."

"All indications are that he managed that part just fine." Conall tugged his hood closer around his head.

"It's also within the realm of possibility that he was killed elsewhere and the body was dumped in the trough after the fact," Gareth said. "Admittedly, moving Erik's body requires at least two people, if not four."

"Why would anyone do such a thing? How could it not be better to leave him where he died?" Conall narrowed his eyes at Gareth.

"Because where he died was not a place he could be left, and by its very location would incriminate the killer."

Conall's expression lit. "Such as would be the case if he died in someone's home, perhaps? We could be looking for an unfaithful wife and an angry husband."

Gareth laughed under his breath. "That would have been my first thought if we were discussing Prince Hywel in his younger days, but I don't know Erik well enough to tell how likely such a scenario might be."

"From your description of him, he was a large and powerful man. Many women find that attractive." Conall spoke matter-of-factly, even as he headed for the ladder that would take him up to where the hay was stored. "I'll check the loft. If he was as large as you say, then it would have been all the more difficult for him to remain hidden."

It was just as well Conall had taken that task for himself because Gareth was having trouble raising his left arm. Pulling himself hand over hand up a straight ladder would be uncomfortable. Not for the first time, he regretted his injuries and cursed under his breath at the men who'd caused them. Most of the culprits in Shrewsbury were either dead or awaiting the justice of the sheriff when he returned from serving King Stephen, but the men who'd hurt Gareth here had yet to pay. Gareth wasn't a vengeful man normally, but he wouldn't be sorry to see justice meted out to them too.

With Conall in the loft, Gareth could turn his attention to the tedious task of searching the area around the trough for a sign of whom Erik might have been with the previous night. The only thing Gareth knew for certain out of this entire investigation so far was that Erik didn't commit suicide as Anselm had suggested. It was just too bad that the prior had smallish and undamaged hands, as befitted the prior of a monastery, or Gareth would have been happy to wrap up this investigation today. As it was, Anselm's hands would not fit around Erik's neck, so they must look elsewhere for their killer.

When Gareth stood in the barn's back doorway that led to the paddock, the trough lay to his left. When Erik had been in the trough, his bulk had displaced a significant amount of water, such that once they'd taken him out of it, the trough had been left half full. Now, thanks to the unending rain, it was near to overflowing again.

Gareth's head came up, and he rubbed his chin as he turned in a circle, feeling like he was being watched but unable to pinpoint where the impression was coming from. Neither he nor Conall was quite up for charging off in a random direction to see if he could surprise an observer. And maybe Gareth was wrong anyway, and the watcher was merely a curious cow that had slipped through the gate.

The ground all around the trough was thick with mud, churned by cows' hooves and men's boots. Although Abbot Rhys had tried to preserve the scene before Gareth and Gwen had arrived, the men who'd pulled Erik from the trough had stomped all around the paddock. At the time, they'd had no choice. Gareth hadn't noticed anything useful on the ground or in the trough then—and a more detailed inspection didn't reveal anything of interest now either.

Gareth turned to look up at the hayloft door and projected his voice so Conall could hear him. "Anything up there?"

Conall poked his head out over the lower half of the door, which was latched while the upper half swung free. "Someone has been up here all right. He left muddy footprints."

"Do you have a piece of rope handy? I'd like to know the length of the shoeprint in case we ever see Erik again. If I know how long the prints are, I might be able to match them to his boots and determine if he was up there." Gareth was glad now that Hywel had asked about Conall's investigative experience—or lack thereof. He didn't feel now that he was telling Conall something that he should already know or how to do his job. "We'll test the rope against Mathonwy's feet too, since they could just as easily be his."

Conall grunted his understanding. "I'll see what I can do." He disappeared for a count of ten and then returned to the door. "There's also an indentation in the hay that indicates someone settled down for a time to sleep or to wait."

"So, we might wonder if that man was Erik or if it was the man who killed him, knowing he was coming."

"Or a third man whom one or the other was coming here to meet," Conall said, "or followed them to spy upon them, or one who could have been sleeping in the barn and happened upon their meeting unexpectedly."

Gareth let out an exasperated puff of air. "Exactly. We're speculating with far too little to go on."

Conall nodded. "I'll measure the footprint." He disappeared again.

Gareth paced around the trough, seeing nothing of interest, getting progressively wetter, and thinking that—injury or no injury—he might do well to climb into the loft to see what Conall had found. Then a glint of silver caught his eye, and he frowned.

His first instinct was to pass it off as a few bits of hay, but then he crouched to the ground and brushed aside the clod of dirt that covered the glint. Five silver pennies, each the width of the tip of his pinky finger, lay in a cluster in the mud.

Gareth wasn't surprised they'd missed the coins in the dark last night. As he crouched in the mud and the rain, the question before him was if the pennies belonged to Erik, to the murderer, or to a third person whose identity they'd just fruitlessly speculated upon. Regardless, their loss to their owner would be grievous—unless, of course, he was Erik. The coins might be small and only five, but sixty could buy a man a cow. A typical peasant in Wales might not possess a single coin even once in his entire life, since goods were bought with services rendered, or services rendered were paid for with goods.

Another man might have been tempted to say nothing in hopes of keeping them for himself, but Gareth didn't have a single heartbeat of greed. He'd sinned enough in his life that he wasn't even tempted to add such a gross addition to his collection. With the trust of his lord and a wife who loved him, Gareth was already the richest man in Wales.

8

Hywel

Hywel couldn't help feeling pride at riding towards the encampment at his father's side. He would never, ever get over Rhun's death, but he was growing used to being the *edling,* the son his father trusted and relied upon above all others. He couldn't think of anything that could have pleased him more than arriving at Aber Castle three days ago to find his father not only on his feet, but welcoming him with open arms. When Hywel had left Owain last to ride to Mold Castle, he'd had no expectation that his father would ever be happy to see him again because he could never forgive Hywel for being the son who lived.

"I gather you knew the dead man?"

Hywel shot a startled look at his father. King Owain hardly ever involved himself in Hywel's investigations beyond ordering him to see to them. He didn't want to know, because he understood that Hywel sometimes walked on the darker side of running the kingdom. Owain had certainly kept Rhun from involvement, though Rhun had involved himself anyway, at times without his father's knowledge.

Resigned to having this conversation, even though he would have preferred to keep his father entirely out of his doings—and not remind him of the past, which any discussion of Erik would have to—Hywel gave a slight jerk of his head in assent and took the *crwth* by the fingerboard: "Uncle Cadwaladr used Erik as a spy for a time, and when he abandoned Erik in Ceredigion, I took him on." He braced himself for his father's reaction to what he was going to say next. "This was before we took Mold."

"Before Rhun's death, you mean."

"Yes, Father." Hywel took in a breath. He didn't regret bringing Erik into his service, but he felt in his heart that Rhun wouldn't have done it, or if he had, it would have been for entirely different reasons—because he would have thought it a mercy, rather than because he wanted to use Erik as a weapon. "I sent Erik to Ireland in case Cadwaladr had retreated there again. It is only since we took Mold that we learned that he'd gone to England, but it had already been months, and I had no means to call Erik back. I did not know that Erik had returned to Wales until this morning when he turned up dead."

Hywel's father made a *huh* sound deep in his chest. "I want to know everything you've learned about Cadwaladr's movements since Rhun's death."

Hywel stared at his father, somewhat taken aback. "You do?"

Owain turned on his son. "Of course I do!" Then he calmed, taking a deep breath through his mouth and letting it out his nose as he often did when he knew he needed to rein in his temper. "I feel somehow that this feud with Madog is a distraction from the main issue, which is the whereabouts of my brother and his latest treacherous plot."

Hywel cleared his throat. "May I ask a question? Several actually?"

"You want to know why I haven't deprived Cadwaladr of all of his holdings—why his wife sits as she does at Aberffraw," Owain said, not as a question. "You want to understand why I have acted as I have, knowing full well Cadwaladr's misdeeds."

"Yes," Hywel said. "I want to know that."

"You think that I have behaved unjustly—not only to you, who loved Rhun so well, but to Cadwaladr himself. You know that the manner in which I have punished Cadwaladr up until now is a far cry from what he truly deserves, and that if I allow him to roam free in England while Alice oversees his lands on Anglesey, it sets a poor precedent." Owain laughed harshly. "You believe that the way I forgave him earlier, for the death of King Anarawd in particular, sent him the wrong message. He saw my mercy as weakness and that made him behave worse."

Hywel nodded his head, suddenly feeling far less righteous than he'd felt a moment ago—and maybe a little foolish. He'd questioned his father's sanity and doubted his fitness to lead. But for all that his father had lain abed for the last four months, here he was speaking rationally. In fact, he was speaking like a king.

"You are not wrong, but you know as well as I that running a kingdom means compromising sometimes. Alice's father is dead, but when Cadwaladr married her, he married one of the most sought after women in England, if what a man values in a wife is the power and influence she can bring him."

"Which Cadwaladr does."

"Which Cadwaladr does," Owain agreed. "May I remind you that her uncle is Ranulf, Earl of Chester, who is himself married to Robert of Gloucester's daughter. In addition, Alice's brother is the Earl of Hertford, another uncle is the Earl of Pembroke, and her brother-in-law is the Earl of Lincoln."

"You're telling me that I was mistaken to think that Cadwaladr would hide in Ireland. He'd tried that already. Likely he's hiding in an earl's household." Hywel ground his teeth at the thought of Cadwaladr cowering amongst his Norman relations.

"You're missing my point, son," King Owain said. "I have to assume that Cadwaladr has leagued with Ranulf again or with one of these other barons. He would league with them even if he still held Ceredigion. I am far more concerned that if I were to deprive Cadwaladr of all of his lands, it means I would also deprive Alice, and that is an affront that her powerful family would not ignore. We already know that Ranulf of Chester has spent his entire adult life looking covetously at Wales. He would like nothing more than to use my supposed mistreatment of Cadwaladr—and by extension Alice—as an excuse to launch a war on Wales."

It took no stretch of the imagination at all to contemplate the enormous resources any of these lords could bring to bear on

Gwynedd should they choose to. The fact that only Ranulf had posed a real threat up until now was in large part because all of England was caught up in the war between King Stephen and Empress Maud. At the same time, the war also provided the perfect opportunity to make incursions into Wales while the rest of England was distracted. Ranulf had already done so. Hywel's father was right that these other Normans might need very little prompting to try it too.

Hywel ran his hand through his hair. "I knew this of course. All politics are a family matter, whether here or in England. What is the war in England now but a fight between cousins?"

Owain paused to study his son's face, and his expression was so serious, Hywel feared what was coming ... and for good reason since next his father added, "What's happening in Ceredigion and Deheubarth is a family matter too—one in which the Earl of Pembroke plays a role. My sister married Cadell's father and died defending Aberystwyth. We are bonded not only by blood ties but by blood spilled."

Hywel swallowed hard at the shift in their conversation. Both Cadell, King of Deheubarth and Clare, Earl of Pembroke, coveted Ceredigion, lands Owain had taken from Cadwaladr and given to Hywel. The fact that Cadell's father had controlled Ceredigion before the war there ten years ago put Hywel's rule in a precarious position. Hywel himself had left Aberystwyth at the end of the summer, called by his father to defend eastern Gwynedd from Ranulf of Chester.

But with the events that followed—Rhun's death and the taking of Mold among them—Hywel had not returned to Ceredigion. He'd even moved Mari and his sons north to Dolwyddelan Castle. Because of Rhun's death, Hywel's duties had changed, and he hadn't known how long it would be until he could return.

Unfortunately, such a long absence meant that Hywel had been required to choose a steward to defend his seat at Aberystwyth. After weighing his options carefully, he'd appointed a local nobleman, hoping that this man's promotion would assuage any concerns the populace might have about how much Hywel cared for them. The new steward, Seisyll, was a capable man, but he wasn't Hywel. While the people feared and distrusted northerners, they also would resent being neglected in favor of Hywel's other holdings in Gwynedd.

Hywel's father saw the uncertainty in him and put out a hand. "I am concerned about Ceredigion but not your stewardship of it. If you have neglected the principality, it is because I have been selfish and kept you in the north too long. When this is over, you should go south again. In particular, you should make peace with King Cadell."

"I have already made overtures in that regard, my lord," Hywel said, feeling suddenly as if he needed to speak formally. "We are making plans to—ah—encroach on Wiston Castle."

King Owain released a disdainful laugh. "Walter the Fleming's possession."

The Normans, in their relentless quest to defeat the southern Welsh, had brought in a host of settlers from Flanders, assigning them Welsh lands and dislocating the local people. The lord who ruled the Flemish knew absolutely that these settlers would never side with the native Welsh and, surrounded by strangers as they were, would fight to the death to keep what they'd been given. As a strong fighting force, they had so far been impossible to dislodge.

The conversation about Cadwaladr had taken them nearly to the forward sentries of the encampment, which lay less than a mile to the southeast of the monastery. With Madog of Powys setting up his own encampment in the nearby fields, the men of Gwynedd had decided to keep their distance, lest fighting break out among the common men. If they were going to war, it wouldn't be by accident.

"Now, I have questions for you, which you have very successfully managed to divert me from for almost the whole of this journey." King Owain waggled his finger at his son. "But they will have to wait." Then King Owain turned in the saddle and waved an arm at Taran, his closest friend and the steward of Aber Castle. "I'm not surprised that Madog agreed to this peace conference, since he is clearly in the wrong, but I suspect treachery too. He should never have tried to murder you, and the only reason he did so is because he thought he could get away with it. I want to know why he thought he could before I walk into that chapter house tomorrow."

Taran urged his horse closer. He'd been riding behind the king and to his right during Hywel's conversation with his father, giving them the space and privacy they needed to talk, father to son. That Taran had left Aber testified to the breach that had opened up between Hywel's father and Cristina, Hywel's stepmother, and Hywel wondered again what had finally broken her and the king apart. *That* was a question Hywel didn't yet dare ask of his father.

When Taran came abreast, Owain said, "I will hear what Madog has to say, for Susanna's sake, if for no other reason."

"Yes, my lord," Taran said.

Susanna was Hywel's aunt, his father's sister—and also Madog's wife. Hywel had given Madog the benefit of the doubt too because of her, and it had almost cost him his life. At the same time, it was she who'd saved him at Dinas Bran, so he didn't object to his father's decree.

As they approached the encampment, located in the curve of the river Clwyd to the southeast of St. Asaph, a shout rose up from the watchers, and then Cynan, Hywel's younger brother, came to greet them, buttressed by Cadifor, Hywel's foster father, and two of Cadifor's sons.

"We are prepared, sir," Cynan said without preamble, "ready to march today, if you wish."

"What do the scouts report?" King Owain dropped to the ground in a smooth motion. Hywel had feared that his father had neglected his health in the months since Rhun's death, but now that he was looking at him objectively, his father was slimmer than he had been last autumn and certainly appeared fitter than when Hywel had last seen him.

"King Madog should be here soon, if he isn't already at the monastery." Cynan held the bridle of Hywel's horse, and he dismounted too. "He rides with his *teulu* and a small army, but he has left the bulk of his men at home to defend Powys."

"He really might not want a war today," Hywel said.

Cadifor folded his arms across his chest and contemplated his foster son. "Then he shouldn't have tried to kill you, should he?"

"Madog has always been ready and willing to fight us," Cynan said. "Why sue for peace? It's unprecedented."

Hywel pursed his lips. "We need more information than we have now. It could be that he's feeling pressure from somewhere else that has nothing to do with us. How far have your scouts ranged east into England, Cynan?"

Cynan gave Hywel a blank look before answering, "Not far, my prince. I didn't want Ranulf of Chester to think we were encroaching on his holdings."

Hywel pursed his lips at Cynan's use of his title, but it was how Cynan would have spoken to Rhun at times.

"Has there been some new development in the war between Stephen and Maud?" Taran urged his horse a few steps forward and dismounted too. "Last we heard, King Stephen had engaged Earl Ranulf in the east."

Owain nodded. "I promised King Stephen I would send men to fight against Ranulf, but until now I perceived my obligation to counter Madog as the greater. Perhaps we should be warier about fighting too."

"You may have the right of it, Father," Cynan said. "A messenger arrived today from my brother at Mold informing me that Stephen has released Gilbert de Clare, Earl of Hertford and nephew to Ranulf, whom he was holding hostage to Ranulf's good behavior." He gestured apologetically to the others in case he was telling them something they already knew. "His freedom was predicated on the surrendering of a number of his castles, which Hertford did. But when his other uncle, Gilbert de Clare, Earl of Pembroke, who up until now has been loyal to Stephen, asked that the castles be given to him in trust, Stephen refused. Now both Gilberts have sided with Ranulf against Stephen. The whole of the west now stands for Maud, with the lone exception of Shrewsbury."

Hywel and his father exchanged a significant glance. They'd been speaking about these three Norman earls, close relations of Cadwaladr's wife, Alice, only moments ago.

"If Chester, Hertford, and Pembroke are fighting Stephen, then their territories are fair game to an incursion by Powys," Hywel said. "Madog knows that any war with us isn't going to end well for him. He'd much rather take his chances with an undefended Chester."

"Plus, with Robert's health failing, his son controls more and more of his domains," Cynan said. "We don't know if he will continue Robert's staunch support for Maud beyond Robert's death."

"The son is not the father." King Owain tapped a finger to his lips. "Robert of Gloucester's suffering through Ranulf's many defections may be as great as my own dealings with Cadwaladr."

Nobody had a reply to that observation—all the more because it was true.

"My lord." Cynan bowed deeply to his father. "Your pavilion is prepared and a meal ready."

"Again. You have my thanks." King Owain made a slight motion with his head in Taran's direction. Taran was the one who'd make sure that everything really was prepared for the king's arrival. The steward nodded, understanding that the thanks had been a dismissal. He departed with Cynan and the others, including Cadifor, who shot a look heavy with meaning at Hywel. Cadifor was a warrior and a straightforward thinker. It wasn't that he didn't understand the need to negotiate or the strategy involved, but he didn't like it, and Hywel expected to hear his foster father's objections later. Rather than feeling caught between his two fathers, he felt comforted that both had his best interests at heart, even if their approach to caring for him differed.

Thus, Owain was left alone again with Hywel, and Hywel marveled that his father was taking him into his confidence in this way. It wasn't as if he never had, but for the first time since he'd become a man, Hywel felt like his father was consulting with him, not simply telling him what to do.

"I assume Gareth is the one heading up the inquiry into Erik's demise?" Owain said, coming back around to their first topic of conversation. Hywel was seeing only now that his father rarely forgot anything. Beneath his expansive gestures, his hearty laugh, and his fearsome temper lay the mind that had kept him on the throne of Gwynedd for the last ten years. Except for Cadwaladr, until Rhun's death, no lord had challenged his fitness to stay there. Even more than a war, Hywel hoped this peace conference would show Gwynedd's doubting barons that the Owain they'd followed all this time was back.

"Yes."

King Owain nodded. "A good use of him, since he is injured. I imagine if he didn't have an investigation to lead, he would be wanting to lead your *teulu* in this fight against Madog."

"He most definitely would. In fact, he would see it as his duty, and I would be hard pressed to dissuade him."

"Then it is good that we take the time to watch and wait. Madog isn't going anywhere, and I intend to wrest concessions from him at this conference that will leave no doubt as to who got the better of the negotiations." King Owain gave a sharp nod. "I'm counting on you to stand with me in this."

"Of course, Father. I have no problem biding my time and lulling Madog into a false sense of security."

Owain turned one more time to look at his son. "Do not think that a decision to accept Abbot Rhys's overtures of peace is an indication that I feel Madog's offense against you is unimportant."

"I know that." Hywel canted his head as he studied his father. "I came here with you with fire in my heart against Madog. But perhaps this fight isn't in our best interests any more than it is in Madog's. While revenge would be sweet in the short term, I can see the benefit of watching and waiting for the right moment to strike."

King Owain guffawed. "You are learning, my son." Then he sobered. "And then we *will* strike." Owain clapped one fist into the palm of the other hand. "Never say that Gwynedd doesn't finish what it starts. I swear to you now that one way or another, we will bring Madog to heel. He may not want to fight me, but that does not mean his treachery will go unanswered."

9

Gareth

"**W**hat's your opinion of coincidences?" Conall climbed down the ladder and moved to stand beside Gareth to look down with him at the coins as they lay in the mud. "It seems strangely coincidental that Erik is killed on the very day we arrive at St. Asaph."

Gareth scoffed. "They happen, but I don't trust them."

"Nor do I." Conall gazed around the paddock, his eyes searching. "If I had been more mindful of them in Shrewsbury, I might not have been captured." He glanced at Gareth out of the corner of his eye. "But then, we would not have met, and I am wondering more and more if what we might see as a chance meeting was destined from the start."

Gareth grunted. "It is at times hard to discern the difference between coincidence, chance, and destiny."

Conall turned to look directly at Gareth. "I attribute the fact that I live to your stubborn refusal to accept coincidence. If I haven't thanked you properly for my life, I apologize. Words are inadequate to convey what I owe you."

Gareth made a dismissive motion with his hand, but Conall wasn't done.

"If you need anything of me, you have only to ask."

Gareth swallowed hard, realizing that Conall's reasons for staying in Wales might have more to do with the life debt he felt he owed Gareth than curiosity or possible diplomacy with Gwynedd. In retrospect, that Conall was too injured for a sea journey was a rather feeble excuse for not returning to Ireland. "I understand the debt you feel you owe me," he found himself saying, matching Conall's grave tone, "and I understand why you feel it, but I did my duty. Finding you in that mill *was* coincidental."

"You were at the mill because you believed the villains had made it their hideout."

"True—"

"The debt remains," Conall said. "As you said a moment ago, it is hard to discern at the time when it is destiny sitting on your right shoulder rather than chance."

Gareth held out a hand to Conall and met his eyes. Among the Irish and Welsh, a life debt was never to be taken lightly by either party. Conall might think he owed Gareth his life, and Gareth couldn't deny the truth of it, but saving a man's life incurred a responsibility in the other direction too. A connection had been formed between the two men, and Gareth now had a responsibility for the life Conall led from this point on. All of this Conall knew without either of them needing to articulate it, and he grasped Gareth's forearm and shook.

But then Gareth grinned. "We are both alive, and that's what matters. Work beside me for long, and you may find any debt paid off very quickly."

Conall smiled with his eyes and shook his head. "I'm beginning to understand why that might be. You could no more turn away when you are needed than you could stop breathing."

"I'm thinking I could say the same about you."

Conall opened his mouth, prepared to protest, but Gareth forestalled him with another laugh. He moved his right hand to Conall's left shoulder and shook him a little, careful not to hurt him. "Friends."

Conall canted his head thoughtfully, but he put an even more gentle hand on Gareth's left shoulder. "Friends."

Satisfied that the exchange had cleared the air between them, Gareth released Conall and gestured to the coins. "I don't know about you, but I find it very hard to believe that finding silver coins in the mud near where the body of a servant to a prince of Wales was found is a matter of chance." He finally bent to pluck the coins from the mud. Straightening, he rubbed the dirt off with his thumb and turned one over in order to peer at the faded lettering and image. "This is seventy years old, issued under King William." He held it out to Conall.

Conall gingerly took the coin. "It's a long way from home."

Gareth waggled his head back and forth. "Maybe. Few Welsh kings have issued coins. If a Welshman is to have one, it is likely to be English in origin."

The rain hadn't at all lessened, but the pounding of hooves of a horse ridden hard along the track to the barn could be easily heard, coming from the south, the direction in which the monastery lay. Gareth didn't actually say *what now?* because it seemed a pointless question, and a moment later, a young monk reined in near the fence. "My lords! My lords! I have a summons from the abbot!"

Gareth and Conall exchanged a look—resigned and wary at the same time. The monastery had few riding horses, so even without the monk's urgent words, Gareth would have known that the reason he'd been sent was important. Abbot Rhys wouldn't have known how far his messenger might have to ride before he found them.

"Just tell me." Gareth took the horse's bridle to hold him steady and looked up at the monk, who was breathing hard with excitement and the effort of his ride.

"Another dead man." The monk put his hand to his heart. "He was found in a field to the north of here. The abbot is already on his way, and he asked that you meet him there."

"We will follow you," Gareth said.

With a whistle, Gareth rounded up Llelo and Dai, who were already on their way to him, having heard the horse's hooves too. It seemed pointless to leave the boys on guard at an empty barn, and their purpose was to watch Gareth's and Conall's backs, not the murder site. As befitting the sons of Hywel's captain of the guard, Llelo and Dai had their own mounts and, in short order, they all cantered after the young monk.

The spot where the body had been found was a mile and a half from the barn and, as promised, Abbot Rhys was already there when they arrived. Neither Lwc nor Anselm was beside him: Lwc might still be helping Gwen question the monks, and the position of the sun indicated that mid-afternoon prayers might have started. As with dawn prayers, Anselm would be needed to lead them.

Two oxen and a plow were stopped ten yards from where Abbot Rhys was standing, having curved from the straight path they'd been laying. It seemed the monk who tended this field had been going over the ground for planting when he'd come upon the body lying in the dirt on the edge of the field.

Their small party reined in and dismounted near the oxen. With a jerk of his head, Gareth indicated that Llelo and Dai should make a circuit of the area, as they had at the barn. Then he and Conall walked to where Rhys waited for them next to the body, which was wrapped in a rough sheet. The dirt was loose from the plowing, but if the men who'd left the body had tried to bury it, their attempts had been half-hearted at best. More likely, they'd simply dumped it. Rhys flicked out a hand indicating that the monk who'd escorted Gareth and Conall should move back. He obeyed with alacrity.

"The plowman saw the body when he turned at the corner of the field." Rhys bent to the wrappings and flicked back the sheet where it covered the dead man's face.

Gareth let out a burst of air, unable to contain his disbelief. "Erik!"

"Indeed." Rhys's tone was as dry as a king's wine.

Conall went into a crouch beside Erik, studying the dead man's face.

Gareth stepped closer too, remembering that Conall hadn't been in attendance that morning when they'd been called to the barn the first time. "Have you ever seen him before?"

"No, I don't believe so. He may have come to Ireland, but not to a place where I was. Then again, he may have been there most of the time I was here." Somewhat absently, Conall lifted up the edge of the sheet, but then he drew in a sharp breath and recoiled. Dropping the sheet, he looked up at Abbot Rhys. "What madness is this?"

"Madness is right," Rhys said. Some of the onlookers had stepped closer to better hear the conversation, and Rhys motioned with his hand as he'd done to the messenger to shoo them away. Once his underlings obeyed, Rhys gestured Gareth closer and pulled back the cloth, exposing Erik's torso.

Gareth drew back with a gasp. He wasn't often shocked, but what had been done to Erik's midsection was unsettling to say the least. The men who'd stolen him had expanded on the stab wound Gareth had seen, cut him down the middle, pulled back the outer layers of skin and muscle, and sliced into his stomach and intestines.

Conall cleared his throat. "I gather he didn't look like this the last time you saw him?"

"No," Rhys said curtly.

Conall was still crouched beside the body. After collecting himself, Gareth knelt to get a closer look, even though that was the last thing he wanted to do. "It's a desecration, but at least he didn't suffer." The wounds were ragged, but since Erik had already been dead, they hadn't bled. It was still raining too, and with the dampness all around—on the trees, the ground, and the grass that grew against the stones of the field—whatever smell Erik was putting out was minimal.

Gareth grimaced. "I confess in all my years of service to my prince, I have never seen anything like this before." He rose to his feet, sickened by what had been done to Erik. Murder was one thing, but being hacked apart was another. It wasn't as if Gareth didn't have experience with the criminal mind, but the man who did this was as cold and foreign to Gareth as any villain he'd ever encountered.

Conall took in a careful breath. "I have."

"I have also." Abbot Rhys turned away from the body to stare east. "In the course of my duties in past days, I came upon a courier from Empress Maud, who'd been captured by the enemy. He'd swallowed the Empress's ring rather than allow it to be taken from him. They cut it out of him. Unlike Erik, they hadn't bothered with killing him first. He suffered." Rhys cleared his throat, disturbed by the memory.

"I have seen something similar, though in Ireland." Conall looked at Gareth. "I didn't know Erik nor his duties for Prince Hywel, but—"

Gareth cut Conall off. He wasn't angry at Conall but at the situation, which had the hairs on the back of his neck standing straight up, and his stomach was churning worse than Gwen's in the morning. "Erik would have known to swallow evidence that he worked for Prince Hywel if he was hard pressed. He was expert at hiding his identity and allegiance, though I don't know if Prince Hywel gave him a token as proof that he was under his command."

"You might ask the prince, when next you see him," Conall said. "It would be unfortunate if his token has fallen into the hands of evildoers. They could do great harm in the prince's name."

Gareth himself had been impersonated at the behest of Prince Cadwaladr last autumn, though the ruse had been far more elaborate, in that the man had been made to look like Gareth. Many men would pay a significant sum to acquire a ring or signet of an enemy lord. It was why such tokens were guarded closely. A man with the seal of the king spoke for the king.

Gareth frowned at the abbot, who was still looking away. "I can tell there's something else. What is it?"

Rhys turned back, his lips pressed together, and then his eyes skated past Gareth and went straight to Conall. "I know of two other reasons for a man to be so mutilated."

Conall had risen to his feet by now, and the way he was looking intently at Rhys had Gareth feeling like he was missing something. Then, when Rhys didn't continue speaking, Conall bobbed his head. "I have encountered such blasphemy in Ireland, but those monsters eviscerate animals not—"

Gareth found his head swiveling from Conall to Rhys and back again. "What are you two talking about?"

"For one, pagans." Conall spat on the ground. "Those who worship the old gods split open an animal and use his entrails to predict the future." He pointed with his chin to Rhys. "I've never seen it done to a man before, though."

"Sacrilege is everywhere," Rhys said, "especially in times such as these when a man feels uncertain in his own home and the four horsemen of the apocalypse ride unchecked. The war in England has unleashed the devil in many men's hearts."

Gareth had no patience for this kind of talk, especially coming from two otherwise reasonable men. "Someone murdered Erik, stole him from us, cut him open, and then dumped him here. Why they did any of that remains a mystery, but it was a human hand that held the knife—and that is the man I will apprehend."

Rhys's expression cleared. "If any of the good people of St. Asaph were involved in something so sinister, I would know of it."

"Of course you would," Gareth said. "Erik wasn't a druid. He didn't care for rituals, satanic or otherwise. He was a spy for Prince Hywel and was killed because of it. Our task is to find out who—and then why. The souls of the men responsible I leave to you."

Rhys nodded jerkily at Gareth. "Of course. You are right."

Conall gave a low laugh. "Perhaps some of the Devil's Weed our captors gave me has addled my mind."

"You see clearly enough most times." Gareth was disturbed by the condition of Erik's body, but even more so at how much the sight of it had shaken his friends. He narrowed his eyes at Rhys. "You said *two reasons*. What is the second?"

"Certain men are fascinated by the human form. Men have been known to dig up the newly dead in order to cut into their bodies. They say the purpose is to better understand what goes on inside, leading to an improved ability to heal the sick." Rhys pursed his lips, just marginally less disapproving than he'd been when they'd discussed pagans.

For Gareth's part, he could understand the quest for knowledge, and he knew something of the innards of men because he'd fought in wars and tried to save the lives of companions on the field of battle. He himself wouldn't be opposed to knowing more about how the body worked and could see its use in healing and in his investigations. Given the gruesome state of Erik's body, however, he wasn't going to say as much to Rhys, who, for all his worldly ways, was still a churchman and would not want to see anyone's body so defiled.

They'd fallen down the trapdoor of speculation again, and it was time to get on with the real business of investigating murder. He pulled the coins from his purse and showed them to Rhys. "We found these in your paddock. I think they give us a far better and more mundane motivation for Erik's death: greed."

Rhys accepted the coins, eyebrows raised. "Five silver pennies? The monastery keeps a bag of coins in our treasury—" He broke off, his face paling and his mind going to a place Gareth's hadn't yet traveled. "If these came from our—" He spun on one heel and pointed to one of the other brothers who'd been lurking twenty feet away. "Brother Fidelus, I need you!"

The monk hastened forward, and Rhys spoke to him in succinct sentences, asking him to take another brother and the horse and return to the monastery posthaste. If the coins had come from the treasury, it was already robbed, but if the treasury was unlocked, someone needed to stand in front of it. Anything else would be a gross neglect of duty. At the same time, Gareth's thoughts went again to Conall's supposition that Erik could have been killed for Hywel's ring. The coins could have been offered in payment, and when Erik spurned them, he was killed instead.

Rhys held out the coins to Gareth.

"What if they're yours?" Gareth asked.

"Keep them until I'm sure," Rhys said.

Conall tipped his head towards the body. "Shall we escort Erik together?"

"Likely he's safe from predation now," Gareth said, "but it's the least he deserves."

10

Gwen

"Gwen! My goodness, I can't believe it's you!"

At the sight of Saran, her long ago friend and mentor, coming towards her out of the gloomy late afternoon, Gwen stopped dead in the middle of the monastery courtyard. She'd known Saran at Carreg Cennan, in the years after Gwen had lost Gareth while her family had been wandering the roads of Wales, singing for their supper.

"What are you doing here?" Gwen hastened forward and wrapped her arms around Saran, finding tears of happiness pricking at the corners of her eyes. She had often thought about Saran over the years, wondering how she was faring, but Carreg Cennan was on the other end of Wales, and Gwen had never gone back. "You're walking into the middle of a war, you know."

"I understood that this one might be averted, but war is why I'm here, of course," Saran said.

Gwen took a step back. "What do you mean?"

"Deheubarth has descended into turmoil, with King Cadell and the Normans at each other's throats. Carreg Cennan has been caught in the middle of the fighting, and because of it, I thought this would be a fine time to visit my sister in Corwen. But the farther north I came, the worse the news was. I'm sorry to hear that Powys and Gwynedd are at each other's throats as well."

In her early fifties, Saran was one of those women who, after she reached a certain age, never seemed to grow older. Admittedly, her hair had more gray in it than when Gwen had known her in the south, and perhaps her face and body were somewhat rounder, but her smile was the same, and her brown eyes gazed at Gwen with the same knowledge and wisdom that had prompted Gwen to make changes in her own life eight years ago.

Gwen pulled her friend into another hug. "St. Asaph is not Corwen, Saran."

"I know, but when I arrived at Corwen, my sister and her son were not there. The villagers told me that Rhodri had come north to fight for Gwynedd, and Derwena had gone after him. Rhodri intended to join King Owain's forces, and she thought to cook and clean for him and those from Corwen who went with him."

Gwen frowned. "Truly, I have encountered no women here at all other than me. The guesthouse was emptied yesterday in preparation for the arrival of King Owain's retinue. Have you checked for her at the encampment?"

"Not yet."

Gwen relaxed a little. "That's a much more likely place to find them, but I'll keep a lookout for them for you. What do they look like?" Not for the first time, Gwen wished she had Gareth's skill with a piece of charcoal.

"Derwena looks like me, so for you she might be hard to miss! Rhodri is tall and gangly—taller than any man I know, with brown hair and eyes."

"And you're sure they came all the way to St. Asaph? Perhaps they stopped at Denbigh."

"I passed through there on the way here. While one man remembered Rhodri, nobody remembers seeing Derwena at all."

To Gwen, Saran was completely memorable, but Gwen could see why—to someone who didn't know her—she would be appear to be just another middle-aged woman. They wouldn't know to look for the sharp mind beneath her rounded shoulders and pleasant demeanor, and if Derwena looked just like Saran, perhaps the same could be said of her.

While Gwen had been talking to Saran, Tangwen had been tucked in Gwen's skirts, half-hiding from the stranger, and now she patted Gwen's belly, asking to be picked up. The personality of a two-year-old was ever changing, and this shyness was a new thing for the little girl, developing in the aftermath of Shrewsbury. Gwen had tried very hard to keep Tangwen out of what had gone on there, but children were perceptive in ways that adults didn't always credit, and Gwen felt that Tangwen must have picked up on the fact that her mother and father had been in danger.

Regardless of the reason, since then, Tangwen balked whenever Gwen suggested that someone else look after her. Gwen had gotten away with a lengthy absence today, first because

Tangwen was asleep and then because Tangwen adored Gwalchmai and had been willing to play with him for most of the afternoon. Gwen had also allowed them out into the monastery gardens to stomp in puddles and thoroughly soak themselves. But Gwalchmai shouldn't have to be burdened with his niece all day when he had tasks of his own to perform. He and Gwen's father would be singing at the onset of the peace conference tomorrow, and they needed to prepare.

Rather than fight Tangwen's need, Gwen had resolved to bring her everywhere, in the hope that the constant reassurance would eventually convince Tangwen that she could be left. It hadn't happened yet, however, so Gwen bent to her daughter and swung her onto her left hip.

"And who is this?" Saran reached out a hand and caught the little girl's finger.

A month ago, Tangwen would have loudly proclaimed her identity, but today she turned away and pressed her face into Gwen's upper arm, so Gwen answered for her. "Tangwen." Gwen couldn't stop the grin that blossomed on her face. "I have another on the way too. Saran, I married Gareth."

For a moment Saran looked at Gwen open-mouthed, and then she laughed with Gwen. "Does he serve King Owain?"

"He is the captain of Prince Hywel's *teulu*," Gwen said.

Saran pressed her lips together, unsuccessfully suppressing a satisfied smile, as if she'd had something to do with the match and with Gareth's success. "He landed on his feet, then."

"That's exactly what my father said to him when they met again a few years ago," Gwen said.

Saran raised her eyebrows. "Meilyr is here?"

"Yes, and Gwalchmai too, now a man in his own right. Meilyr is King Owain's court bard."

"So he really did go back to the king." Saran made a *heh* sound. "We'd heard that he'd finally swallowed his pride and apologized, but I didn't necessarily believe it."

Gwen didn't think Meilyr would be terribly fond of that description of the course of events that had transpired between him and King Owain. But even if unflattering, it wasn't far off from the truth. Still, in the end both men had managed to come to terms to their mutual satisfaction and with their pride intact—in part because Meilyr *was* an accomplished bard and Gwalchmai might well prove to be better. Since that day, her father had learned to say not only *I'm sorry* but also *I love you.*

As if he was aware he was being discussed, Meilyr chose that moment to leave the guesthouse, heading across the courtyard towards the stable with purposeful steps. But at the sight of Gwen with Tangwen in her arms, he changed direction and strode towards them. He had a pipe-horn in his hand and was frowning at it more than truly looking at them. "Gwen, when is Gareth to return—" he broke off, gaping at Saran, having not recognized her until he actually stopped in front of her.

"Hello, Meilyr," Saran said. "You look well."

Meilyr recovered his voice. "What are you doing here?"

"I am looking for my sister and nephew."

"Derwena and Rhodri are here?"

"I have hope they might be in Gwynedd's encampment." Saran lifted her chin to indicate Gwen. "From what Gwen said, that is where the bulk of King Owain's men have gathered."

"Yes, it is." Meilyr cocked his head. "Perhaps I can escort you? I was just heading there myself." He looked at Gwen. "Llelo mentioned hearing one of the soldiers singing and believes he's been trained as a bard. I must find him."

Gwen smiled, but her father had already stuck out his elbow to Saran. "Shall we?"

"We shall." Saran took Meilyr's arm and smiled over her shoulder at Gwen.

Gwen shook her head, laughing as she watched them walk away. The pair were similar in age, and she had no doubt that by the time her father returned to the monastery, Saran would have elicited everything that could be gotten out of him regarding what they'd been doing since they left Carreg Cennan. Her father had always been gruff, but the very fact that he had offered Saran his arm indicated that his desire to escort her was genuine. In his old age, her father liked intelligent women, ones who didn't fuss and could be relied upon in a crisis. Saran was all of those things.

Gwen's duties at the moment were far more prosaic and had nothing to do with the investigation. Tangwen needed to be fed, never mind that dinner would be served in another hour. But the pair had just sat down at the table in the guesthouse dining room, having found the monk in the kitchen obliging to Tangwen's needs, when Gareth entered the room, Conall in tow.

"Erik's body has been returned to us."

Gwen scooted back her bench, intending to rise, but Gareth put a heavy hand on her shoulder.

"Don't. This is one body I'm not going to let you see." He pulled out the other end of the bench and sat.

"Why would that be?" Gwen glanced up at Conall, but he was giving nothing away. Instead, he gave her a quick bow and departed, his boots echoing loudly on the floorboards on the way to the door of the guesthouse, a clear indication that he didn't want to be part of this conversation if he could help it.

Gwen watched him go, her eyes narrowing, and then she returned her gaze to her husband's face. With Tangwen eating happily at the table, the words they could use to describe what had passed in the hours since they'd seen each other were going to be limited. In addition, Gwalchmai had disappeared, so she couldn't call upon him to mind his niece, and Gwen hadn't seen Evan since they'd spoken under the gatehouse.

Gareth pursed his lips, and she could see him casting around in his mind for the right way to phrase what he wanted to say. "Erik is not in a condition that I want you to see. The people who took him from me—" his eyes skated to Tangwen and then back to Gwen's face, "—cut him open."

That was not what Gwen had been expecting to hear. She raised her eyebrows, but didn't repeat the words as might have been her natural response if Tangwen had not been present. "Why would they do that?"

"Our working theory is that they were looking for a token Prince Hywel might have given to him. As you saw at the barn, they'd already taken all of Erik's possessions away with them, but it could be that when the item they were looking for wasn't on his body—" again the glance at Tangwen, whose eyes were fixed on her father's face. Gareth smiled and bent forward to chuck her under the chin. "Is that good, *cariad*?"

Tangwen nodded.

Gwen smiled at her daughter and spoke to Gareth out of the side of her mouth. "It occurred to them only after they'd left him at the barn that he might have swallowed it? Have you spoken with Hywel? Did he give Erik a signet or another token?

Gareth pulled Tangwen into his lap. "I don't know yet. He hasn't returned from the encampment. I did, however, find five silver coins near the water trough." Gareth kissed the side of his daughter's head. "What did you find?"

"Puddles," Tangwen said, thinking he was speaking to her.

Gareth's eyes widened dramatically. "Did you stomp in them?"

"Gwalchmai and I did. We got wet."

Gareth sat Tangwen at her place again and then motioned with his head to Gwen that they might confer a few feet away. One eye on Tangwen in case she protested her mother's departure, even if it was only a few feet, Gwen stood.

Gareth put his arm around her shoulders and kissed her temple as he'd kissed Tangwen's. "Anything from your end?"

"A monk, Brother Deiniol, who claims that his monastery was sacked by men wearing Gwynedd's colors, has arrived from Wrexham."

"What?" Gareth gawked at her. "You're not serious?"

"I am perfectly serious, or at least he is. He arrived during mid-afternoon prayers, and Anselm took him away to wait for Abbot Rhys's return."

Gareth paced around the small space between the dining room table and the door. "It can't have been our men."

"Of course it wasn't, but I'm inclined to believe Deiniol that they wore Gwynedd's colors."

Gareth stopped his pacing. "This is a complication we didn't need today. The peace conference begins tomorrow morning. How will Madog feel to learn that men from Gwynedd raided a monastery in his kingdom?"

"Since he is clearly in the wrong regarding Prince Hywel, it will give his own grievances some weight." Gwen wrinkled her nose "I have more news, and maybe you'll like this better: Deiniol met Erik on the road."

Gareth reared back. "Where?"

"In a village north of Llangollen. Erik had a companion with him, a tall lanky fellow." As she spoke, Gwen frowned, because the description of Erik's friend wasn't far off from the way Saran had described Rhodri, and she said as much to Gareth.

Gareth made a *huh* sound under his breath. "That ruins our theory that Erik had just returned from Ireland, since he was coming to St. Asaph from the wrong direction." He shook his head.

"We need to find this friend—and anyone else who might have seen them together. I need to question that monk."

"He's not going to like that. You should have seen the look on his face when Evan was talking to him. It was all he could do to avert his eyes from Evan's surcoat."

A boot scraped on the threshold. Conall was back. "Perhaps this Rhodri fellow has unusually large hands and a missing finger, and he was the one who killed Erik." Conall shot a glance at Gwen and put up a hand, asking her pardon for speaking about murder when Tangwen was present. "A falling out between friends, if you will."

Gwen glanced at her daughter, who fortunately was intent on her slice of apple. Gwen lifted one shoulder in unspoken acceptance of his apology. She hoped, too, that Conall wasn't right about Rhodri, for to learn that her nephew was a murderer would break Saran's heart.

Conall gestured back the way he'd come. "Abbot Rhys would speak to us now." He looked at Gwen. "Including you, if you will come."

11

Gareth

Since Gwen had resolved not to leave Tangwen behind if she could help it, and since Rhys had asked for Gwen specifically, Gareth carried his daughter into Rhys's office, with the caveat that Gwen would take her away if the conversation involved too much of what she shouldn't hear. Abbot Rhys's eyes lit at the sight of the little girl, however, and in a moment Tangwen was playing at Gareth's feet with a set of wooden blocks that Rhys had pulled out of a chest in the corner. The man had hidden depths—and Gareth had thought he was deep before.

A second monk, one Gareth hadn't yet met, stood off to one side by the window. A good ten years older than Gareth, he was long and lean and far fitter-looking than most men, regardless of their age, without the round belly that often afflicted older men. Gareth didn't have to work hard to guess his identity: this was Deiniol, the stranger, whom Gwen had already encountered and who had arrived at the monastery earlier that day.

While Gareth and Gwen took seats near Rhys's desk, Conall crossed his arms and leaned a shoulder against the inner wall. Gareth could just see him out of the corner of his eye, which Conall had probably intended. The man calculated every angle, and he would know that Gareth would feel uncomfortable having someone standing behind him, even if he was a friend. Gareth also suspected that Conall wasn't standing to be intimidating, but to disguise the fact that his ribs hurt more when he sat than when he stood.

For Gareth's part, he was afraid that if he sat, he might never rise again, but he sat anyway. He let out an involuntary sigh at the pain in his shoulder and stretched out his legs in front of him.

Rhys politely ignored Gareth's discomfort and gestured to the newcomer. "I have asked Brother Deiniol to join us. As I'm sure you've heard by now, he met Erik on the road, and I'm hoping that he has some insight into our larger problem."

Gareth focused on the abbot, his brow furrowing. "We have a larger problem?"

Rhys folded his hands on the desk in front of him. "His monastery was sacked by men wearing Gwynedd's colors."

"They *were* men of Gwynedd." Deiniol's hands were tucked into the sleeves of his robe, the right in his left and vice versa, a familiar stance among monks, and his chin stuck out obstinately.

Gareth looked at him for a moment and then returned his attention to Rhys, who gazed back at Gareth with an unreadable expression. At another time, Deiniol's certainty might have been somewhat amusing, but Rhys was the one who had called the peace conference between Powys and Gwynedd. Deiniol was a man of Powys, and Wrexham monastery was located in Powys. Deiniol's assertion that Gwynedd was responsible for the banditry had now put Rhys in an awkward position. If he outright denied the possibility of Gwynedd's involvement, Madog—when he found out about the theft, which he would soon if he didn't know already—would see any assumption of Gwynedd's innocence as taking sides.

That meant the necessary denial was up to Gareth. "Men of Gwynedd didn't do this—or at least not any in the king's service."

"How do you know?" Deiniol said.

"I am the captain of Prince Hywel's *teulu*, so I know my own men, and King Owain's men have been preoccupied either with the recent conquest of Mold Castle or in preparation for the coming war against Powys."

"You're telling me that you can account for the movements of every man in the royal guard over the last few weeks?" Deiniol said.

Gareth's jaw clenched. *He* couldn't. He'd spent the last few weeks either in Shrewsbury or traveling between Aber and Shrewsbury with a small complement of men. He'd left Prince Hywel's *teulu* in the charge of staunch companions, however, Evan among them, and their whereabouts could be accounted for. "Perhaps not every man, but I can tell you that no large company has been absent long enough to ride to Wrexham, rob your monastery, and return."

Deiniol let out a *humph* and then turned to Abbot Rhys. "I stand by what I saw."

Rhys put out a calming hand. "I believe you."

Gareth decided that he might as well gather what information he could from Deiniol while he was here, which was surely what Rhys had intended in bringing them all together. "Your monastery employed no soldiers to protect you?"

"The favor of King Madog of Powys has always been sufficient, but he marches for war. Any man who patrolled the roads has been withdrawn from his duty. Madog looks to England, and it is because of that war that our monastery was vulnerable to a raid from Gwynedd."

Gareth didn't rise to the bait and deny the accusation again. He realized by now that it would do no good. Deiniol was fixed in his opinion, and Gareth could hardly blame him. If his home was attacked by men wearing Chester's colors, it would take a great deal to convince him that he was being deliberately deceived. Though it was considered unchivalrous, this would hardly be the first time that men used the surcoats of an enemy lord to disguise their identity. That didn't mean, however, that the disguise wasn't effective.

Deiniol frowned in concentration. "While travelers do bring news from England and Wales, and of course we are well acquainted with the war between Stephen and Maud, it is the nature of our order to be a retreat from the world, to be of it but not in it." He paused to check the comprehension of his audience. Nobody was having any trouble understanding what he meant.

He continued, "We see how the war has unleashed the devil in men, who have known nothing but violence for ten years now. With the failing health of Robert of Gloucester, Maud's influence in the west lessens, and that lack has spurred King Stephen to press the advantage wherever he can, most recently against Chester. That has put our monastery in the crossroads between the Earl of Chester, who supports Maud, and the Earl of Ludlow, who supports Stephen, but as they are fighting farther to the east, it leaves the border with Wales unprotected."

At the general nods all around, Deiniol added, "I know as much as I do because my abbot told me of it before sending me on my way."

"Abbot Tudur is an old friend," Rhys said for the benefit of Gareth and Gwen. "The brothers have been scattered to several monasteries, but a party of twenty are on their way here." Rhys sent a wry smile in Gareth's direction. "A handful intended to ask for sanctuary in Shrewsbury."

"I can accept that as a coincidence," Gareth said.

Deiniol made a helpless gesture with one hand. "How this may change with the recent defection from Stephen of the Earls of Hertford and Pembroke, I don't know. I know only that my abbot entrusted me with the task of finding a home for my brothers."

Abbot Rhys met Gareth's gaze. "Lawless men are free to roam wild when kings and barons are distracted by a quest for power."

"Thus we found in Shrewsbury," Conall said.

"We don't—" Gwen looked from one man to another and tried again, "—we aren't thinking that what happened in Shrewsbury is happening here, are we?"

Gareth put out a hand to reassure her. "Perhaps not slavery. No. But organized thievery? I would believe that."

"The men who sacked our monastery were organized," Deiniol said. "They came in broad daylight when we were at our prayers and most of the buildings were unoccupied. Before we knew it, they'd barricaded us inside the church. They gave us the opportunity to flee only when they realized most everything of value was in the church."

Gareth drew in a long breath through his nose. "I suspect you are less than pleased to have found sanctuary in Gwynedd, but I hope you can see it now as a blessing. No group of armed men, no matter how well organized, no matter what their allegiance, would dare attack St. Kentigern's while we are here."

"But you *are* men of Gwynedd," Deiniol said. "King Owain could simply order his men to take what is here."

Gareth's chin firmed. "It is just barely possible that men of Gwynedd did, in fact, destroy your monastery, but they did not do so on the orders of King Owain. When you speak of the king, you will do so with respect."

Deiniol swallowed hard.

Gareth realized that as he'd spoken, he'd leaned forward in a way that Deiniol might perceive as menacing. Gingerly, he leaned back before Abbot Rhys had to tell him to calm down.

Gwen shot him a worried look before adding, "Prince Hywel and King Owain themselves, when they hear of these events, will insist that the perpetrators be brought to justice, no matter whom they serve."

Rhys looked directly at Gareth. "We need to know if there is a link between what happened in Wrexham—and what is happening around it—" he gave special emphasis to these words with a flick of his eyes in Deiniol's direction, "—and Erik's death."

Deiniol started at that and turned to Gwen. "My lady, when you showed me the picture, you didn't tell me the man was dead!"

Gwen gave him a small smile. "I know. That you didn't know until now implies that you didn't kill him."

Deiniol's jaw dropped. "Well, of course—"

At a motion from Rhys, he stopped talking. "You may leave us now, Deiniol. If Gareth has more questions about what happened to your brothers, I hope that you will accommodate him by answering as completely and truthfully as possible."

"Of course." Deiniol bobbed his head in Gareth's direction. "I can say, my lord, that I do not believe that you were among the culprits."

That Gareth could be so accused at all rankled him, and he struggled to be gracious. He did manage to say, "I'm sorry for what happened to you and your brothers. I assure you that if men of Gwynedd are responsible, I will do everything in my power to find them and see that not only are they punished, but that the valuables taken from Wrexham are returned."

"Thank you." Deiniol left the room.

Once the door closed behind him, Rhys leaned forward, implying that now that Deiniol was gone, the real discussion could begin. "I did an accounting of our treasury. It is possible that the coins you found belong to this monastery. My records indicate that we are missing six silver coins, plus three other items: two gold crosses and a ring. I wouldn't have known to look closely—or thought to do so until the next accounting—had you not found the coins, since on the surface nothing has been disturbed." He shrugged in a somewhat self-deprecating way. "Perhaps I am even mistaken that we are missing anything."

Gareth scoffed. "If the monastery were run by anyone but you, I might consider the possibility. Tell me the truth—are you mistaken?"

Rhys took in a breath, and Gareth sensed his hesitation was less because he was searching for patience but that he was trying to control anger. "No. Someone has been in the treasury."

In Wales, the wealth of a monastery was in its sheep, cattle, and land, not in gold or silver. At times, however, wealthy barons endowed the monastery with their temporal goods. They might donate money, jewelry, candlesticks, chalices, or other movable items. They did so out of Christian devotion, in an effort to find absolution for a long life poorly lived, or simply because they had no suitable heir to whom to bequeath their wealth and didn't want it to go either to a distant relative they didn't know or simply revert to the king.

"What I don't like," Gareth said, "is that Deiniol's monastery and yours have lost wealth—his more than yours obviously."

Gwen was tapping a finger to her lips as she thought. "Deiniol's monastery was robbed and burned outright."

"My immediate thought is to agree that these are two very different circumstances," Rhys said, "and that they could not possibly be perpetrated by the same men."

Conall, who had so far remained completely silent, spoke for the first time. "That's the kind of coincidence we don't like."

Rhys nodded. "I agree, thus the notion that what is happening here is part of a larger tapestry."

"How long has it been since you did an accounting of the treasury?" Gareth said.

"Five days. I reconcile the ledger with all the items once a month, though the schedule isn't necessarily that rigidly regular. It is an unseemly task for a monk, but somebody has to do it."

"Were you alone?" Gwen said.

There was a pause. And when Rhys didn't answer immediately, Gareth leaned forward, gazing at him intently. "Father?"

Rhys made a motion with his head implying that he didn't want to say, but knew that he must. "It is always the abbot and the prior who do the accounting, along with a third monk, chosen at random. In keeping with the traditions established by my predecessor, I never choose the same man twice."

Gareth's eyes narrowed as he thought. "So the men involved were you, Prior Anselm, even though he must have just arrived—"

"He'd been here only two days," Rhys said.

"And a third man. Who?" Gareth said.

Rhys scratched the top of his head, clearly still reluctant to say, but as Gwen, Gareth, and Conall looked at him, he gave a sharp nod. "Brother Mathonwy, the milkman."

Gareth rocked back in his chair. "That changes everything."

Rhys sighed. "You'll have to talk to him again."

Gareth looked over at Conall, asking with his eyes if Conall was ready for another visit to the barn. The Irishman nodded and then looked at Rhys. "Does anyone else know about the missing items?"

"Since I sent Brother Fidelus back earlier in such haste, by now most of the monastery will know something is amiss," Rhys said. "They don't know exactly what is wrong, however."

"Not even Prior Anselm?" Gwen said.

Rhys shook his head. "But with Erik's death, the theft and rediscovery of his body, and the condition in which it was found, rumors are swirling around the monastery. In fact—" he rose to his feet, "Vespers is upon us and I must see to my flock. Many of them have spent their entire lives in the monastery and do not have the emotional ballast to accommodate these events."

A knock came at the door, and at Rhys's call of "Come!" Brother Lwc opened it and poked in his head. His eyes were wide, excited by the news he had to share. "Father Abbot. King Madog of Powys has come."

12

Hywel

Hywel had thought he'd understood how angry, hurt, and fearful Gwen had been after his uncle had abducted her to Ireland. Now, as he stood beside Gareth and stared down from the top of the gatehouse tower upon the King of Powys in the monastery courtyard, his stomach tied in knots, he realized that he hadn't understood at all. Not really.

This man tried to kill me! Hywel had faced death in the past. He'd fought in many battles, and he and his uncle, Cadwaladr, hated each other with a passion that was hard to measure. But this betrayal was unlike those others. Madog had violated the sacred oath of hospitality that was the backbone of every interaction between Welshmen.

Thankfully, simply having that thought pass through his head was enough to put Hywel's mind to work again. The fact that Madog could betray not only his alliance with Gwynedd but the very basis of Welsh society suggested that Madog had been spending so much time with Normans of late that he had forgotten who he was.

Hywel's eyes narrowed as he studied his uncle. The King of Powys was of middle height with the growing girth of middle age. He had neither mustache nor beard and wore his dark but graying curly hair somewhat long and loose. He had dressed as the king he was in a fur-lined cloak and highly polished knee-high boots, but he also wore the full regalia of a Powysian knight: armor, sword, and all.

"How am I to dine at the same table as Madog? How are Father and I to sit across from him tomorrow at the conference?"

"The same way men in your position always have," Gareth said, "with grace, and because you have to."

"I hate him. I almost hate him more than Cadwaladr, though that's probably going too far."

"I know."

As Madog dismounted in the courtyard of the monastery, he was greeted by Abbot Rhys. Unfortunately, seeing as how he was only allowed to watch the formalities from the top of the gatehouse, Hywel was too far away to hear what was being said. Hywel's father had delayed returning to the monastery so he wouldn't be tempted to do exactly what Hywel was doing. In fact, his father had chosen to remove himself from St. Kentigern's guesthouse rather than sleep in the same building as Madog, should the Powysian king choose to stay at the monastery. As loath as Hywel was to sleep anywhere near Madog ever again, he had decided to stay. It was an act of defiance and a refusal to be intimidated.

Hywel's Aunt Susanna had ridden with Madog, along with their son, Llywelyn, whom Hywel had bested in his escape from Dinas Bran. Small, blonde, and slender, Susanna was a few years younger than her husband. Without her help, Hywel could not have escaped from Dinas Bran, but the solicitous way Madog helped her from her horse implied that he didn't know the role she had played. She was in an impossible position—torn between loyalty to her brother, the King of Gwynedd, and her husband, the King of Powys. Hywel wondered if the true hand behind the peace conference was actually hers more than Abbot Rhys's.

He shook his head. "How does he do it?"

"Who?"

"Abbot Rhys. He's speaking to Madog as if he trusts him and his motives. It's exactly the same way he spoke to my father this morning."

"Rhys is one of those men with the ability to perfectly understand another's position and convey it without any of the hearers being aware that he doesn't share that opinion," Gareth said. "It isn't that he doesn't have one, but his purpose here is to come to a peaceful solution to the current dispute between Gwynedd and Powys—even if only for a time. To do that, he has to be trusted by both sides, and that can't happen if Madog thinks Rhys is on our side."

"It makes him impossible to read," Hywel said. "Looking at him now, I'm wondering if he believes that the marauders could have been from Gwynedd."

"He was a spy. That's his job. As abbot, those skills are put to daily use. He governs a hundred men, is seen as the source of wisdom for an entire cantref, and is now in a position to broker peace between kings."

"About that." Hywel made a *hmm* sound deep in his throat. Then he glanced around the wall-walk and even went so far as to step into the stairwell behind them to make sure they were alone. Then he came back to Gareth. "I never told you that after Newcastle-under-Lyme, I came to see him."

Gareth rubbed his chin as he studied Hywel, who noted the wariness that had suddenly come over his friend. "Why did you do that?"

"Because I had questions about the role he'd played in our adventure there, and I needed to ask them."

"Did he answer?"

"Yes."

Gareth just looked at Hywel, quietly waiting.

"Rhys was a spy for Empress Maud, but before that, he worked for Geoffrey of Anjou, her husband."

Gareth raised his eyebrows. "I did not know that."

"In the course of our conversation, Rhys told me that King Henry did not die from eating too many lampreys. He was murdered at the behest of Geoffrey of Anjou, Empress Maud's husband."

Gareth took in a breath. "Who else knows that he knows?"

"A handful of men at most, all spies."

"You say Geoffrey was responsible, not Maud?"

"According to Rhys, it was done without her knowledge."

Gareth rubbed his chin. "That wouldn't matter if the truth about Henry's death became known. Stephen's claim to the throne would be instantly validated. Nobody would believe in her innocence, and nobody would allow her to take the throne over the dead body of her predecessor."

"No, they would not."

"It would end the war." Gareth barked a laugh. "Your father wouldn't be happy about that. It is only the war in England that is preventing every Norman in England *and* the king from turning his attention to Wales, thinking we've been a thorn in England's side for too long."

"Especially if Cadwaladr gives them reason to fight. The end of the war would mean that he finally gets what he wants."

"Your father's head on a pike." Gareth made a guttural sound deep in his throat.

Hywel frowned. "More immediately, in the wake of Erik's murder, I'm concerned about Rhys's personal safety. With him rising to his current status, he is no longer living a retiring life. Someone at some point might remember who he once was and worry about his conscience. He should never have accepted such an elevated position, knowing what he knows and the secrets he's keeping."

Gareth swore. "My God, the man's a danger to himself—but good luck convincing him of that."

Hywel put out a hand. "There's more, Gareth. I must speak to you of Cadoc, the archer Rhys vouched for and we accepted into our company after Newcastle."

"What about him? He's your best archer bar none."

"He was Rhys's assassin when he worked for Maud."

Gareth whistled low. "So that's his story. Why are you telling me this now?"

Hywel pointed into the courtyard with his chin. "Look at Madog."

Gareth's expression hardened. "You're not thinking of assassinating Madog, are you? Promise me you wouldn't violate Rhys's trust that way!"

"No, that isn't what I meant. Cadoc is the best archer I have, and he has proven himself worthy these last three years. I was thinking that he might serve me now as Erik did."

Gareth snorted. "As long as you don't tell him that serving you got Erik killed."

Down in the courtyard, Rhys was now speaking to Llywelyn while Madog was conferring with his captain. Gareth kept his eyes fixed on them, but Hywel didn't think he was really seeing them, which proved to be the case a moment later when his friend added, "I've been thinking about what you said back in the guesthouse—about finding your own men, your own allies. Now that you've brought up Cadoc, I'd like to … suggest a venture."

"What kind of venture?"

"You have your *teulu*, as befitting a prince of Gwynedd, but I'd like to separate out another small force of men who aren't noblemen or knights and train them specially."

"Train them how?" Hywel kept his eyes on his captain.

"Quite frankly, to be—" Gareth seemed to be having trouble articulating his thoughts.

"Killers? Spies?"

Gareth let out a burst of air. "Yes and no. I wasn't thinking so much of them being like Erik, but more akin to what Rhys was for Geoffrey and Maud. Part of an elite force—a small group of men who can infiltrate a castle, or rescue a hostage, or—"

"Or win a war before it starts."

Gareth nodded.

Every now and then Gareth, who because of his strong sense of rightness many thought to be the most predictable of men, surprised even Hywel with the way his mind worked.

"Yes."

Gareth blinked. "Yes? Just like that?"

Hywel nodded. "Would you have Cadoc as their leader?"

"I was thinking of Gruffydd, Rhun's former captain."

"He might view it as a come down from his former station."

Gareth shook his head. "He has already fallen as far as a man can fall short of losing his own life. He will see it as the opportunity it is."

Hywel was more glad than he could say—or would say—to have Gareth standing at his right shoulder again. The trip to Shrewsbury had seemed necessary at the time, but Hywel needed

Gareth's clear vision and common sense—Gareth's *and* Gwen's. Hywel might be just selfish enough to ensure that any attempts to go off on their own in the foreseeable future were curtailed.

"I also need to speak to you of what we've discovered about Erik," Gareth said.

"I hear the body is returned."

"Yes, but not in the condition in which it was originally found. His stomach was cut open."

Hywel was aghast. "Why?"

"We fear he was killed because his assailant knew he was working for you. All of his belongings were taken, and we are wondering if the killer could have been hoping to acquire a token that you gave to Erik."

The conversation had distracted Hywel from his hatred of Madog, but now his stomach twisted again. "I did give him a ring. I didn't think of it before. You haven't found it?"

"No, my lord. What does it look like?"

"Gold, stamped with my crest." Hywel stared unseeing over the battlement. What a stranger could be doing with Hywel's signet ring, pretending to be his agent, didn't bear thinking about. And yet, he would have to think about it—and worse, he'd have to tell his father of the danger.

Then, as if Gareth could read Hywel's thoughts, he tipped his head towards the other side of the battlement. "Here comes your father for the evening mass. You should be at his side when he enters the courtyard."

Hywel gave a jerky nod and took the stairs from the gatehouse tower down to the gate. He strode out of the monastery without a backward glance and caught his father's bridle the moment that he reined in.

"He's here?" King Owain said by way of a greeting.

Hywel nodded. "With Susanna and young Llywelyn."

His father took in a long breath through his nose and let it out. Then he dismounted, landing on his feet in front of his son. "Are you ready for this?"

Hywel simply looked at his father for a heartbeat.

Owain nodded and took another deep breath. "I know. I've lost one son this year already, and he meant to deprive me of another. I can't think about it, Hywel, because if I do, I will be unable to speak with him."

Hywel tipped his head. "We don't have to do this. We could still walk away."

"No." Owain sighed. "I promised Susanna and Abbot Rhys that I would try. Besides, my counselors tell me that fewer of my barons have turned up than I might wish. If we fight Madog, it won't be with the full strength of Gwynedd."

"We aren't the only ones who are watching and waiting," Hywel said with a bit of acid in his mouth. "To answer your question, Father: Yes, I am ready. As ready as I'll ever be."

"It isn't her fault that my father gave her to Madog," Owain said, as an aside as they walked together underneath the gatehouse tower. "She paid the price for our need for peace. I will not begrudge her the right to keep it."

As they entered the courtyard, Hywel acknowledged that this was why his father was a great king. He had an army at his back—not as large a one as they might have wished, but big enough—and he was able to turn away from war because not only was it the right thing to do for his family, but it might be the right thing to do for Wales. They had taken Mold Castle finally, as some outlet for their grief at the loss of Rhun. An attack on Powys would have given them a similar feeling of vengeance—but vengeance could take a king only so far—and it wasn't wise to rule with vengeance in mind. It was far better to be strategic, as they'd discussed on the way to the encampment.

Hywel had lurked at his father's side, usually a few paces behind Rhun, his whole life. He'd learned rudimentary strategy before he was ten years old simply by watching what his father did. He fully intended to keep watching and learning as long as his father was willing to teach him.

"I will follow your lead, Father."

13

Gareth

Gareth had been neglecting his duties to Hywel for some time now, ever since he'd left his company to journey to Shrewsbury. That Prince Hywel had wanted Gareth to go and that the journey had resulted in news about Cadwaladr's whereabouts had been all to the good—and one of the purposes of the trip—but he was the captain of Hywel's guard, and he had men to see to.

He was worried, in particular, that some might have started to resent his elevation when so many of his duties had to be borne by others in his absence, and now because he was injured. To that end, with Evan at his side, he left Hywel and the king to their awkward reunion with Madog and his family, and began a circuit of the monastery grounds, starting at the back in the northeast corner, to the east of the rear gate. The rain had momentarily stopped, and some of the clouds had cleared, revealing a patchwork of stars.

"Did Erik's body tell you anything?" Evan said.

Gareth suppressed the frown that formed on his lips at the memory of Erik's mutilated body. He sighed. "Someone held him down in the trough below the water level. Whether he died from strangulation or from drowning, I can't say for sure unless I cut him open even more than the men who stole him already did."

What Gareth didn't feel like talking about—and was more information than Evan needed—was that he'd pressed down on Erik's chest and the characteristic pink foam that formed in a man's lungs when he drowned had come up. Still, Gareth had seen the same pink foam in strangulations. On a certain level, it didn't matter which method had killed Erik, only that he was dead.

As they walked their inspection circuit, the first man they came upon was the least expected. Gruffydd had been the captain of Prince Rhun's *teulu*; he was a knight and a landowner in his own right. He had a wife and child Gareth had never met, and the loss of Rhun had meant that he and many of the men he'd led had been folded into Prince Hywel's retinue, while others had been added to King Owain's. *Teulu* was the Welsh word for *family,* and in this context it meant exactly that. Thus, Gruffydd had lost a portion of his family, his lord, and a large dose of his authority in one go. It was why Gareth had proposed giving him the task of leading Hywel's special force. Even with his changed status, however, sentry duty was not among his usual chores.

The immediate grounds of the monastery were surrounded by a stone wall, which started out ten feet high at the gatehouse, where the main road ran east to west through St. Asaph, and also along the road by the river, which Gareth had traveled in his aborted attempt to bring Erik's body to the chapel. By the time the wall had run around two-thirds of the monastery, however, it was more like six feet high—about Gareth's height—and more of a deterrence to trespass than an actual barrier to an invader.

Gruffydd stood atop the wall, a dark shape against the lighter evening sky, straddling the exact corner of the wall with his legs spread wide, one foot on the wall running east-west and the other on the one running north-south. The wall was only two feet thick here, and there was no wall-walk or steps up. Gruffydd wasn't holding a torch, which was only to be expected if he wanted to see anything beyond the margins of the monastery, and Gareth and Evan hadn't chosen to carry one either. If they had, they might have missed Gruffydd in the dark.

Gareth and Evan stopped a few paces away and looked up at him. "See anything?"

"Sheep. Many sheep. And a party of men I'm not liking at all."

"Whose men?" Gareth cast around for a way to climb onto the wall, and Gruffydd pointed to a tree to Gareth's right. If he grasped one of the lower branches, he could swing himself up into the tree and then step over to the wall. Doing so might be painful, but he let Evan go first to show him that it could be done, and he used his good right arm to heave himself into the tree. He tried not to think about the fact that Gwalchmai could have done this without a second thought. Growing old wasn't for the faint of heart. Then again, he wasn't ready for his death bed either, even if during this last week he'd felt sometimes like he was already on it.

Evan steadied him once he was up, and the two men picked their way along the top of the wall to where Gruffydd stood, still unmoving, his arms folded across his chest.

Torches flared in the distance, perhaps three hundred yards away across the orchards and fields that formed this part of the monastery's property.

The monastery itself was laid out in a long rectangle, with the main gate facing south along the east-west road that ran through St. Asaph. The gatehouse protected the primary buildings of the monastery, which lay beyond the cobbled courtyard and were approximately a hundred yards at the widest and perhaps a hundred and fifty yards deep north to south. All of this was enclosed by the stone wall, which protected the most vital portions of the monastery's gardens and upon which Gareth and the others were currently standing.

From here, however, the monastery's lands fanned out, with the river running north to south on the far western side, and the eastern road making a wide curve around a portion of the monastery's expansive pastureland, fields, and orchards.

From his position on the wall, Gareth could see the flames of at least a dozen campfires, and he realized what he was seeing. "It's Madog's camp."

Gruffydd grunted. "I thought they had set up their tents farther to the east."

"Apparently not." Gareth peered into the distance as shouts echoed across the fields. "Perhaps Madog hopes to flank us."

"I would have preferred to go to war against them," Gruffydd said.

Gruffydd had been with Hywel when Madog had tried to burn them alive, so he had every right to his anger, even if it wasn't a very fruitful emotion and clouded a man's judgment.

"These men didn't do anything but be born in Powys," Gareth said matter-of-factly. He didn't want Gruffydd to think he was being condescending, but if he was going to be useful to Hywel, he needed to rein that anger in—as they all did. "It isn't their fault their lord is a treacherous bastard."

Then a shout came from much closer by, followed by a woman's shriek, "Stay away from me!" The words echoed to them from a small stand of fruit trees on a low hill between fields two hundred feet from where they stood. Gareth thought he even heard a somewhat ominous *thud* as something heavy—like a body—hit the ground.

The three men looked at each other and, without needing to say anything about it, Gruffydd and Evan jumped off the wall. A six-foot drop was going to jar Gareth's shoulder, so he took the long way down, this time using the overhanging branch of the same tree as a brace to ease himself down to the ground outside the monastery wall. By the time he reached level ground, Evan and Gruffydd were well ahead of him.

He ran after them, holding his left arm close to his body and cursing. He pulled up at the edge of the trees, finding the darkness under them a sharp contrast to the brighter sky outside, and followed his friends into the woods. The rich smell of apple blossoms filled the air.

Someone moaned up ahead, allowing him to more accurately pinpoint where he was supposed to go, and then he bumped into someone's back.

"Careful." Evan put out a hand. "It's Conall."

Sure enough, beyond Evan, a strand of moonlight made it through the leafy canopy overhead, and shone down on Conall, who was moaning as he pushed himself to all fours. Gruffydd put a hand under his arm and helped him to his feet, at which point Gareth stepped out from behind Evan. "What happened?"

"I have no idea."

With an exasperated *tsk,* Gareth went to Conall's other side and steadied him. He weaved a bit, and between Gareth and Gruffydd, they helped him hobble out of the trees to a low wall that surrounded the next pasture and sat him on it.

Conall hung his head, his arm across his belly, breathing hard. "This I did not need today."

"What were you doing in the trees?" Gareth said.

"I was watching Madog's camp." Conall lifted his head. "I don't see any of you celebrating mass with the two kings either."

Gareth laughed under his breath. "No. We left that to men greater—and possibly braver—than ourselves."

Conall bobbed a nod. "Your politics are just like ours—full of intrigue between close family members. The last thing I want to do is involve myself or Leinster in that, but since I was here, I thought I could be of use in one of the few ways I know how."

"Scouting," Evan guessed.

Another bob, though Conall arrested the movement halfway through as it seemed to hurt him. "I was minding my own business—or rather, Madog's—when I bumped into a woman. She screamed and hit me."

None of the other men could keep the smirks off their faces.

"It did sound like a woman," Evan said.

Conall groaned and rolled his eyes. "I will never live this down. In my weakened condition—" Conall's tone was full of ironic laughter, "—I couldn't defend myself."

"In other words, she got the jump on you, and you let her go rather than stab her with your belt knife," Gruffydd said.

Conall scoffed. "She was plump and older." He lifted his chin to point at Gareth. "You would have done the same."

"I would have squealed too." Gareth relented a little from his smirking laughter.

But then a caterwauling scream from a real female's voice rose up near the lights in the distance. "No! No! He didn't do anything! He came here in good faith. You can't take him!"

The woman continued to lament, but her cries faded to a more generalized weeping. "You two stay here." Gruffydd pointed at Gareth and Conall, and then he and Evan sprinted off.

Conall groaned again, straightening while still leaning against the wall. "Come on. You don't take orders from him, right?"

Shaking his head and laughing, Gareth wrapped his good arm around Conall's waist to help him to the other side of the wall. They crossed two fields, following Gruffydd and Evan, who'd leapt the walls athletically. Conall and Gareth chose to detour both times to a nearby stile and eventually came out onto a road that ran between the monastery fields and a rising hill upon which Madog's men had pitched their tents.

A woman knelt in the center of the road, hunched over with her arms around her waist, sobbing. She was alone now because the party of men to whom she'd directed her protests was moving away from her towards the camp and even now was passing the first sentry points. Though the road was completely dark, torches lit up the camp, and Gareth could make out the silhouettes of at least eight men, one of whom had his wrists bound behind his back, which Gareth could tell because the two men on either side of him had grasped his elbows and were hauling him along.

Gruffydd and Evan had stopped beside the woman, looking between her and the men and hesitating.

Gareth called ahead to them. "Don't. Wait." He and Conall hurried the last few paces to where they waited. Gareth was breathing hard from his effort. Annoyingly, Evan and Gruffydd seemed completely unaffected by their run.

Gareth stopped beside Gruffydd and spoke in an undertone. "We are men of Gwynedd, and those are Madog's soldiers. We can't involve ourselves in whatever this is about—not without learning more first. King Owain wouldn't thank us for that." Then he turned to the woman, whom Conall was helping to her feet. "We heard you cry out. What's this about?"

"They took my son!"

All the men looked again to the camp. Madog's soldiers and their prisoner had disappeared into its depths.

"Why would they do that?" Gareth said.

"I don't know!" Her answer came out a wail. "All they said was that he was a wanted man."

"But they didn't say what he was wanted for?" Gruffydd said.

"No!" Again the wail, but this time there was a tone to the protest that didn't ring entirely true.

Gareth's eyes narrowed. "He must have done something."

The woman put a hand to her heart and took in a breath. "I don't—I don't think so. I don't know." Then her attention went to Conall as if seeing him for the first time, even though he'd been the one to help her to her feet. Her eyes widened, and she pointed at him with a trembling hand. "That's the man who attacked me in the woods!"

"I didn't attack you, woman," Conall said. "You ran into me."

She glared at him. "What were you doing in the woods?"

"The same as you, I imagine. Spying on Madog's camp."

"I wasn't spying!" Her response was heated, but when the men around her simply looked at her, she settled down. "All right. I was following my son. But that's not really *spying*. It's being a good mother."

Gareth found himself on the edge of patience. By now the party of men and the woman's son were long gone, and the camp emitted only the usual noises of men talking and laughing as they ate and drank. The men weren't necessarily prepared for imminent war, but Gareth counted at least six sentries, spread out on the perimeter of this side of the camp—and those were just the ones he could see. "Let's start at the beginning. What is your name and the name of your son?"

"I'm Derwena, and that's my son Rhodri."

14

Gwen

The four men heard the whole story from Derwena on the way back to the monastery, and she (quite willingly) went through it all again in the dining room of the guesthouse for the benefit of Gwen, Meilyr, and Saran, who had returned by then. The sisters had been jubilant at their reunion, even if both women were dismayed to know that Rhodri was a captive in Madog's camp.

Gwen had seen to Conall's injuries already and put him to bed with a warm compress and a carafe of mead. As it turned out, the retinues of neither king had chosen to stay in the guesthouse, except for Hywel, who at the moment was dining at the Gwynedd camp, and Susanna, who'd gone to bed with a sick headache. Gruffydd, Evan, and Gareth had done a quick canter around each man's obligations and responsibilities, ending with Gruffydd departing to speak to Hywel of the night's events. Tangwen was asleep, and Gwalchmai had gone to the church to sing for Compline. Abbot Rhys knew well Gwalchmai's worth, and Gwen suspected that he would employ him to the fullest capacity as long as the young bard was a guest in his house.

Thus it was Evan, Gareth, Saran, and Gwen who gathered around Derwena to listen to the story. Meilyr was there too, but he'd found a seat in the corner with his lyre and was playing a gentle melody. Gwen assumed that he was listening, but he had deliberately set himself apart so as not to become involved in their business or the investigation until he was wanted.

"The part you haven't yet explained is *why* exactly Madog's men arrested Rhodri," Gwen said, trying to keep the exasperation out of her voice but undoubtedly failing.

Derwena looked down at her feet. So far, Gwen had been willing to give her the benefit of the doubt because she was Saran's sister and obviously under great duress. But there was something shifty about her wide-eyed innocence, and when she talked, she didn't always look directly at anyone. It could have been that she was embarrassed, but equally, it could be because she wasn't telling the entire truth. Saran was one of the most intelligent people Gwen knew, man or woman, but it was possible that Derwena hadn't been given the same gifts.

"Rhodri has been secretive of late. He didn't want me to come north with him, but I put that off as simply his concern for his mother's wellbeing." Derwena shook her head. "But now I fear it was something more."

Gwen didn't know everything there was to know about young men—less than many women, certainly—but she suspected that few wanted their mothers along on their adventures even if they weren't doing anything that would put them in prison. Again, it was a naiveté on Derwena's part that Gwen found disconcerting. She didn't say anything, though—just allowed Derwena to keep talking.

"What sort of *more* are you thinking of?" Gareth said.

Derwena's eyes flicked around the room. "I'm afraid I don't know."

Saran had her arms folded across her chest and was studying her sister. "Anything at all will help us to understand what's happening here and maybe to get Rhodri back."

Gwen was glad it was Saran who'd said that, because it felt like Derwena was a hair's-breadth away from closing up.

Derwena shook her head, her eyes back on her feet. "It could be that Rhodri was passing information. Maybe."

"From whom to whom?" Saran said. "Rhodri serves King Owain, but he was arrested by King Madog's men. Are you saying he spied for King Owain?"

Saran's assessment seemed to leave her sister speechless. She shook her head again, her eyes on the floor, and then shrugged helplessly. "I don't know."

Saran went down to a crouch in front of her sister, like Gwen might in front of Tangwen when her daughter was having a hard time conveying her thoughts. "None of us believe that Rhodri spies for Owain, Derwena. Whom did he really serve?"

But even Saran couldn't get anything more out of Derwena. She'd gone mute, and just shook her head.

"Derwena, do you have a place to stay tonight?" Gwen broke in.

"She can stay with me," Saran said before Derwena could answer. "Earlier I spoke with the healer here in St. Asaph, and she made me welcome."

"No—" Derwena put out a hand. "I would be glad to stay with you, but I will not be an unwanted guest." Saran opened her mouth—perhaps to protest—but Derwena overrode her. "She invited you, not me. I have a place with some of the other women in the encampment." Derwena stood and brushed her hands down her skirt, smoothing the fabric. "I'll just go." And with a few hasty steps, she was out the door and gone.

Gareth jerked his head towards the door. "Evan and I should follow."

There was a time when Gwen would have wanted to go with him, maybe as recently as two weeks ago in Shrewsbury when she *did* go with him, but she had duties here, not the least of which was Saran herself. From the way Saran was holding her arms around her middle, she was less than pleased with how the evening had gone.

Once Gwen, Meilyr, and Saran were alone, Meilyr stopped the music and put down the instrument he was holding. Saran paced in front of the fire, the fingers of one hand playing with the end of her long braid, which was otherwise coiled around her head. When Gwen had known her in Carreg Cennan, her hair had been coal-black, but a startling white streak now rose from her widow's peak, and elsewhere the black was shot with strands of white.

"What are you thinking, Saran?" Gwen said after Saran had paced around a little more.

"She's my sister." Saran took in a deep breath and let it out.

Meilyr pulled one of the stools closer to him and put his feet up on it. "We know she's your sister, Saran, and that you want to think the best of her—and want the best for her. Even if it's been a long time since you've seen us, you should know that you can tell us what troubles you."

She gave him a genuine smile. "I *have* seen you at your worst."

Meilyr nodded, his eyes on Saran's face. "Yes, you have. Things are better now."

"I can see that." Saran's eyes went to Gwen. "My sister is two years younger than I. She was the baby of the family, prettier than I, and she has always used her prettiness to get what she wanted."

"I would not have said that Derwena is prettier than you now," Gwen said.

"She's had a hard life, and any woman who reaches middle age as we have has lost her beauty by now. She had more beauty to lose. Her husband died when Rhodri was a child, and since then she has struggled to support them with her small flock of sheep." Saran sighed. "Rhodri grew up clever but not wise or intelligent, if you know the difference?"

Meilyr and Gwen nodded, because how could they not? It was a common condition.

"Perhaps he inherited that from his mother." Saran looked down for a moment. "Derwena has always been calculating. You saw that when she was here. She tries to fall back on innocence and her beauty, but it's gone now and all that's left is the cleverness."

"What is it that you think she is being clever about?" Gwen said. "Do you think she knows what Rhodri is up to?"

"She knows," Saran said. "I have no doubt that she knows, and she doesn't want to tell us because we won't approve or because it will implicate him in some genuine wrongdoing."

Meilyr pushed to his feet. "Let me escort you to the healer's house, Saran. Perhaps if we two go over it again, we can figure out what she's hiding."

Saran smiled. "Thank you, Meilyr. I would like that." She nodded to Gwen. "Tomorrow, my dear."

Gwen stood to hug Saran, and stayed behind as they departed as her father had clearly wanted. This was again one of those moments when an investigation intersected with her and Gareth's personal lives, and Gwen didn't see how she could stop it from happening. At the moment, given how pleased with life her father seemed to be all of a sudden, Gwen wasn't going to interfere with his developing relationship with Saran.

It was odd to be completely alone for once, and for a moment Gwen didn't know what to do with herself. But the monks who attended the guesthouse had gone to Compline before cleaning up from dinner, so she began collecting cups and stacking empty dishes on a tray to return to the kitchen. When the first load was ready, she carried it through a narrow doorway, along a covered but open-air walkway for a few steps, and then into the kitchen. It was empty but for one man, who was just pushing open the back door.

Both he and she hesitated in their respective doorways, each equally surprised to see the other, and then Gwen took a few steps forward to set the heavy tray on a nearby table. "Father Alun!"

The old man beamed. "My dear Gwen." He walked towards her and put his hands on her shoulders in a partial hug. "You look absolutely radiant!"

Gwen didn't know about that, but she smiled anyway. Father Alun was the priest of the church in Cilcain, a town ten miles as the crow flies east of St. Asaph. Alun had been unlucky enough to find the body of a woman who looked like Gwen half-buried in his graveyard last autumn. That finding had ultimately set Gareth and Gwen on a course for Shrewsbury. While she couldn't regret knowing that the girl who'd died had been her cousin, she was sorry that Father Alun had been caught up in murder.

"I am well." She leaned forward to speak to him conspiratorially. "Gareth and I are expecting another child later this year."

He squeezed her shoulders. "I'm so happy for you, especially after all that has happened." He shook his head and looked down for a moment. He was thinking of the loss of Prince Rhun, as they all still did, many times a day.

"But why are you here?" Gwen said.

He looked up. "The peace conference, of course. I was invited as a witness."

Though Gwen would never say it, she thought it was kind of Abbot Rhys to invite the older man. She didn't think Alun was exactly lonely in Cilcain, given the busy life of a parish priest, but it must be nice to be among other churchmen every once in a while, men he could truly relate to as friends, rather than as confessor and parishioner. Rhys had implied as much earlier when they were discussing why Rhys already knew about the events of the previous year without Gwen or Gareth having to tell him.

"Come. Sit." Gwen moved a stool from beside the fire to the table. "You must be hungry after such a long journey."

"I am. I am."

For a moment Gwen frowned. "Why did you come to the guesthouse instead of the monastery kitchen? Surely they have a spot for you there."

"They do; they do." Alun spoke heartily, but then he leaned forward and said in a loud whisper, "The food over here is better."

Gwen smiled. "I'll fix you something."

"I hope you serve it with news from Gwynedd. We know of the taking of Mold, of course, but recent events often pass us by in Cilcain."

"I do have much to tell you." While she talked, Gwen bustled about, getting the old priest dinner. The pot over the fire had a few cups of mutton stew left in it, and half a loaf of bread remained on the sideboard. She set the meal in front of him, poured them each a glass of mead, and then pulled up a stool to sit beside him.

"Where is your husband? I hope he is not so unwell that he is abed?" Alun said.

Gwen smiled ruefully. "I'm waiting for him to return. I'm afraid that we have another death to investigate."

"You don't say! My dear, that's terrible."

Gwen pursed her lips, reminded of her encounter with Deiniol, and pulled the sketch of Erik from her purse. "Do you recognize him?"

Alun squinted at the page. "Is he the murderer or the victim?"

"The victim." And she described his overall size and shape beyond simply what his faced looked like.

Alun stood and took the paper closer to the fire, which was blazing brightly. "My eyes aren't what they used to be, but I saw this man earlier this week."

Gwen spun around on her seat. "In Cilcain?"

Alun nodded. "Passing through. He stopped at the church to ask if I knew where Prince Hywel was now, as he wasn't at Mold Castle where he was supposed to be."

Gwen's eyes lit. "So he was looking for the prince. I don't suppose he said what for?"

Alun shook his head sadly. "No."

"Did he have anyone with him?"

"Not that I saw." Then Alun frowned. "He asked if my church was missing any relics. I told him that we had so little here, there was nothing to miss, and if a thief was so desperate that he needed to rob us, he was welcome to what he took."

Gwen studied the priest. It was just like Alun to say that. More importantly, his testimony was the first link between Erik and the thefts. Then her stomach dropped into her boots as fear surged through her. It could even be that Erik had been looking into what had happened in Wrexham, as she and Gareth now were, and someone had killed him for it.

15

Gareth

Even as Gareth trailed after Derwena, he was cursing himself for following yet another new thread when he'd been dropping the old ones left and right. First and foremost, if Rhodri was the same man who'd ridden to St. Asaph with Erik, they needed to get Deiniol and Rhodri in the same room together to see if they knew each other. He also had yet to question Mathonwy, the milkman, about his visit to the treasury.

Gareth didn't necessarily think that Mathonwy had anything to do with the theft. If he had, he would have run, not calmly returned to his milking—but he might have spoken incautious words to someone else, which had then led to the theft. And as always, Gareth told himself not to presume anything without evidence until he had no more threads to pull.

Evan loped beside him across the courtyard, trying to avoid the puddles that had formed among the dips in the cobbles. It wasn't raining right now, thankfully, and Derwena was hurrying along at a rapid clip such that by the time they left the guesthouse, she'd already entered underneath the gatehouse.

"Moves fast for an older woman, doesn't she?" Evan said under his breath.

"She does seem to be in a hurry, doesn't she?" Gareth said.

Evan checked the location of the moon. "Prince Hywel's dinner with his father and the other lords who have come should be ending soon."

"I should have been among them," Gareth said.

Evan scoffed. "You didn't want to be there any more than you wanted to attend the mass. The last thing you need right now is to involve yourself in politics."

Gareth gave a low laugh. "You have the right of that."

They reached the gatehouse, passed through it easily because the gate was still open, and Gareth lifted a hand to the gatekeeper as he went by. Derwena had, in fact, turned east as if she intended to go the encampment, but once she passed the corner of the stone wall of the monastery that fronted the main road, she turned left in order to head northeast down the side road, heading back to the place where they'd found her by Madog's camp.

The older woman trotted along at a rapid clip, and because the road was otherwise deserted, Gareth and Evan had to stay well back lest she look over her shoulder and see them. If this had been mid-afternoon when the monastery was a busy place, they perhaps could have remained undetected, but it was late evening, and there wasn't another soul but them about. The moon reflected off the puddles and the clouds, allowing them to see well enough to follow. If it had been raining, they couldn't have seen anything without a torch.

No longer jesting with one another, Gareth and Evan followed the western margin of the road, trying to keep to the trees. Just past Madog's encampment, which was considerably quieter than it had been an hour earlier, Derwena slowed. Gareth and Evan held back, thinking they should get no closer than two hundred feet but having no idea why Derwena had returned here. Then a woman holding a torch, the flame of which was blowing hard in the wind, stepped out from a side-path—one that ran through the monastery grounds and intersected the road Derwena had come down. She was followed by a man on horseback.

Gareth and Evan froze, and their ears strained to hear what the three people were saying. Unfortunately, the wind that was blowing through the newly leafed trees that lined the road prevented them from hearing anything else. It was darker under the trees than on the road too, so Gareth bent over in a half crouch and began to pick his way through the grass and bushes. He'd gone only a dozen feet, however, before the man on the horse reached down and pulled Derwena up behind him. Turning the horse's head, he cantered away north. The woman, watched them go for a moment and then turned away and hastened back down the path by which she'd come.

Gareth picked up the pace, though still trying to keep to the soft grass beside the road to disguise the sound of his boots hitting the earth. He called over his shoulder to Evan, "We may have lost Derwena but let's not lose this other woman!" Even injured as he was, the two hundred feet took Gareth no time at all, though he found himself annoyed again when Evan eventually beat him to the crossroads.

Earlier, when they'd helped Conall after Derwena had knocked him down, Evan and Gareth had come off the northeast corner of the monastery's protective stone wall, crossed the cleared space between the wall and an orchard, and then crossed two pastures in order to reach Madog's camp. They hadn't used the road the woman had disappeared along, since it was farther north. But as they followed it back through the monastery grounds, Gareth realized it was leading them west towards the barn where Erik's body had been found.

Sure enough, the road eventually intersected the cart track that Gareth had been on several times today already and which started at the back gate of the monastery. The woman with the torch was just barely in sight, and Gareth and Evan hustled after her, turning south to follow the cart way. She reached the back entrance, passed through it, and then the gate shut behind her.

The monks didn't normally post a guard at the gate, but since the peace conference would start tomorrow and a murderer was on the loose, Hywel had sentried one of his own men here. Gareth and Evan pulled on the latch and found it locked, as it should have been. Thus, as the woman must have done, they knocked on the wooden door. A heartbeat later a little window opened in the door, revealing one eye and the nose of the guard. "Da!"

"How did you end up pulling this duty, Dai?" And then Gareth waved a hand dismissively. "Never mind. Let us in."

"Yes, sir." The door swung wide.

Gareth and Evan stepped through it in time to see the skirts of the woman who'd preceded them disappearing around a hedge up ahead. While on the road, she had covered her hair with a veil, but now the covering hung loosely around her shoulders, and the moon glinted off her blonde hair. Gareth pointed with his chin at her retreating back, asking the question of Dai, even though he already knew the answer. "Who was that?"

"Queen Susanna."

Evan would have hurried after her, but Gareth caught his arm and stopped him. "Wait."

Evan subsided, and Gareth looked at his son. "Did she say anything to you about where she'd been?"

"No."

"Will you tell me what she did?"

He gave an elaborate shrug. "She took one of the torches that lit the gate and headed off east."

"How long did you have to wait for her return?" Gareth said.

Dai shook his head and looked down at the ground while mumbling, "I don't know. A while."

Something was wrong. Dai hadn't wanted to answer that question. "Did you see with whom she met?"

Dai's eyes skated towards the left for an instant and then came back to his father. "No."

Gareth looked at his son. "Dai."

Dai wavered, but he was an honest boy at heart, and capitulated without Gareth having to order him again to speak. "It was my duty to guard the door, but I was curious about what the Queen of Powys was doing outside the monastery so late in the evening, so I followed her. It was easy because of the torch."

"Leaving the gate unguarded *and* open," Gareth said.

Dai returned his eyes to his feet.

Gareth ran a hand through his hair and scrubbed at it before dropping his hand. "Pray something good comes of this. What did you see?"

"Queen Susanna met a man on horseback who was waiting for her in the middle of the track that led east. He pulled her up behind him, after which I had to run to keep up. Then just before they reached the crossroads, Susanna dismounted, and they waited, hardly speaking, for a long time. I was wavering, knowing that I'd left the door unguarded and feeling guilty about it, when a woman stopped on the road to talk to the queen."

"We saw that last part," Gareth said. "Could you identify the man if you saw him again?"

"He wore a hat pulled down low over his head, but—" Dai frowned.

"But what?" Gareth waited. His son had always been more observant than most.

Dai turned his body this way and that, motioning with his left hand. And then his expression cleared. "Both when he helped Queen Susanna mount and when he pulled the woman onto his horse, he held out his left hand to them, and—" He stopped again, clearly still puzzled as to whether or not what he saw could be true.

Gareth placed a hand on Dai's shoulder. "And what?"

"He was missing the last finger on his left hand."

16

Hywel

That his Aunt Susanna was involved in the intrigue swirling around the monastery surprised Hywel when he heard about it, which wasn't until the next morning as he was preparing for the conference. Or rather, he wasn't surprised that she was involved in intrigue—only that she would sully her hands with murder. Then again, her relationship with Derwena and the defingered man remained to be established. Hywel needed to confront her with it—he couldn't leave that task to Gareth—but like the rest of the investigation, it would have to wait until after today's meetings.

The men who would speak of peace were gathering in the chapter house, which was the largest room in the monastery outside the dormitory or the church itself. This was where the monks met every day to listen to their Rule read and to discuss monastery business. Conall loitered by the gatehouse, watching the riders as they came in. After each one passed, he would signal to Hywel and Gareth with one or two fingers or a raised fist to indicate whether they wore their weapons and how many he noted, or if the man had left them at home as promised.

So far, though no man openly wore a sword, Conall had counted three boot knives among Madog's men, and seven men who wore dart sheathes up their sleeves. Conall himself had a knife hidden ingeniously in his bracer, a design Hywel was determined to ask his armorer to copy next he saw him. Unfortunately for Conall, he hadn't been wearing his bracers when he'd been captured back in Shrewsbury, which was what had given him the thought to look for weapons among Madog's men.

Hywel stood in the courtyard, Gareth at his left shoulder. Gwen fussed over them both, making sure their belts were straight and their surcoats smoothed across their chests. For the fifth time, she adjusted the way Hywel's cloak draped around his shoulders, and he caught her hands before she could twitch the fabric again. "It's fine, Gwen. You shouldn't be nervous. You don't have to attend."

"It would be easier if I were attending! I hate waiting."

Gareth put a hand on her shoulder. "Perhaps you can take Tangwen for a walk into the village. Saran should be there, and—"

Gwen subsided, something of a grim set to her chin. "I suppose I could ask around about Erik again. You found nothing, but you couldn't have talked to everyone. I want to be of use."

Hywel met Gareth's eyes for an instant over Gwen's head, and his captain gave him a brief nod. Showing Erik's image around the village in broad daylight was a better occupation for her than nearly anything else they could think of, and Gareth was silently saying that having approval come from Hywel himself was better than from Gareth. "That's a good idea, Gwen. Let us know when we adjourn if you discover anything."

"Of course." Gwen bent to pick up Tangwen from where she was crouched with a stick over a puddle. When she straightened, Conall, whom Gareth had already signaled to approach, was standing beside her. At the sight of him, she shook her head and tsked. "And I suppose you're coming with me?"

"It seems so." Conall always had an air about him that implied both that he couldn't care less about something and a certain resigned amusement. But he smiled genuinely at Gwen. Gwen rolled her eyes at her husband, but with Tangwen on her hip and well-guarded by Conall, she left the monastery courtyard.

Hywel turned to Gareth. "You don't have to be here either."

"Yes, I do. If ever you needed the support of your captains, it is now."

"I'm fine."

"He tried to have you murdered."

"That is true." Hywel gave Gareth a jerky nod and then turned to face his father, who'd just entered the courtyard through the gatehouse.

The King of Gwynedd was surrounded by his guard, among them Ithel, his captain and Cadifor's eldest son, and Cynan, Hywel's younger brother and the castellan of Denbigh Castle. The next oldest brother, Madoc, wasn't here because he held Mold for Owain, and it wasn't so long since they'd taken it that Owain felt they could leave it with a steward. The king's eldest legitimate son,

Iorwerth, now a thinly muscled seventeen-year-old man, was serving in Cynan's train, just as Gareth's sons, Llelo and Dai, were.

King Owain stumped up to Hywel and halted in front of him. "You ready?"

"Yes, sir."

"Where's Madog?"

"Already inside, sir. Abbot Rhys suggested that the two of them speak privately for a moment before the conference started." Hywel cleared his throat. "I think it was so you and he wouldn't be left to your own devices in the courtyard again."

Owain grunted. "I was civil last night. We'll see about now."

Hywel had hoped that the arrival of his father would be somewhat calming to the overall tension in the air, but that had been a faint hope. His father was as agitated as Hywel had ever seen him. That meant that Hywel himself had to be the calm one. With no help for it, he straightened his shoulders and strode into the chapter house at his father's side.

Madog and Rhys were standing in an open space beyond which row after row of wooden benches formed an extended half-circle around this central area. There was room for two hundred men to sit, and each party had been accorded roughly half the seats, with a few extras going to monks and associates of the monastery. Hywel nodded at Father Alun, who was standing against the wall behind the lectern, from which on another day the Rule and the news of the day would be read.

Owain's boots scraped on the stone floor as he stopped three paces from the King of Powys. "Madog." The menace in his tone caused Rhys's eyes to widen slightly, and though Madog didn't betray himself by rocking back on his heels, his nostrils flared.

Hywel kicked himself for not having said something to his father when he came in about toning down his aggression, but perhaps it would have only agitated him more. Not for the first time, Hywel wished himself far away, thinking of his boys and wife at Dolwyddelan, where he'd spent far too little time of late. He also spared a thought for his castle at Aberystwyth and instantly put that thought away. He would attend to Ceredigion when he had fulfilled his duties to his father here.

As it was, Rhys put out a hand to the party from Gwynedd. "Please, if you would sit here and Powys will sit there." He stabbed a finger to indicate where each king should sit, across from each other at the ends of a long table that took up the center of the open space, with Rhys sitting in the middle of one side, facing the audience.

Gareth leaned into Hywel. "Is this a peace conference or a courtroom?"

Hywel smiled wryly. "There's never been much difference between them, has there? Each side presents its grievances, its counter-arguments, and its witnesses, and then the conclave decides the verdict as guided by the convener, in this case, Abbot Rhys. My father has presided over assemblies like this a thousand times, though not usually with quite so many lords in attendance."

He bumped Gareth's shoulder with his own. "Why did you leave Cadwaladr's service? Was it because cutting off that boy's hand was unjust? Of course. But it was also because the boy wasn't given his day in court as required by the law."

By now Owain had turned to where Rhys pointed and taken the chair opposite Madog's. Hywel was not allowed to stand behind his father, since that would block the view of the men behind him, so he chose a seat to his father's right that would allow him to see the faces of both kings. With a suppressed groan, Gareth settled on the bench next to him, giving Hywel a pang of guilt for not sending his friend away. Still, the tension in the room had the hair on the back of Hywel's neck standing straight up, and he couldn't be sorry that Gareth was beside him if—when—things went bad. If the conference went on for the full two hours between now and the bell for noon prayers, he would find a way to ease Gareth's discomfort.

Wasting no time, Rhys didn't seat himself just yet but stood at the lectern, raised a hand, and the room quieted. "We all know why we are here. While both sides are much aggrieved, war should be the last resort of reasonable men, who should be able to sort out their differences without killing each other, as is forbidden by our Lord."

This was shockingly plain speaking, and while some of the men on the benches around Hywel shifted uncomfortably, Hywel leaned forward, interested now more than worried.

"We pray as our Lord in heaven instructed that we might find the strength to live as Godly men." He bent his head and began to pray, first in Latin and then in Welsh.

Hywel listened at first, but with so many people in the room, each with his own agenda and ideas about how this should go, he couldn't help but lift his head slightly to survey the room. Every other man had his head bowed, which gave Hywel free rein to observe them. He was more glad than he could say that Rhys had forbidden the wearing of even a knife today. The prayers might be heartfelt, but the mood of the room was ugly. Rhys was right that both sides had longstanding grievances, and Madog didn't think his were any less serious than Gwynedd's.

Hywel was tired of war, but he understood that sometimes a king had to resort to it when an opponent wouldn't listen to reason. That Madog had tried to murder him was still incomprehensible to Hywel. It made no political sense that he could discern, and for that reason, he had to think there was a greater issue underlying the act. He regretted how little time he'd had to explore the issue since it happened, but the key question he had to answer if his father was to come out of this conference unbowed was why Madog had seen Hywel's death as a means to an end. And exactly what that end was.

17

Gareth

Sitting next to Hywel as the conference continued could have been more uncomfortable, though Gareth wasn't entirely sure how—and it wasn't just because his body ached. He'd lived in Powys for a time, and he recognized many of the men at Madog's side, including a former employer, Bergam of Dyffryn Ceiriog. Bergam's lands were located to the southwest of Llangollen and part of Powys, so Bergam had come to St. Asaph at Madog's behest. Gareth had left Bergam's employment in the same way he'd left Cadwaladr's—under a cloud because the tasks he'd been asked to perform were impossible to stomach. The man's spoiled son was not here, for which Gareth could only be grateful. Ten years on, Gareth was wiser, but he didn't have faith that the man's son would be.

For Bergam's part, he hadn't recognized Gareth, or if he had, he gave no sign of it as his eyes passed over him without stopping.

At first, Rhys did most of the talking, which was fine. There were few men alive who made as much sense when they spoke as

Rhys. Then Gwalchmai and Meilyr sang—not war songs, but ones of peace and tranquility to soften the mood—and then the moment came for airing grievances. King Owain went first.

Somewhat laboriously, though in hindsight Gareth had seen him move with agility of late, so it had to have been a bit of an act, Owain rose to his feet. What would happen next was as much for his own barons' benefit as for Madog's. Owain had to prove he was a fit king.

King Owain finally reached his feet, and once he did, he stood completely upright, his chin held high and his shoulders straight. "You tried to kill my son."

He sat down again.

His accusation was met first with shocked silence, then with disbelief that those few words were all he'd said, and then as Owain gazed impassively at Madog, a murmur of consternation swept through the room. Everyone had expected Owain to enumerate a variety of affronts to Gwynedd, from incursions across the border to disputes over cattle, and conclude with the attempted murder only after these others had been examined.

Petty crimes like the former could be negotiated, and even put to one side with enough talking, but the attempted murder of the *edling* was a crime clearly laid out in Welsh law as punishable by the payment of an enormous *galanas*, a life debt. It hardly mattered that Madog hadn't succeeded, because the punishment, the *sarhad,* would be essentially the same. That is, it would be the same if Owain had the authority to order Madog to make such a payment, which he didn't. These were two kings, equal in stature.

With an unprosecutable crime such as this, Owain's only other choice had been to go to war.

Gareth's earlier comment about this being a courtroom instead of a peace conference had been dead on. It could never have been anything else, not with the attempted murder of Gwynedd's *edling* at the center of the discussion.

When Cadwaladr had ordered the murder of King Anarawd of Deheubarth—and for all intents and purposes admitted to it—he should have made such a payment to Cadell, Anarawd's brother. King Owain had forced him instead to spend most of his wealth to pay off the Danes whom he'd brought to Gwynedd, and Owain had never demanded that Cadwaladr pay Cadell anything. That debt still lay between Gwynedd and Deheubarth, and even if the fault was entirely Cadwaladr's, not Owain's, and Cadwaladr himself was now in exile, the debt remained. Cadell had allied himself with Cadwaladr last summer—and it could even be that Cadell wasn't asking for *sarhad* because he'd colluded with Cadwaladr to kill his brother—but that didn't mean anyone else had forgotten what he was owed.

Abbot Rhys studied Owain for a moment, his lips pressed together in a thin line. This was not a good beginning. Owain had come to the peace conference, but Rhys was feeling now that he hadn't come in good faith. But he straightened his shoulders, acknowledging what couldn't be changed, and turned resolutely to Madog. "Since Gwynedd has said all that it has to say, it is your turn to air your grievances."

Beside Gareth, Hywel nodded his head, acknowledging the proper procedures were being followed: first both sides spoke of their grievances without rebuttal by the other side. Thus Madog was not obligated to respond to Owain's charge until the time came for it, presumably during the afternoon session so that both sides could take some time to confer among themselves and develop a strategy for answering the charges against them.

Madog's eyes were fixed on Owain, who did not look away. He rose to his feet in much the same ponderous style Owain had used and then snapped his fingers to a man standing off to one side, holding a rolled parchment. The man was short and white-haired, with hunched shoulders but bright blue eyes that blinked rapidly as he focused on Madog. Then he stepped forward and bobbed his head in a bow.

"Who are you?" Rhys said.

"Derfel, the king's steward."

Rhys leaned back in his chair and gestured to one of the scribes behind him. "Make a note that Derfel read the grievances." Rhys returned his gaze to Madog's steward. "Continue."

In a sonorous voice, though not quite bard-like, Derfel began with a list of Madog's titles, which seemed to go on for a full page, and then at the point Gareth began to have trouble focusing, he launched into the long list of complaints that Powys had against Gwynedd, beginning with incursions dating back to the 1130s, mostly under the auspices of Cadwallon, Owain's deceased older brother—who in fact died fighting against Powys in 1132. The grievances ended with Gwynedd's conquest of Mold Castle.

Throughout it all, Owain simply watched Madog, and Madog watched Owain back. Rhys was gazing down at the table in front of him, looking at nobody and appearing to be listening intently, while the scribes scribbled furiously behind him. Later, each of their versions of events would be carefully examined and a single definitive document created.

After Derfel read all this out, he paused for a moment, which caused Rhys to look up expectantly, thinking he was finished. But then Derfel lifted his chin. "Powys has one final grievance to put forth to the assembly, one that is so heinous, so misguided, that it supersedes all other grievances."

Madog's expression had turned smug, which made Gareth suddenly very nervous. Hywel stirred beside him and leaned in close. "Do you know what's coming?"

"Yes, and you do too."

Hywel sighed and spoke even more softly, "The sacking of the Wrexham monastery."

Gareth had time only to nod before Derfel proved Hywel's words prescient: "We charge Gwynedd with taking advantage of the anarchy in England to enrich itself at the expense not only of Powys, but of the Church! We accuse Gwynedd of sending men to raid and destroy St. Dunawd's Monastery, southeast of Wrexham, of which King Madog has been a benefactor for many years!"

Taran, who'd been sitting on Gareth's other side, directly behind King Owain, leaned forward and stabbed a finger in Madog's direction, more agitated than Gareth had ever seen him. "That's absurd—"

Rhys made a chopping motion with his hand. "This is not the time for refutation."

Madog's expression as he looked at Owain was triumphant. "I have a witness." He spun around in his chair.

Rhys put out a hand to him too. "This is not the time for witnesses either—"

But two men had already entered the room, a third man held between them. The man's face was bruised in places and his lip bloodied. He didn't exactly struggle, but then again, he didn't seem entirely conscious, as his eyes were unfocused, and his hands bound behind his back.

Rhys was on his feet now, looking daggers at the newcomers, but Madog was standing too, and he wasn't taking no for an answer. He made an expansive gesture with one arm. "I present Rhodri ap Tudur of Corwen. He will testify that he was among the band of men who sacked the Wrexham monastery on King Owain's orders."

The last words rang throughout the chapter house, loud enough to overcome the uproar. Taran's face was red up to his hairline, but he seemed struck speechless. King Owain remained in his chair, contemplating Madog and Rhodri. He'd known about the sacking, having heard the story from both Hywel and Abbot Rhys in turn. Thanks to Deiniol's arrival, everybody at the monastery knew about it.

Rhodri's attention remained on his boots, but Madog's eyes were hot with passion, revenge, and glee. For once Owain's legendary temper was dampened, however, and he sat somewhat canted in his chair, one leg crossed over the other, and his elbow on the arm of the chair. A single finger tapped his lower lip.

Hywel, too, had remained completely calm, and both he and Gareth moved out of their seats at the same time: Gareth to take Taran, who'd long since risen to his feet, by the arm and pull him away from the table at which the two kings were sitting, and Hywel to whisper in his father's ear. King Owain listened, nodded, and then rose to his feet. Straightening his tunic with a jerk, he tipped his head to Rhys. "Gwynedd will adjourn until after Sext."

"Agreed." Rhys bowed to Owain and then turned with equal gravity to Madog.

Madog glared at the abbot. "Why adjourn? We have discussed nothing yet!"

King Owain arms were folded across his chest in a classic stance of disagreement and defiance. "There's nothing to discuss. I could have told you that from the beginning."

Rhys put out both hands, one to each king, in a soothing gesture. "Gwynedd has much to consider. They will meet with you again after a meal." He tipped his head at the two men holding Rhodri. "Whether or not the council finds Gwynedd guilty of what you suggest, we will keep Rhodri in a cell here until such a time as he can be brought forward again to testify."

Madog continued to glare at Owain even as he pointed at Rhodri. "That man is my prisoner!"

"He is a witness to a crime," Abbot Rhys said. "He will be safe enough in our charge."

Madog grunted and waved a hand at his guards, who let go of Rhodri. Rhodri's chin stuck out, and he seemed to be slightly less bleary than a moment ago, but he didn't fight the two monks who came to take his elbows and direct him from the room. Madog watched them go, and then, eyes blazing, returned his gaze to Owain. He was doing a fine job of implying that he was truly angry for the sacking of the monastery. Perhaps he even believed Owain guilty. But Gareth couldn't forget the image of Susanna speaking to Derwena, Rhodri's mother, and the lone rider with nine fingers. So far in this investigation there were far too many people who knew more than they were telling.

18

Gwen

"Have you seen your sister?" Gwen decided that speaking frankly to Saran was the best way to go about finding the truth. Saran had been helpful years ago in Carreg Cennan when Gwen's father had been accused of murder. She might find it odd that Gwen continued to involve herself in investigations, since it was an unusual occupation for a woman, but Saran was far from usual herself.

"No. Not since she left us last night." Saran put down her knife. She was standing at the healer's work table, chopping roots Gwen couldn't identify from where she stood. "Have you?"

The healer had gone to see to a newborn baby and his mother, and Conall was lounging somewhere outside, as he liked to do. The man was more self-contained than almost anyone Gwen knew outside of Prince Hywel himself—and she knew him well enough to know that much of his behavior was a mask to hide what he was really feeling. She had to assume that Conall's was too—except she didn't know him well enough to see beneath his mask.

Gwen looked down at her feet. She wanted to tell Saran what Dai, Gareth, and Evan had seen last night. The words were on the tip of her tongue, but they stuck there. It wasn't that she didn't trust her friend, but things were far less simple now than they'd been when she'd lived at Carreg Cennan and been trying to save her father.

"You don't have to tell me what is going on, Gwen, but I might be able to help."

"It isn't that I don't trust you, Saran, but—" Gwen raised her eyes to the ceiling. "It's possible that Derwena is involved in something unsavory, and if our suspicions are correct, I don't want you to feel that you have to choose between me, because I took you into my confidence, and her."

"What do you mean by unsavory?"

Gwen ground her teeth. She'd gone and said more than she should have even though she'd just told Saran that she wouldn't. Saran had that effect on her, and she should have known to be warier before coming here. "After you left with my father, Derwena rode off with a man whom we think might be involved in Erik's—"

Gwen made a grab for the cup of water that Tangwen held in her right hand. Saran had set the little girl up on a stool at the table with a cup of water and a variety of tiny seed dishes. Tangwen had lined them up in front of a small whisk broom, which the healer used for sweeping up the residue of her preparations, and a carafe around which Saran had tied a ribbon. They, along with Tangwen's stuffed cloth doll that she took everywhere with her, were pretend guests whom Tangwen had invited to a meal. She'd been talking to them in her sweet two-year-old lisp while Saran and Gwen had been discussing the investigation.

Saran studied Gwen with somber eyes. "Involved how?"

Gwen sighed and carefully poured half the water in Tangwen's cup into a more stable container. "There are indications that the man in question might have actually killed him." She put out a hand to her friend. "I can't say more. Gareth won't be pleased that I said this much."

"He sent you to me, didn't he? Maybe that was because he thought I could help."

Gwen licked her lips. "Can you tell me what your sister has been doing these last few years? Has she lived all her life in Corwen?"

"No." Saran let out a burst of laughter. "No, of course not. She went there because of Rhodri, who was to have married a local girl. I don't know what happened there, but even after the wedding was called off they stayed. Before that, she lived in Llangollen. That was where her man was from."

"But he died," Gwen said.

Saran nodded. "When Rhodri was still a babe."

"Was she ever at the castle?" Gwen held her breath.

"She worked as a maid for a time after her husband died. Why?"

"That I can't tell you, not without permission."

Saran went back to her chopping, and the set of her shoulders told Gwen that she was irritated. "Then I can't help you further."

"I'm sorry." Gwen put a hand on Tangwen's back. "It's time to go, *cariad.*"

Saran pointed at Tangwen with her chin. "No need for that! We're just getting to know each other, aren't we?"

Gwen looked doubtfully at Tangwen, who was looking at Saran rather than at Gwen.

"Would you like to stay with me a while? As soon as you're ready, I'll take you right back to your mother." Saran kept her tone light. Gwen was almost afraid to speak, but she raised her eyebrows at Saran, who nodded.

"I'll see you later then." Gwen bent to drop a quick kiss on her daughter's cheek and then backed away towards the door.

Saran leaned forward across the worktable, a dried cherry from last year's crop on her palm. Perhaps she'd been saving it for just this moment. "Would you like to eat this?"

Tangwen reached out a hand, grabbed the fruit, and popped it into her mouth, giggling as she did so.

As Gwen slipped through the doorway, she heard Saran say, "Cherries are good, aren't they?"

Tangwen had many adults in her life, but she had no grandmothers, and Gwen was happy for her to discover what she'd been missing. Saran herself had no grandchildren, so it was as if they'd been waiting for each other.

Conall straightened at the sight of Gwen exiting the healer's hut. As she'd supposed, he'd been lounging against a low stone wall that surrounded the house across the street and kept its family pig from running wild. What she hadn't expected was to find him holding the reins of a woman's horse while conversing with the woman—or rather, girl—on its back.

The girl was escorted by two other men. One stood fifty feet away, out of earshot, but the other was Iorwerth, King Owain's seventeen-year-old son. At the men's shift in attention, the girl turned to look at Gwen, who halted too, struck dumb by her beauty. She didn't wear a coif, so tendrils of her light brown hair hung around her face, shimmering in the morning sun with red and gold highlights. Her features were perfect—from her bow of a mouth, to her upturned nose with its dash of tiny brown freckles, to her large gray eyes with long, dark lashes. No wonder Conall had affected an air of casual interest, and Iorwerth, who was much more innocent, was gazing at her with wide-eyed appreciation. The men would have to be blind not to be interested in this girl.

Conall put out a hand. "Gwen, I'd like to introduce you to Marared, Madog's daughter."

Gwen smiled at the girl and curtsied. Marared wasn't Susanna's daughter, so she had to have been born illegitimately. Gwen had no expectation that Madog was a faithful husband, but he had far fewer illegitimate children filling his court than Owain. It was very hard to tell how old the girl was, given the tendency of girls to mature early, but if Gwen had to guess, she would have said Marared was a year or two younger than Iorwerth—roughly Gwalchmai's age, and he would be sixteen later this year.

Marared looked gravely down at Gwen from her seat on her horse. "It is a pleasure to meet you."

Gwen looked from Marared to Conall. "I don't mean to interrupt."

"It is no trouble." Marared put out a hand. "I was just waiting for my mother."

Gwen tried to think of a tactful way to ask who her mother was and failed. "Do you mean Queen Susanna?"

Marared smiled. "Of course. My mother died when I was born, so my father took me to live at Dinas Bran. Susanna is the only mother I have ever known."

Raising her husband's bastard was not a task every woman would take on willingly, but Susanna seemed to have done so—and done an excellent job with this girl for her to be so bright and charming.

"Where is she?" Gwen looked around, not seeing either Susanna or a riderless horse.

But a moment later, Susanna appeared on foot with two manservants in attendance, coming onto the main road from a side street beyond the healer's hut where Saran remained with Tangwen. It appeared that she had walked from the monastery as Gwen and Conall had. Susanna smiled as she saw Marared, who lifted a hand to her mother, and Susanna's smile widened even more when her attention landed on Gwen.

"My goodness, Gwen!" Queen Susanna spoke melodiously and moved the last fifty feet towards Gwen with such grace she might have been skating on ice. She stopped in front of Gwen and put her hands to Gwen's upper arms. "It is a wonder to see you all grown and beautiful. I had heard that your family had returned to Aber. I'm sorry I have been unable to visit there in so long."

Gwen had last seen Susanna many years ago, when Gwen herself was just a girl. In fact, now that Gwen thought about it, that encounter had taken place at the funeral of Cadwallon, Susanna and Owain's brother, who'd died fighting men of Powys near Llangollen. The bad blood between Gwynedd and Powys had a long history, and Susanna had been caught in the middle of it for her whole marriage. In fact, the fighting had been the reason *for* her marriage, even if the truce it engendered had been merely temporary.

And while it had never occurred to Gwen before, Gareth had probably been at the funeral too, since his uncle had died the same day as Cadwallon. At the time, Gwen had been eleven years old and Gareth eighteen, so they wouldn't have looked at each other twice.

Then Susanna added, as if reading Gwen's thoughts, "I was just speaking to Conall of those days."

Gwen just managed not to gape at Conall, who was looking as impossibly amused as always. "Excuse me, my lady, but how is it that you knew Conall before today?"

"At one time, my father considered a match for me with Diarmait of Leinster. I lived in his court for a few months before my father decided to marry me to Madog and brought me home. Conall was one of my guards while I was in Ireland."

The corner of Conall's mouth lifted. "I was fourteen years old and completely smitten. I wouldn't have thought you'd remember me, and I am honored that you did."

Susanna raised her eyebrows. "You were completely smitten, and I hated everything about Ireland except you. Of course I wouldn't forget you."

Conall bowed like a courtier. "My lady."

Now it was Susanna's mouth that was twitching. Marared and Iorwerth were looking on with identical astonished expressions on their faces. In the bloom of youth as they both were, they had trouble picturing either Conall or Susanna so young. Meanwhile, Gwen was trying to calculate when this visit had taken place, and realizing in the process that Conall was not Gareth's age as she'd thought, but quite a bit older.

"My lady, did you come to the village for a particular purpose?" Gwen said.

"I came to see the healer. Before I could knock, Conall informed me that she was not at home, and thus I didn't disturb you and your friend."

Gwen shot a look at Conall, who winked back at Gwen. How Susanna had recognized Gwen was now apparent. She had walked by in the time Gwen and Tangwen had been inside the healer's hut, so when Susanna returned to find Gwen on the street, she knew instantly who she was.

"Did you get what you needed from the healer?" Gwen desperately wanted to ask what Susanna had come to the village for—and even more to ask what she'd been doing with Derwena and the nine-fingered man last night, but it was impossible to do either under these circumstances. These questions were for Hywel—and Hywel alone—to ask.

But Susanna waved a hand dismissively and told her what she wanted to know without her asking. "A sick headache laid me low all of last night. I took poppy juice, retired immediately after I arrived at the monastery, and didn't rise until this morning. I used the last of the tincture I had, however, and came looking for more, in case I'm as desperate tonight as last night."

Gwen took a small step forward. "Poppy juice is dangerous but can be very helpful at times."

"Carys told me where she keeps it. I'll just collect it and be on my way." Susanna nodded at Gwen, in a clear dismissal, and turned towards the hut.

Gwen stood hesitantly in the road, watching her go, and then turned to look at Conall. For the first time this morning, his eyes had narrowed. Marared hadn't noticed the change in the air, however, and was still smiling, though rather than at the world at large as before, she was looking directly at Iorwerth. Acknowledging that his attentions were surplus to requirements, Conall put his heels together and bowed. "It was a delight to make your acquaintance."

"Likewise." Marared batted her eyes at Conall, eliciting a smile from him and a frown from Iorwerth.

Feeling that they needed to be gone before Susanna came out again or Iorwerth decided he needed to defend Marared's honor, Gwen set off at a brisk pace back towards the monastery. Conall hastened to catch up. "Where are you going in such a hurry?"

Gwen glanced at him. "I know you think very highly of Susanna, but she lied just now when there was no need to do so. She was establishing her whereabouts. Did you tell her about the investigation into Erik's death?"

"No." Then he frowned. "She did ask what I was doing here, so I had to tell her something."

"What did you say?"

"That I was associated with the company from Gwynedd because of an unrelated matter Gareth and I had worked on together in Shrewsbury. I had been wounded and was healing before I returned home to Leinster. When she pressed further, I told her I was simply escorting you to the village."

Gwen chewed on her lower lip as she thought. "Susanna is a very intelligent woman. What's more, she's had to survive for the whole of her marriage on the cusp of Powys and Gwynedd. She knew that Hywel was going to Shrewsbury because he told her he was when he was at Dinas Bran. It's an easy leap to the idea that your presence there was related not only to Hywel's, but to Cadwaladr's doings."

"I'm sorry." Conall really did sound contrite. "It isn't often I'm surprised by anyone into revealing more than I should."

"Much less a woman?" Gwen looked at him sideways.

"I wasn't going to say it."

"Never mind," Gwen said. "She could have learned all of that simply by asking any man in Hywel's *teulu*. She probably already knows about Erik's death and all the particulars. We haven't spoken of it, but monks gossip as much as anyone and a monastery is like a small village in that way."

They'd arrived back at the monastery. The conference was ongoing, and she crossed the courtyard at a quickened pace to enter the guesthouse. She pulled up in the doorway, inordinately pleased to find Susanna's maid sitting by the fire, looking rather limp. She was a woman in her middle forties, with a slender build and gray hair that fell loosely around her shoulders—an unusual style for a woman of her age.

Gwen crossed the floor to peer down at her. "Are you all right?"

The woman looked up, sweeping a lock of hair out of her face as she did so. "Do I know you?"

"I'm sorry." Gwen put a hand to her heart. "I am Gwen ferch Meilyr, wife to Gareth. We are staying in the guesthouse too."

"You are from Gwynedd."

"Yes."

The woman sniffed and returned her gaze to the fire. "I am unsure what is wrong with me. My lady was ill last night with a headache, and I meant to sit beside her bed in case she needed me, but I was so tired myself I slept the whole night through."

Without waiting to be invited, Gwen plopped herself down onto a nearby stool and took the woman's hand. "I am so sorry to hear that. Is there anything I can do?"

In the face of Gwen's relentless kindness, the woman couldn't remain aloof. "No, thank you. I really am much better." She gestured to her hair. "I know I must be a sight."

Gwen tucked one of the loose strands behind the woman's ear. "Your hair is lovely."

The woman smiled despite herself. "Thank you."

"I'll fetch you a warm posset. Maybe that will help until the queen returns." Gwen rose to her feet, intending to head for the guesthouse kitchen. Conall had been standing to one side of the door, his arms folded across his chest and one ankle crossed over the other, looking amused again, but he frowned and put out a hand to her before she could. "Do you hear—" He stopped and went to the door.

Gwen followed to find that men were spilling out of the chapter house, and they were in something of an uproar.

"That doesn't look good." Conall shook his head and started down the steps. "I admire Abbot Rhys, but Powys and Gwynedd have ever been at each other's throats. There was no real reason to think it would be any different this time."

Gwen followed after him. "He felt he had to try."

The first bunch of men in Powysian surcoats stalked towards the gatehouse, while a smaller group from Gwynedd milled about, glaring after them. The level of rancor in the courtyard was high. Gwen searched for Gareth, standing on tiptoes so she could see better.

Then a young monk hurtled into the courtyard, coming from the gardens. He skidded to a halt at the sight of so many noblemen, and Conall grabbed him around the shoulders to steady him. "I was sent to find help—" he put his hand to his chest, breathing hard, "—the barn is on fire."

19

Hywel

The messenger spoke to Abbot Rhys, and the news of the burning barn swept through the conclave with hardly a pause from speaker to listener. He'd barely opened his mouth to announce what was happening before the chapter house was deserted.

Hywel instantly sent Gareth off with Gwen and Conall. The barn was where Erik had died, so they might truly regret its loss, depending upon what they'd missed seeing inside it the first time around. Within a few moments, the only people who remained in the chapter house were members of Hywel's own family. Abbot Rhys himself had walked away with Madog, bending his ear with soothing tones, thanking him for sending his own men to assist in fighting the fire.

Hywel had never experienced quite this amount of disarray at the end of any meeting in which his father had participated.

Eventually, the only people left in the room were King Owain, Hywel, Taran, Cynan, and a few retainers, including Gruffydd, who stood at the door, as far away from the action as possible. After sitting back in his chair with a sigh, King Owain looked down for a moment, one hand smoothing his mustache, and then he started to laugh. Hywel looked at Cynan, whose eyes widened as he stared at their father, and then Cynan shook his head, making clear that he had no idea why Owain was laughing, and he wasn't going to be the one to ask.

Hywel sighed. Such was the fate of the *edling*. That thought, again today, made him smile rather than despair. If nothing else, his father's amusement was contagious. He pulled out the chair Rhys had abandoned and sat in it, his eyes on the king.

By now, King Owain was laughing so hard that tears were leaking out of the corners of his eyes. It wasn't until he put both hands on the top of his head and leaned back to look up at the ceiling, trying to gain control of his laughter, that he finally managed to speak. "Old Madog really pulled that one out of the sack, didn't he? Whoo!" He rocked back in his chair, still struggling for control.

"What are you finding so funny?" Hywel said.

Owain wiped his eyes. "We had him, you know. We had him completely in our net." Within the space of a heartbeat, the amusement vanished entirely, and Owain leaned forward to look intently at Hywel. "He tried to kill you. You. My. Son." He poked a finger on the table to emphasize the last three words.

But then he calmed and sat back again. "There really should have been no counter to that. He gambled with your life, and he lost. He should have had to pay a price for his ambition."

Hywel opened his mouth to speak, but his father put up a hand to stop him.

"Cadwaladr's ambition. I know that's what you think." He sighed. "I think it too."

"That wasn't exactly what I was about to say," Hywel said. "You know—and Rhys knows—about what happened in Shrewsbury. But Madog doesn't know that we know it. That Madog and Cadwaladr conspired to sell Madog's people as a quick way for Cadwaladr to raise money so that he can pay someone—Ranulf, perhaps, or one of Alice's other brothers or cousins—to attack Gwynedd remains Cadwaladr's end game. He still wants the throne. Madog must have seen my arrival at Dinas Bran as a way to clear away one more impediment."

"Not that either Madog or Ranulf needs an excuse to attack Gwynedd," Owain added. "We did just take Mold and the surrounding lands."

Hywel nodded. "Nevertheless, though we shouldn't assume it quite yet, I truly believe that Madog himself hired these men to attack that monastery in order to come to the conference with a grievance that was credible and new. Bringing up the death of his father or what happened fifteen years ago before Uncle Cadwallon died might be relevant in the long run—and Madog surely keeps those grievances against Gwynedd fresh—but they would not be enough to convince the conclave that you are in the wrong in the matter of the attack on me."

King Owain tapped his fingers rhythmically on the table. "And that is why Madog truly came to this conference, isn't it? Not for peace, per se."

"It was to convince outsiders, Normans, maybe even King Stephen or Robert of Gloucester, that you are out of control."

"With grief, still, you mean?"

Hywel canted his head to one side, saying yes without saying it.

"Rhun's death has repercussions far beyond the actual loss of him, which is distressing enough," Owain said. "It is time, however, that the other lords of Wales and the March stopped thinking I'm in my dotage. I have many years of rule in me yet."

"I don't doubt it," Hywel said. "In truth, I hope for it."

His father shot him a piercing look. "You mean that."

"Of course I mean it!"

"Not all sons would," Owain said.

Hywel snorted in disgust. "This son has always felt that way. If something were to happen to you, I would lead, and I would want to, but I'm patient. Rhun was too, you know."

"I know." Owain rubbed at his chin. "So, how do we get the better of Madog?"

Hywel smiled. Intrigue was to him like mead was to another man—his lifeblood, even if he'd been neglectful of that side of him of late. "First of all, there are a few things you don't know." He proceeded to relate everything they knew about the investigation into Erik's death, which on the surface appeared peripheral to the situation with Madog, up until last night, when

Susanna had seen Derwena away with the man who might be his killer.

"And this is the sister of the woman Gwen knows, who came here looking for her?" Owain said.

"Yes. It feels coincidental that Gareth, Conall, and Gruffydd witnessed Rhodri's capture last night. If Rhodri really was a member of the marauders, paid for by Madog, then he should have been with them already. Why arrest him and abuse him now? But if I'm wrong, and Madog didn't set this all up, how did they know that Rhodri—a common boy from Corwen—was involved?"

"Puzzling, but not insurmountable," Owain said. "We need to get to Rhodri."

Hywel rose to his feet. "I'll do it. He knows more than he's telling, that is certain. If he will confess to the raid on the conclave, and if he was the one who rode to St. Asaph with Erik, then perhaps he will tell me some detail that will help us discover who murdered Erik and why. In fact, I'll go see him now before anyone else has time to start thinking about what he knows and while most everyone is still at this fire."

Owain pushed to his feet too and jerked his head at Cynan. "With me, son. We will make our unhappiness known to everyone within hailing distance. They will remember us, and nobody will wonder what has become of Hywel."

Cynan grinned. "It will be my pleasure, sir."

The two men transformed their faces into the very epitome of discontent and stalked from the room, mirror images of each other except that Cynan was several inches shorter than his father.

Hywel went out the other way, in the direction the monks had taken Rhodri when they'd left the chapter house.

Hywel had been to the monastery before and had made it his business to know how it was laid out. The monks' dormitory was on the second floor above the chapter house and attached to the church at the north transept, so during the night offices the monks could descend into the church by the night stair without having to go outside. At the same time, while the vast majority of monks participated in the daily life of the monastery, there were times when a brother wanted solitude or was under penance, and such a man moved into a cell in the northern range of buildings, adjacent to the infirmary block.

The cells weren't really cells in the prison sense of the word, but while the dormitory was exactly that—a long, open room where the monks at the monastery slept—the cells were private, each with its own door. There were three of them, tucked between the infirmary pantry and the warming room for the sick. They had their own anteroom, to protect the inhabitants of the cells from weather and the wind that might blow through the window, perhaps a foot square, in their individual wooden doors. Each cell had a second window high up in the back wall. It meant they couldn't see out of it, but daylight could light the cell and save on candles.

Rhodri's cell was being watched by the same two monks who had taken him away. Either Madog really did trust Abbot Rhys to keep Rhodri safe, or he'd been distracted by the fire and hadn't yet given thought to how thoroughly his prisoner might be guarded. Last Hywel had seen, Madog been walking away with Rhys, and somewhere in the back of Hywel's mind, he had a stray thought that Rhys had meant to distract Madog and his men so they left the field clear for Hywel. But then he gave a dismissive shake of his head. Rhys was an old soldier and spy, but he wasn't omnipotent.

The two monks who guarded Rhodri wore hooded robes, hands hidden inside their sleeves. Both were dark and lean in their middle twenties, and they could have been brothers in life as well as vocation. Perhaps they were.

Hywel's boots scraped on the threshold to the anteroom, calling the attention of the two monks to him. "May I speak to the prisoner?"

The expression on the monks' faces would have made Hywel laugh if things were a bit less serious. The brothers knew who Hywel was, and they didn't want to deny him, but they hadn't been given orders regarding who might talk to Rhodri.

"I will be only a moment."

When the two men still hesitated, Hywel put up his hands. "I assure you that I won't harm him! And if anyone asks, you are free to tell him that I came calling."

"Yes, my lord." The two monks left the cell anteroom, instead posting themselves on either side of the exterior door, which remained open. Hywel didn't mind. This wasn't a secret meeting, since the monks had obviously seen him. If word got back to Madog that he'd been here, he wanted there to be no questions about what he'd come for.

The window shutter in the door that blocked Rhodri's cell could be opened from either side, and Rhodri's window lay open flat against the outside of the door, allowing his guards to see what he was doing inside. At the moment, that was nothing, other than sitting on his pallet on the floor, looking, if anything, more miserable than he had in the conclave.

Hywel put his nose to the window. "Come here, boy."

Rhodri looked up. He couldn't have missed Hywel's conversation with the monks, but he was putting on the appearance of caring little for it one way or the other. "I was told to speak to nobody."

"Told by whom?"

"King Madog." As Rhodri said the king's name, he lifted his left hand in a dismissive gesture, and Hywel instantly revised his approach. Though the last finger on Rhodri's left hand was completely normal, his hands were the size of serving platters. Hywel had been going to try to sweet-talk him, but now he decided that amused dismissiveness was a better tactic.

"I don't want to talk to you about the sacking at Wrexham. I already know you weren't paid by my father to do it."

Rhodri was on his feet in an instant. "But I was! We all were! I swear it!"

Hywel was again derisive. "How much did Madog pay you to swear it?"

Rhodri's expression went blank for a moment as he tried to figure out what Hywel had just asked, and then he launched himself at the door. "Nothing!"

Hywel backed off. "How much did Owain pay you, then?"

"Ten pennies each!" That was a fortune for a peasant.

"Do you have those pennies on you now?"

Rhodri stuck out his chin in stubborn defiance. "I spent them."

"Is that why you're here? To get more money out of King Owain?"

"No! He summoned me!"

Hywel looked darkly at Rhodri. "How so?"

"I received a message to meet my contact here at St. Asaph. He had another task for me, one that didn't mean sacking a monastery. That was why I was on the road north of the monastery last night." Rhodri looked down at his feet, seemingly having forgotten about not talking to anyone. "I was supposed to meet one of King Owain's captains there, but King Madog's men appeared instead."

"What was the name of Owain's captain who paid you?"

Rhodri's head came up. "So you believe me?"

"I believe that you were paid, and if it was one of my captains who did it, then I want his name so I can get to the bottom of this quickly—hopefully before the conclave starts again this afternoon."

The boy finally remembered to look mulish again. "I shouldn't tell you."

"You really should. Perhaps it will mean that we go easy on you when you're accused of murder."

Rhodri jerked backwards. "I didn't kill anyone!"

"Your own hands say otherwise."

Rhodri held his hands out in front of him, turning them back and forth.

"I have a dead body in the chapel, one of my men. He was strangled by someone with unusually large hands, and yours would fit around his neck perfectly. And then, a noose will fit around yours."

"A-a-a noose!" Rhodri's horror and confusion seemed genuine.

"In addition, I have a man who will swear that he saw you in the dead man's company three days ago." Hywel's words were a mix of half-lies and outright untruths, but he didn't care as long as they got a reaction out of Rhodri.

Which they did.

"No!" Rhodri staggered away from the door. "I-I-"

"If it wasn't you, then you should tell me the name of the man who paid you, and maybe we can discover together what is really going on here."

Rhodri was still staring at Hywel. Then he moved forward and grasped the sill of the window with both hands. "This is a church! I claim sanctuary!"

"You can claim sanctuary all you want, but only after you tell me this man's name." If Hywel had been inside the room, he would have thrown Rhodri against the wall, and Rhodri seemed to know it, because he cowered before Hywel's wrath, both arms moving to cover his head as if Hywel was about to hit him, which wasn't an illogical assumption. "Gareth! His name was Gareth!"

Hywel so wanted to laugh, but now that the name had been given, he realized he was completely unsurprised to hear it, and that was why he was able to keep his expression serene. Rhodri had just told him far more than a name. He'd given him the identity of the man behind the plot, even if that was a name Rhodri didn't know. Hywel bobbed his chin in thanks and stepped back from the door.

Rhodri lowered his arms, his eyes on Hywel and disbelieving that the questioning was over. "What about me?"

Hywel studied him from several paces away. "Tell your story to the conclave just as you told me. I won't interfere."

"You really do believe me." Rhodri's shoulders sagged.

Hywel scoffed. "Every word you've told me is a lie, but that lie didn't come from you, and *I* believe that *you* believe yourself to be telling the truth. Go ahead and tell it. Obey Madog, do as you are bid, and you will survive this."

"Thank you." Rhodri breathed in and out as if he'd just run a mile.

"No." Hywel gave a low laugh as he turned away. "Thank *you.*"

20

Gwen

Though the men in Madog's party had been leaving the monastery in anger, the fire had effectively distracted them. In short order, everybody—monks, men of Gwynedd and Powys, and half the village, who'd somehow heard about it too—was heading towards the barn. Saran and Tangwen were not among them, Gwen was glad to see. Saran might be new to being grandmother, but she knew when a spectacle was something a two-year-old girl needed to see and when it wasn't.

Gwen gazed around the courtyard, looking for Gwalchmai or her father, but neither was present either. Both knew better than to offer to fight the fire anyway, since to do so could threaten a bard's livelihood. If he took in too much smoke, it affected his voice, and if he helped with the buckets, he could get blisters on his hands—or worse, get them burned. Gwalchmai had loved foolish hijinks when he was a boy, but now that he was a man, he took his responsibilities to his profession and his family seriously.

It took extra time to saddle the horses, but the men thought it was worth it to have transportation. And the time it took also allowed Gareth to give Gwen and Conall a brief summary of the disaster the peace conference had turned into. It was too bad that the rain of yesterday was gone, since they surely could have used a downpour. The night had been relatively clear, and though low clouds hung on the horizon, promising more rain in the future, for now the sky directly above them was windswept blue.

Llelo and Dai met them on the road on the way to the barn, riding towards them from the other direction. Gwen had greeted the boys the day before, but she took a moment to inspect them more closely now. While it had been only a few weeks since she'd seen them, it looked to her like they'd each grown another inch or two while she was in Shrewsbury. They sat in the saddle with the bearing of men, not the boys they'd been six months ago. It made her think about the child in her belly and wonder if it was a boy, knowing if it was he would one day look like them.

By the time they arrived at the barn, more than four dozen men—monks, soldiers, and villagers—had formed a line in order to pass buckets of water to the barn from the river, which lay fifty yards to the west beyond the road. Gareth reined in to the left of the road on the river side. Gwen, who'd been riding double behind him, slid off the back of Braith, and then Gareth dismounted and tied Braith's reins to a small tree. The horse wouldn't typically wander off, but the fire could spook her, and they didn't want her to race away or get tangled in the brush in her fear. At least the wind was blowing from the west, so the smoke was directed the other way and didn't choke them where they stood.

The people who were fighting the fire were doing so valiantly, but a few moments of watching showed Gwen that whatever they were doing would serve only to stop the flames from spreading. There was no hope of saving the barn, not with the walls all but consumed already. There might not have been any hope within a few moments of it starting. The monks had stored hay here and not much else, and hay was the best tinder there was.

A person couldn't grow to adulthood without witnessing at least one house fire. They were extremely common because they could be started so easily. A log could roll out of a fireplace or grate and light the whole house. A lantern could tip over and spill its oil, fueling a quick-burning fire. Stable or barn fires were generally started one of three ways: a lightning strike on the roof, a carelessly placed torch, or an overturned lantern. Gwen had never been to the barn herself, but Gareth had told her that the roof was the most structurally sound part of the building, and even though it was thatch, the fire was only just getting started in it while the rest of the barn had already been half-consumed beneath it. It did seem that the rain of yesterday had made some difference, in that one day with thin March sunlight wasn't enough time to dry it out.

"Nothing like a good fire to unite warring factions." Conall's eyes were fixed on the smoke and flames pouring from the loft.

"Do you genuinely think that's what this is?" Gwen said. "That it was set on purpose?"

"It wasn't a lightning strike. We've had no rain today." Gareth's eyes were equally assessing as he took in the destruction. "But the abbot would never countenance this."

"What about your king?" Conall said.

Gareth rubbed his chin. "This isn't like him."

"But it's like Hywel," Gwen said in an undertone. "You know it is."

Gareth shook his head. "Not this time."

"I'm not the only one who might think it, though." Conall turned to look at Gareth. "Hywel couldn't have known that the conference would fall to pieces so easily, but he had to have considered the possibility and what might be the outcome if it did."

Gwen didn't like the idea that Hywel might be making moves without them again. He'd sworn not to lie to Gwen anymore. Gareth, on the other hand, seemed unconcerned by the suspicion—or maybe he just didn't want to think about it. He motioned towards the men with buckets and said to Conall, "Aren't you going to help?"

Conall coughed dryly. "I'm right behind you."

Neither man moved, which had Gwen fighting the giggles, not that either their injuries or the burning barn were in any way funny. Llelo and Dai hadn't hesitated and had already joined the line. Gwen took one step forward, intending to follow them, but in the same moment that Gareth reached for her elbow to stop her, a monk detached himself from the front of the line, where he'd been directing the men as to where to toss the water, and came towards them. Once he arrived, Gareth introduced her to him, and he turned out to be Mathonwy, the milkman.

Mathonwy gestured helplessly to the barn. "It's just terrible."

"It seems that we have involved ourselves in something beyond the usual, and this is not your fault unless you were the one to set the fire," Gareth said.

Mathonwy gaped at him. "No, my lord! Of course not!"

"Do you have any idea how it started?" Gwen said. "Did you leave a lantern behind?"

He ducked his head in a quick, though not entirely perfunctory, obeisance. "Madam. I don't bring fire to barns if I can help it. That's why I'm always anxious to finish the milking before the sun sets." He smiled ruefully. "I don't mean to be rude, my lord, but you and Sir Conall would be better off asking these questions of yourselves. Other than my presence last night and this morning, you two were the only men to visit the barn since we found the body."

Conall raised his eyebrows. "You think so? I highly doubt it."

Mathonwy turned towards him. "Why? What do you mean?"

The question elicited a laugh from Conall, though his expression was somewhat morose. "I strongly suspect the barn has been visited on and off for two days." He glanced at Gareth. "I didn't think it was important to set a watch to take an accounting of those who visited."

Gareth shook his head. "I didn't either."

Mathonwy was bewildered. "Why would anyone come here?"

Gwen knew the answer to that. "To gawk. Murder was done here, and evil draws people to it."

Gareth added, "It is possible that the murderer was among them."

Conall scoffed under his breath. "Certainly the man who set the fire was."

That made Mathonwy frown. "The fire could have been an accident."

Gareth, Gwen, and Conall just looked at him, not bothering to actually express their disbelief in words.

Conall sighed. "We hate coincidences, Brother Mathonwy. How likely is it that the day after a body is discovered in the barn, it burns to the ground?"

Mathonwy spread his hands wide. "Coincidences are not unheard of. They happen all the time."

"Maybe in your line of work," Gareth said.

Gwen put a hand on Gareth's arm, quelling his uncharacteristic abruptness. His wounds must really be paining him. "Speaking of coincidences, we have a few questions to ask you about your visit to the treasury with Abbot Rhys the other day."

Mathonwy blinked at the change of subject. Gwen had to admit that from Mathonwy's perspective, it was an odd question to be asking with the barn burning behind him.

"Uh … what is it that you want to ask me?"

"What was your role in the accounting?"

"I went through the items in the treasury side by side with Abbot Rhys while he checked the items off his list."

"What was Prior Anselm's role?" Gareth said.

Mathonwy shrugged. "He counted the coins, and then Abbot Rhys and I counted the coins. I think one of the reasons the abbot chose me that day was because I can count."

"From your years of counting cows in order to keep track of them?" Gwen said.

"Cows, sheep, chickens." Mathonwy nodded. "I'm not much good for reading or writing, but I like numbers, and I remember them."

"At the time did the number of coins in the record match the number of coins counted?" Gareth said.

"Yes." Mathonwy was very sure, though as he spoke he looked warily at Gareth, who'd just implied that they no longer did. Mathonwy didn't ask for more information, however—just had a look in his eye as if he was putting that thought away to take out later to examine further.

"Thank you." Gareth nodded at Mathonwy, who returned to the line of monks and his bucket.

Gwen still had the idea that she should be working alongside them, but Gareth kept her hand in his. "It's a lost cause, Gwen."

"They're working on it as a matter of principle." Conall yawned and immediately bent over in a fit of coughing.

Gwen moved to him concerned. He had cracked ribs and possible internal bleeding, so she'd been keeping an eye on him since Shrewsbury, fearful that any one of his numerous wounds would fester.

He put up a hand. "It's just the smoke. I'm all right."

"What do you think?" She turned to look up at Gareth.

"About Conall, Mathonwy, or the barn?"

"Any. All."

Conall straightened. "I'm fine."

Gareth shot him a skeptical look but then answered Gwen's question. "I don't think Mathonwy is lying about either the barn or his work in the treasury. I have met men like him who remember numbers. If he says that the coins matched the record book, it only corroborates what Abbot Rhys himself told us. If Rhys is lying to us, I don't want to know."

Conall made a *huh* sound deep in his chest that wasn't quite a cough, the implication being that Gareth should know better than to dismiss anyone as a suspect.

Gareth gave a noncommittal motion with his head. "Neither Gwen nor I can seriously contemplate wrongdoing on Rhys's part. Some people you just have to trust, and if they betray you in the end, so be it. The love and trust along the way are worth it."

"All right. I was just asking." Conall swallowed hard, and Gwen had an instant thought that Gareth's words weren't only about Rhys—and Conall knew it.

"It seems to me that what we have here is a string of second thoughts," Gwen said. "Erik is murdered and the body discarded, but then stolen later. In the same way, the body is returned, but then the barn is burned after a full day has passed. It's as if someone had what they thought was a good idea at the time, and then reconsidered later."

"That is a devilish idea." Conall actually sounded pleased, his voice full of admiration. "Are you sure you're not a villain yourself, my lady?"

It was another jest, and Gwen obliged him with a laugh, but then coughed herself as smoke wafted in their direction, swirling around as the wind picked up for a moment.

Gareth made a guttural sound deep in his throat. "I should have scouted the area better rather than leaving it to the boys."

"The boys are fine." Gwen put a hand on her husband's arm. "Neither of you are really in top form, Gareth, but even so, from what you've said, you didn't have time. In a way, we have been putting out fires from the moment we arrived in St. Asaph. We've been reacting instead of acting, but I don't know what else we could have done through any of this. It isn't as if we know yet why Erik died. What with dead spies, complicit queens, and long lost friends, none of this makes any sense."

With a roar, the roof of the barn crashed inward, and within two heartbeats, it was a pile of burning rubble. It was really too bad that the rain had stopped, because they could have used it. The only upside to the collapse was that the monks had an easier time reaching the flames, which were getting more under control, now that the roof had smothered much of the fire beneath it.

"We don't know much, but we do know something." Gareth tipped his head to indicate that Gwen and Conall should come with him, and he moved them under the overhang of a tree, another ten paces from the barn. The sound of the fire had been making them speak louder than normal. This way, they were farther away from anyone who might overhear and could speak more softly themselves. "We are looking for at least five men, maybe more, and I don't believe five men moving bodies and burning barns are all that easy to hide. We still haven't shown Rhodri to Deiniol, but if he was Erik's companion, then at least we have one question answered."

"And what Queen Susanna and Derwena have to do with all this we don't know either," Gwen said. "Don't forget that Dai saw Derwena go off with a nine-fingered man, who could have killed Erik."

Gareth looked down at her, a smile twitching at the corner of his mouth. "You really like calling him that, don't you?"

"Because that's what he is!" Her words were protesting, but she laughed again. "I know you have never trusted Erik, Gareth, and that he was a spy, but it looks to me like he knew about the sacking of Deiniol's monastery and was riding to Hywel to tell him about it. Perhaps he stopped in St. Asaph because he'd feared that this monastery was going to be a target too."

Gareth's eyes turned thoughtful. "Wrexham was a raid, and this a quiet theft of a few items. The men who raided there burned it to the ground—" He stopped, his eyes moving towards the destroyed barn.

Conall's jaw hardened. "Then again—"

At that moment, Abbot Rhys, who'd been watching from the other side of the barn, came around to the front and stopped twenty paces away from them to study the destruction. He was deep in conversation with Anselm, both men standing with their arms folded across their chests.

Gwen's brow furrowed. Three had become two. "Where's Lwc? I haven't seen him all day."

"He wasn't at the conclave," Gareth said, "which now that I think about it is somewhat surprising. Up until now, he has hardly left Rhys's side unless he was at yours, Gwen."

"You know, there's a few others who ought to be here but aren't. Deiniol, for one—" Gwen broke off from what she'd been about to say, and all three of them looked towards the monastery.

Gareth began walking rapidly back to where he'd picketed Braith. "Let's go see what we've been missing."

21

Gwalchmai

Gwalchmai had sworn to his father, to Gareth, and to Gwen that he would stay out of their investigations. Unfortunately, this time—as every time, truth be told—that promise was proving impossible to keep. After singing at the beginning of the conference to put everyone in the proper frame of mind, he'd gone to the chapel to practice his scales, while his father had chosen to wander the gardens. King Owain wanted a new song, and it was Meilyr's task to write one. Gwalchmai didn't envy him. Gwalchmai himself had been writing his own songs for years, but he hadn't yet mustered up the courage to share any of them with anyone but Iorwerth, the king's son and Gwalchmai's best friend.

At the moment, Iorwerth crouched beside him in an alcove in the cloister, the eyes of both young men fixed on the west range where the abbot's quarters and the treasury were located. Gwalchmai knew where the treasury was from eavesdropping on Gareth and Gwen, who'd been discussing the progress of the investigation last night when they thought everyone else was asleep. They should have known better.

For his part, Gwalchmai had been involved enough in their cases to know when something nefarious was going on, and from what he understood, nobody was supposed to enter the treasury without the express permission of Abbot Rhys. It could be that his secretary, Lwc, had been given permission, but with everyone else fighting the fire, somehow Gwalchmai doubted it. By rights they should all be at a meal, as noon had come and gone. Gwalchmai's stomach growled, reminding him that he hadn't eaten since breakfast.

Iorwerth heard it too, elbowed him, and spoke in a low whisper, "Don't remind me. I'm hungry too!" In the last year, Iorwerth, who was born the year before Gwalchmai, had grown tall, and the combination of his training to be a knight and his voracious appetite had resulted in a broad chest and thick muscles in his arms.

"Is your father going to be worried about you since you're missing dinner?"

"He went with Taran to the camp. He hardly notices when I'm beside him, so I doubt he'll notice if I'm not. If he chastises me for my absence later, I'm thinking I'll have something to tell him."

The little bit of doubt Gwalchmai and Iorwerth had about what they were doing (spying) and if they'd misunderstood the situation was the only thing keeping them from confronting the young monk. Gwalchmai told himself it was best to watch, follow, and then report to Gwen and Gareth as soon as they returned from the barn. Iorwerth, of course, was all for whatever Gwalchmai had in mind.

Gwalchmai hadn't ever heard the phrase *inside man* until last night, and he hadn't really known what Gareth had meant by the term until he saw it with his own eyes: Lwc was the inside man in the monastery, and he was using his role as the abbot's secretary to steal from him.

The very idea burned Gwalchmai's gut.

"What better way to get everyone out of the monastery than to start a fire?" Iorwerth said in a whisper.

"I was just thinking that too." Gwalchmai put a hand on Iorwerth's arm. "There he goes!"

Lwc came out of the treasury, closed the door behind him, and hastened down the stone passage to the exit near the west entrance to the church. That would take him to the pathway that ran past the guesthouse into the courtyard. Gwalchmai would have thought *someone* would be watching, but even if they were, maybe they wouldn't notice how bulky Lwc had become under his encompassing robe. Gwalchmai probably wouldn't have noticed if he hadn't just seen him come out of the treasury.

"Let's go!" Iorwerth sprang to his feet, and the two boys left their hiding position at a run, making for the same door Lwc had just gone through. When they reached it, however, there was no sign of Lwc. They looked at each other for a heartbeat, acknowledging that there were only two ways Lwc could have gone, and with a nod, split up. Iorwerth took off down the path that led to the monastery gardens, and Gwalchmai headed left towards the courtyard. Either path could take Lwc out of the monastery, and it was just a question of guessing right as to which one Lwc thought would be least watched.

Gwalchmai set off at an easy jog, soon hitting the cobbles that formed the walkway into the courtyard, but when he reached it, nobody was in sight. He warred with himself for a moment as to whether he should keep watch at the gatehouse—the only avenue in and out of the monastery on the south side—or run after Iorwerth. He cursed himself for not having chosen that way to go, because even now he could picture his friend tailing Lwc, discovering what had become of the treasure, and getting all the glory of the discovery.

Still dithering, Gwalchmai ran to the entrance to the monastery and stood in the road outside. Nobody appeared, not even the gatekeeper, who seemed to be snoring where he sat. Gwalchmai turned in a full circle on one heel. Nothing seemed amiss, either in or out of the monastery.

But then, both to Gwalchmai's relief that he hadn't guessed wrong and dismay that he was right to be worried, Deiniol appeared in the stable doorway, leading his horse, followed immediately by Lwc. It wasn't as if either could help noticing Gwalchmai, since he was standing smack in the middle of their way out. However, Deiniol directed his steps towards the gatehouse, a rueful smile on his lips. "A bad business."

In contrast to Deiniol's easy familiarity, Lwc faltered at the sight of Gwalchmai—and it was that falter that renewed Gwalchmai's faith that he was on the right track.

"Where are you going at this hour of the day?" Gwalchmai made sure his tone was full of curiosity, not belligerence.

Deiniol smiled again. "The abbot gave me permission to ride down the road some ways in search of my brothers from Wrexham. I would have thought that they'd be here by now, and I'm worried that something has happened to them along the way."

Before Gwalchmai could think of how to reply to that, first Conall, with Iorwerth behind him on his horse, and then Gareth and Gwen, appeared, riding down the path that led past the front door of the church. Their horses' hooves couldn't help but make a clopping sound on the cobbles. At the sound, both Deiniol and Lwc turned—in Lwc's case with a jerky motion—to look.

Conall paused to let Iorwerth off the horse, and the young prince skirted the perimeter of the courtyard on foot, heading towards the narrow path by the stable that led north out of the courtyard. When he reached it, he simply stood in the middle of it, effectively acting as a barrier in case Deiniol and Lwc thought to flee. Iorwerth posed an actual threat, seeing as how he was taller and more muscled than Gwalchmai, who was a bard, not a warrior.

Both Lwc and Deiniol kept their backs to Gwalchmai, who stayed where he was. If the two monks really had been up to something, they would not want to take their eyes off Conall and Gareth, even injured as both men were. For his part, Conall urged his horse closer to the gatehouse where Deiniol, Lwc, and Gwalchmai waited.

Gwalchmai decided to draw Deiniol's attention back to him to give the others a chance to get closer before anything happened. "Your brothers have a long way to walk. How can you possibly ensure that you'll travel the same path as they?"

"The Lord will guide me." It was a platitude Gwalchmai had heard before, but it didn't seem right coming out of Deiniol's mouth, and it made him hesitate to ask anything else because Deiniol seemed to have an answer for everything. Gwalchmai himself was starting to feel stupid.

Fortunately, by now Gwen and Gareth had dismounted, and Gwen moved to Lwc's side. She stood so close to him that it made Gwalchmai uncomfortable. Gareth leaned casually against the wall of the gatehouse tunnel.

Gwalchmai met Gwen's eyes for a heartbeat, and she gave him a hint of a nod. He took it as an indication that not only did she want him to continue asking questions, but that she and Gareth were on the same track he was.

He looked at Deiniol. "It seems an odd time for you to go, given that the barn is burning down and we're in the middle of an important peace conference."

"That makes it the best time. Abbot Rhys has many responsibilities and hands to do the work, and I will be little missed."

"You may be little missed, but I would have thought that Abbot Rhys needed Lwc now more than ever." Gwen had finally decided to speak. "We saw the abbot standing without you just now, Lwc. It's puzzling to me that you didn't go to the barn with him."

Lwc started. "Brother Deiniol asked for my assistance in preparing for his journey, and I gave it."

Then Conall spoke from behind them. "I'd like to take a look at your bags, Deiniol, before you go."

"Of course you may, but why would you want to?" For the first time, Deiniol's placating smile faltered, and anger flashed in his eyes for a single heartbeat before he mastered it.

"That would be because Prince Iorwerth and I spent the last half-hour watching Lwc carrying the monastery's wealth from the treasury to the stable," Gwalchmai said in a voice loud enough to carry to Iorwerth, who nodded vigorously back.

"Lwc! Why would you do such a thing?" Deiniol took a step to one side, putting space between him and Lwc. Gareth now edged closer, encroaching on Lwc's space as Gwen was on Deiniol's.

For his part, Lwc's face paled and stayed pale, making him far easier to read, even for Gwalchmai. Gwen noticed too, and her lips pressed together tightly as she looked at the young monk.

Deiniol was a good enough mummer for an Easter play, and even Gwalchmai might have been convinced of his innocence if Lwc hadn't taken that moment of distraction to rabbit. He dashed past Gwalchmai, knocking him off balance with a hard shove, and disappeared through the open gate.

Gwalchmai was after him in an instant. "I got him!"

He took off at a hard run, knowing that neither Conall nor Gareth were in any shape to run anywhere.

After leaving the gatehouse, Lwc took a right so as to head west, towards the bridge across the river. Gwalchmai pounded down the road after him, not really gaining but not falling behind either. Then Lwc reached the corner of the monastery and took a right, heading down the road in the direction of the fire. Smoke wafted into the afternoon sky, blowing east. As he ran, Gwalchmai was trying to predict what Lwc thought he was doing, since he was running directly towards a hundred men, any one of whom could stop him simply by standing in the middle of the road and blocking it. Perhaps he hoped to swim the river and escape that way.

After another fifty yards or so, Gwalchmai realized that he was definitely gaining on the young monk, who'd had to hike up his long robes and hold them above his knees to free his legs. Gwalchmai could simply pound along, his arms and legs pumping furiously. He was only a hundred feet behind when Conall passed him on horseback. Another fifty yards farther on, Lwc swerved to the left into the trees that lined the river, except they'd reached the vicinity of the millpond and watermill. The young monk launched himself over the stone wall that marked the mill's domains. With a desultory casualness, Conall's horse leapt it immediately after.

By the time Gwalchmai clambered over the wall himself, Lwc was on the ground in the clearing before the mill where grain carts parked, with Conall's knee in his back and Conall's horse casually chuffing at the margins of the clearing for grass. As

Gwalchmai trotted up, his breath coming less in gasps than it had a moment ago, Conall waved a hand to his saddle bags. "Rope, if you will."

"Yes, sir." Gwalchmai unbuckled the satchel on the back of Conall's horse and rummaged inside until he came up with a length of rope, which he tossed to the Irishman. If anyone asked, Gwalchmai could say with certainty that Conall himself possessed no jewels or coins beyond what was in his purse. Not that Gwalchmai would have expected otherwise, but it was good to be thorough.

Conall quickly tied Lwc's hands behind his back, pulled him to his feet, and gave him a little shake. "You stole from the monastery, yes? Gwalchmai can testify that you did, so don't bother to lie."

"Yes." Lwc's head was down. Every line of his body spoke of misery.

"Is this the first time, or did you steal a few pennies last week?"

"That wasn't me."

Conall frowned and glanced at Gwalchmai, who already knew from his eavesdropping that some money had been missing from the monastery before today. It was odd for Lwc to lie about it, however, since he was well and truly caught. "Where did you put what you stole? Will I find it in Deiniol's bags?"

"No. It's in the stable, hidden in grain sacks."

"Whose idea was it to burn the barn to the ground?" Conall said. "Yours or Deiniol's?"

Lwc's head came up. "That wasn't us! We didn't burn anything!"

"You're trying to tell me that you never planned to steal from the monastery, but the opportunity presented itself so you took it?" Conall's voice was dripping with disdain.

"No! We were going to do it after the peace conference ended. With so many people about, it's easier to keep your head down and do whatever you like. That's what Deiniol said, and it's true! We just had to wait until Abbot Rhys was occupied. It was meant to be tonight at dinner, which is being held at the Powys encampment."

"How about murder?" Conall said. "Was it you who killed Erik to stop him from exposing your plan to steal from the monastery?"

Lwc shook his head frantically back and forth. Gwalchmai felt a little sick to see the fear on his face. "I didn't kill anyone!"

"Why was Deiniol leaving if the gold was still in the stable?" Conall said. "What was supposed to happen next?"

"This evening at dusk, I was to wheel it in a hand barrow out the back gate of the monastery. We figured that with everyone at the dinner, it would be easy to slip by without anyone asking questions."

"And what about you?" Gwalchmai said because he couldn't help himself. His dismay had turned to disgust. "How much were you to keep for yourself?"

Lwc's mouth dropped open, and he looked pleadingly at Conall. "The gold wasn't for me! It was for my monastery. Deiniol was going to give it to our abbot so he could rebuild it!"

Gwalchmai took a step forward. "You came from Wrexham too?"

Lwc nodded frantically.

Conall barked a laugh. "What kind of sense does it make to steal treasure from one monastery to rebuild another?"

Uncertainty entered Lwc's eyes. "Uh ... well ... Deiniol said that the bishop took the gold that should have gone to Wrexham and gave it to Abbot Rhys. Deiniol said that Abbot Rhys didn't deserve his station, that he was grasping and ambitious—" Lwc broke off, head hanging down again.

Conall let his silent disbelief drag out for a count of ten. Lwc refused to look at either of them.

"Are you even a monk?" Gwalchmai said.

That question had his head jerking up again. "Of course I'm a monk! I came as an infant to Wrexham!"

"How is it that you came to St. Asaph to be the abbot's secretary?" Conall said.

"I can read and write. Deiniol told me how to write out the orders so they'd be believed. Deiniol had the bishop's seal to mark it, and then he sent me here in advance of him. After the thefts, I was to stay another week and then head back south." Lwc hung his head again. It was an odd pose for a man who'd just stolen a fortune from a monastery.

Conall noted the irony too. "You have an interesting relationship with the Ten Commandments, son." He canted his head as he looked at Lwc. "How long was Deiniol a monk at Wrexham?"

Lwc's face went blank for a moment, as if it had just occurred to him that Deiniol might be not what he seemed. Gwalchmai wasn't yet sixteen, but he'd sung for kings since he was nine years old. He watched people out of need and habit and because, more often than not, up until they'd returned to Aber four years ago, he'd always been on the outside of every social situation, looking in to what he couldn't have.

"He arrived a fortnight before we were raided, riding from Abbey Cwm Hir." Lwc paused. "Or so he said. The abbot believed him," Lwc ended, somewhat defensively.

Gwalchmai pulled on his lower lip as he thought. "What about Brother Anselm?"

"What about him?"

"I remember Gwen saying that the two of you arrived in St. Asaph together, both sent from the bishop. That was a lie in your case. What about his? Is he working for Deiniol too?"

"No!" Again, Lwc looked horrified. "I joined him on the road, just a few hours out from St. Asaph. He seemed surprised to see me, but because I had a letter from the bishop too, he accepted me."

"This is Bishop Meurig of Bangor, yes?" Conall said.

Lwc nodded. "But he isn't in Bangor right now. He journeyed to Chester on St. Dafydd's day and is still there, meeting with Chester's bishop and visiting Lichfield and Coventry." Lwc spoke these words rapidly, as if he didn't know them to be true for himself but had heard someone else say them.

Conall barked a laugh at Lwc's pedantic tone. "You heard that from Abbot Rhys, did you?"

"Yes, sir."

"You respect him—Abbot Rhys, that is—don't you?" Gwalchmai said. "You know that what Deiniol told you isn't true, don't you? You probably knew it from your first day at the monastery."

Lwc was back to staring at his feet. "I do."

Conall put a gloved finger to Lwc's chin, forcing him to look up. "Then why would you steal the monastery's wealth?"

"I didn't have a choice—" he broke off.

"How so?" Conall said.

Lwc's lower lip stuck out. He was affecting a pose like Gwalchmai might have at five years old when Gwen caught him in wrongdoing. "Deiniol threatened to tell the abbot that I had come here to steal. I didn't want the abbot to think badly of me."

"How did you think he was going to feel when he found the monastery's wealth gone, you gone, and his monastery sacked?" Conall said.

Lwc gaped at him. "What did you say? Who said anything about sacking?"

Conall tsked through his teeth at Lwc's foolishness. "Theft at Wrexham and theft at St. Asaph—and Deiniol and you present at both places. Is anyone going to think that's a coincidence? How long before the band of marauders arrive to take what's left and destroy the monastery?"

"Those were men from Gwynedd! Hired by King Owain! Everybody knows that! Deiniol said that King Madog captured one of the men responsible last night!" Lwc was practically gasping with righteousness at being so falsely accused.

Conall studied him, tugging on one ear again, which Gwalchmai was beginning to recognize as something he did when he was thinking. "What the king is going to believe, rather than anything you've said so far because it defies reason that anyone could be so foolish, is that you've been in league with the bandits all along. You let them into Wrexham, and then you came to St. Asaph to try the same thing here. The peace conference upended your plans, so you set fire to the barn to distract everyone, stole the treasure, and were about to ride away with it." Conall looked at Gwalchmai. "It makes perfect sense, doesn't it?"

Gwalchmai tried to look very serious. "It does." He marveled at how the boy could have been so thoroughly deceived. Of course, he hadn't been raised on the road as Gwalchmai had, but in a monastery. If nothing else, however, Lwc should have known that stealing was wrong, no matter how desperate the need.

"No, no, no! That's not it at all!"

Conall dragged Lwc over to his horse and lashed the end of a second piece of rope around his wrists. He kept tight hold of the other end, even as he boosted Gwalchmai onto the horse's back. "Tell Gareth and Gwen what Lwc has said. We'll be along shortly."

Looking down at the pair of them, Gwalchmai hesitated, wanting to say something, to thank Conall for including him and trusting him. He wanted to sneer at Lwc for being perhaps the stupidest man he'd ever met.

Misunderstanding Gwalchmai's hesitation, Conall said, "Don't worry. I won't hurt him."

Gwalchmai nodded, relieved, and urged the horse towards the stone wall. But just before the horse leapt it, he caught Conall's laughter and added comment, "—much."

22

Hywel

For the last quarter of an hour since he'd left Rhodri's cell and arrived in the courtyard, Hywel had been getting an earful, first from Gareth and Gwen about what had been going on since he'd last spoken to them, and then from Iorwerth, detailing his surveillance of Lwc's theft of the treasury. It was hard to believe so much could have gone wrong in so short a time—hard to believe, that is, if he hadn't been associated with Gareth and Gwen for as long as he had. Deiniol, one of the apparent culprits keeping Hywel from his father's side, had been tied at the wrists and attached by a rope to a post in the stable, out of earshot of Gareth's narration but not out of sight.

Then Conall's horse turned under the gatehouse, Gwalchmai instead of Conall mounted on its back, and trotted up to where the trio were standing.

"Did you catch him?" Gareth said by way of a greeting.

Gwalchmai dropped to the ground with an envious agility. Hywel wasn't injured like Gareth, but he was tired—and growing older. His muscles were stiffer after riding in a way that hadn't been the case a few years ago.

"Conall did. Lwc told us a tale, one worth hearing. It might even be true." Gwalchmai lifted his chin to glare in Deiniol's direction and raised his voice so that it could be heard across the distance. "He says Deiniol murdered Erik."

At the accusation, Deiniol showed a surfeit of emotion, struggling against the rope that bound him so that he could move closer. "He can't have said that! I didn't murder anyone. I didn't steal anything either."

"Did he really say that Deiniol murdered Erik?" Gareth said in an undertone to Gwalchmai.

Gwalchmai turned his face away from Deiniol. "No, but he did blame Deiniol for the idea to steal from the monastery. The treasure is hidden in sacks of feed in the stable. Lwc was going to wheel them out in a handbarrow later tonight."

Gareth put a hand on Gwalchmai's shoulder. "Good work." He strode off, past Deiniol and into the stable.

Gwalchmai and Gwen in tow, Hywel approached Deiniol. "If you didn't murder Erik, do you mean to imply that you convinced Lwc to murder Erik for you?"

"What's this about murder? There's been no murder—not by me!" Deiniol said. "You can't think it!"

Hywel canted his head. "Do you know who I am?"

Gareth had greeted Hywel when he'd arrived as *my prince*, so if Deiniol had been paying attention at all he should know that

Hywel was a man of importance, even if he didn't realize that he was the *edling*.

Deiniol's jaw clenched. Given that Deiniol had been caught with Lwc, and that he was also their only witness to the existence of Erik's friend, they'd gone full circle with him. It was doubtful that they could believe anything he said.

Still, Hywel took his refusal to answer as an assent of a kind and said, "Then you know that I have the power to hang you right now for murder on Lwc's word. We are in the middle of a war, and we don't have time for the niceties of lawyering. Can you produce anyone to vouch for your innocence?"

Deiniol licked his lips, looking more uncertain with every breath. "No, my lord."

"Then you would be wise to admit to the lesser charge of theft and tell us what you did do rather than risk the greater one, don't you think?" Gareth returned from the stable, holding a silver candlestick in one hand and a bag of coins in the other.

Deiniol tugged fruitlessly on his bindings. "I have never seen those before! This is not my doing, but Lwc's! I came into the stable at the same time Lwc was tying closed one of the feed sacks. I had nothing to do with any theft! I was in the wrong place at the wrong time. That's all. You *have* to believe me."

"We really don't," Gareth said.

Deiniol's eyes moved from Gareth's face to something beyond Hywel. Hywel turned to look and saw Conall and Lwc entering under the gatehouse, Lwc on a leading rein. The boy looked appropriately cowed, a little rough around the edges with dirt smearing the front of his robe, but his face showed no bruising.

At the sight of Hywel, Gwen, and Gareth at the entrance to the stable with Deiniol tied to a post, Conall stopped fifty feet away and didn't approach. Hywel jerked his head in the direction of the cloister, thinking it wise to keep Lwc and Deiniol separated until he heard the full story from both of them. Conall tugged Lwc towards the far side of the courtyard, and Hywel turned back to Deiniol, whose eyes had bugged out a little at the sight of the younger monk.

Hywel pursed his lips and then waved a hand. "Watch them, you two," he said, referring to Iorwerth and Gwalchmai, "while we confer."

The four adults moved to the center of the courtyard, equal distance between the two culprits but no closer to understanding what was really going on here.

"What exactly did Lwc say?" Hywel said to Conall.

While Conall gave a summary of his interrogation of Lwc, Hywel's eyes stayed on the boy. He sat on the ground in his dirty robe, his knees pulled up and his chin resting on them. Then he turned to look at Deiniol, whose expression had turned even more apprehensive.

Conall concluded with a lifted chin. "What does Deiniol say?"

"He denies any wrongdoing, up to and including having a hand in the thefts," Gareth said.

"Can we believe either of them?" Gwen said.

Hywel looked at her, thinking her comment uncharacteristically suspicious. "You don't think Lwc speaks the truth?"

"Clearly he's involved since Gwalchmai and Iorwerth saw him stealing from the treasury, and we've recovered what he stole. But it's awfully convenient of him to play the innocent and put all the blame on Deiniol, who we have so far caught in no wrongdoing."

"We simply find him smarmy and off-putting." Conall spoke matter-of-factly, in a manner Hywel had grown accustomed to hearing from him.

"Does it change anything to know that I spoke with Rhodri just now, and he claims that he was paid by my father to be among those who sacked the monastery?" Hywel said. "He accuses Gareth of being his paymaster, and he is prepared to say so in front of everyone at the conclave."

The three others gaped at him, prompting a harsh laugh from Hywel.

"Not again!" Gwen was holding Gareth's hand so tightly her knuckles whitened. "How do we prove otherwise?"

Hywel shook his head dismissively. "Madog has no power over my men, and he knows it. The timeline is easy to disprove, and I will be the one to do it. It's a distraction to impress his own lords, who won't believe a word I say, but it doesn't matter because by naming Gareth, Rhodri has named the real culprit."

"Cadwaladr," Gareth, Gwen, and Conall said together.

Hywel canted his head. "It's likely, but so far unprovable unless someone talks."

"Which brings us back to Deiniol and Lwc," Gwen said.

"The monastery has three cells, and now we have three men to fill them," Hywel said. "I say we let them stew a while. Erik's dead, but so far his is the only death. It's a puzzle, but it's *my* puzzle. I don't want the conclave having anything to do with it."

"Even if when Deiniol sees Rhodri and tells us that he was the man with Erik, we can't believe him, since it would be in his best interests to implicate someone else. And if Deiniol doesn't recognize Rhodri, we can't believe that either," Gareth said.

"I know it doesn't look like it right now, but we are getting closer." Hywel told them about Rhodri's enormous hands, even if he had no broken or missing finger.

"We can't hang a man for having large hands." Gareth ran a hand through his hair. "He feels as innocent in all this as Lwc."

"Which means *not at all.*" Hywel tsked through his teeth. "You'll note that neither Lwc nor Deiniol has a damaged left hand either."

"I noticed," Gareth said sourly.

Hywel looked at Gwen. "Find Abbot Rhys and tell him what's happened. We'll take care of Lwc and Deiniol, secure the treasure, and then meet you back at the guesthouse." He lifted his chin to draw her attention to the sound of returning firefighters, whose chattering could be clearly heard, coming from the monastery gardens. "We need to hurry before the conclave starts again."

Gwen stared at him aghast. "Surely with all that has happened, Abbot Rhys will postpone another session until tomorrow!"

Hywel tsked through his teeth at her innocence. "He won't. He has two factions in his monastery who hate each other. Leaving them to their own devices for the afternoon is a recipe for war, not peace, and he knows it."

23

Gareth

The investigation was becoming more absurd with every hour that passed. That wasn't something Gareth might have said about any murder a month ago, but with his new policy of not allowing these investigations to overburden him, he could see the humor in the situation. Gareth could take some consolation in the fact that Hywel was right that the only body they'd found so far had been Erik's, even if they'd found it twice.

Still, after the meeting with the horrified Abbot Rhys, Gareth went to check that Erik's body, having been washed by now and prepared for burial, was still in the room off the cloister where he'd left it last night—and that the two monks whose job it was to pray over him hadn't raced to put out the burning barn with the rest of their brothers and allowed someone to take it.

At the sight of the two monks sitting where he'd left them, Gareth let out a sigh of relief. They looked up as he entered, but other than a raised hand, Gareth didn't speak to them. This wasn't one of those monasteries where silence was enforced—not like some of the English houses—but unnecessary conversation was frowned upon. Gareth had been spending so much time in monasteries lately that he was growing used to the habit of conversing with gestures rather than words.

He'd been here until very late last night, doing more than his duty, in fact. Every soldier who'd spent any time at war had seen men's insides spill to the ground, ripped open by a blade in the course of battle. But the Church looked askance at cutting open a man for any reason, as well they should, seeing such efforts as rooted in paganism. Gareth had been given permission to examine Erik, however, and he had made the most of it. He'd even put charcoal to paper, sketching the locations of each of Erik's organs—what was left of them, that is. The length of a man's intestines alone was a revelation. Gareth didn't know when such a record might come in useful again, but he was neither squeamish nor one to waste an opportunity to learn more about his craft when it was presented to him.

Having verified that Erik's body was still there, Gareth returned to the monastery guesthouse, where a belated meal was finally being laid out. Gwen, Conall, and Hywel were there when Gareth arrived, along with Meilyr, Gwalchmai, and Iorwerth. Meilyr was looking daggers at Gwalchmai, and Gareth could well guess the reason why.

Gwalchmai hadn't yet reached his adult height, but he carried himself with the ease of a man far older. He was used to the weight of responsibility. He was growing up, whether Meilyr (and Gwen) liked it or not. And if not for his and Iorwerth's curiosity, they would be farther behind in this investigation than they were, so before Meilyr could upbraid his son for involving himself in yet another investigation, Gareth told him so.

Meilyr subsided, somewhat reluctantly, and then set to his food with a will, as they all did. For a quarter of an hour, the room was completely silent as everyone ate and drank. Then Gwen sighed, pushed away her bowl, and tipped her head at her father. "Saran has been keeping Tangwen since this morning. Could I ask you to collect her? I would hate for Tangwen to be a burden on their first day together."

Meilyr narrowed his eyes at his daughter, knowing that she was sending him off so as not to involve him in what they were doing any more than he already was. But there was something else in his manner that almost made Gareth laugh when he realized what it was: Meilyr *wanted* to go. And Gareth didn't think it was because he missed his granddaughter. Gareth would have to ask Gwen, who was better at these things than he, but it came into his head the Meilyr was personally interested in Saran.

Then everyone's ears pricked up at the sound of chattering voices coming through the open window that faced the courtyard. Gareth pushed back from the table. "People are starting to arrive."

Hywel's eyes were sober. "Father should be returning from the encampment at any moment."

Everyone rose to their feet and left the room. As if Hywel's words had been some kind of warning, King Madog's party appeared from underneath the gatehouse within a few moments of them stepping outside. This time Queen Susanna rode beside

Madog, and King Owain and his men followed a few lengths behind.

Evan was among the first to dismount, and he hastened to speak to Gareth. "Where have you been?"

"Busy, as I will tell you in a moment."

"That's him! That's him!"

They all swung around to look at who had spoken. Madog's men held back Rhodri, who was wrenching at his captors' arms and trying to throw himself across the courtyard at Gareth. Everyone stared at the young man as he pointed, "He's the one! He's the one who paid me!"

Every man in the vicinity of Gareth closed ranks at the same moment, blocking any direct path to Gareth. For Gareth's part, he was gratified by the loyalty of his men, but the sickening feeling at being falsely accused came slithering once again into his belly.

King Madog's face was alive with triumph, exactly as it had been in the chapter house several hours earlier. "Arrest that man!"

Alone, Hywel took one step forward. "You will not."

Although Rhodri had put the courtyard into an uproar, there was something about the way Hywel's voice carried—his assurance and clarity of purpose—that closed people's mouths and brought silence to the onlookers.

Then Abbot Rhys appeared from around the church and walked between the parties of opposing men. "Accusations are to be saved for the conclave, which shall commence momentarily."

He looked directly at King Madog and then at King Owain, both of whom nodded at him, accepting his authority.

Madog's enthusiasm diminished slightly, but even so, he radiated an air of righteousness that couldn't be dispelled by having his victory delayed for another quarter-hour. Rhys preceded the kings towards the chapter house, which meant returning the way Rhodri had come, along the path behind the church.

Watching the various groups of men follow, Gareth's eyes narrowed. "Why was Rhodri brought down to the courtyard when it only meant that he would have to retrace his steps a few moments later?"

"To accuse you, of course, in a fine, dramatic fashion." Hywel snorted and looked at those who surrounded him. Gwen had opened her mouth to protest, but Hywel forestalled her with a raised hand. "We know the truth, and it will come out if only we let it."

Gareth put an arm around Gwen's shoulders. "We've been here before, only last November."

Conall raised his eyebrows. "After Shrewsbury, you promised to tell me the full tale."

"Now probably would be the time, since I'm wondering if it pertains to this one," Gareth said.

"I'm wondering many things." Hywel jerked his head at Iorwerth, indicating that he should attend the conclave too.

"Hywel, no! Surely you aren't going to turn Gareth over to Powys!" Iorwerth was horrified in a way only a seventeen-year-old boy could be. He'd missed the unspoken underpinnings of the conversation. He should know about the events of last autumn and why his friend, Gwalchmai, had gone to Shrewsbury, since Gareth couldn't imagine that Gwalchmai hadn't told him, but he was not yet sophisticated enough to make the connection without help.

Though Hywel didn't have the time to do it for him, he did wink at his brother. "Watch and learn, young man. Watch and learn."

24

Gwen

Gwen was alone again in an empty courtyard. It was odd enough that she stood still for a moment considering her options. Her duty was first and foremost to Tangwen, and she debated whether she should follow after her father to collect her daughter. Before she could, however, Brother Ben, the monk who'd been hurt when Erik's body had been taken, evident by the bandage wrapped around his head, loped into the courtyard. He pulled up at the sight of Gwen all alone. "Where is your husband?"

"In the chapter house with the other men." Gwen moved towards him. "What are you doing out of bed?"

"If your husband isn't abed, then I shouldn't be either."

Gwen couldn't argue with that. "Why do you need him?"

Brother Ben dipped his chin. "Mathonwy requests his presence at the barn. We've found—" he coughed apologetically, "—another body."

Gwen didn't often gape. She took pride, in fact, in her ability to remain unshocked, but her mouth fell open as she looked at the monk. "I can't disturb the conclave. It's too important."

Ben turned up one hand. "What should we do?"

Gwen sighed. "Mathonwy will have to make do with me." She tugged her cloak closer around herself. They were well into afternoon now, but instead of being the warmest part of the day as it often was in summer, the wind had picked up and was scattering the last of autumn's dead leaves across the courtyard.

She headed to the stable to get her horse and then was hugely relieved to find Llelo and Dai inside, brushing down the horses who'd come with King Owain's party. Under normal circumstances, Gwen would hardly have said that St. Kentigern's monastery was a dangerous place, but there had been an ominous tone in the courtyard even before Rhodri's accusation. Gareth didn't know about the second body yet, but he wouldn't want her going anywhere without protective men around her, even if the only men available were the youngest in the king's party.

"Are you going to tell us what's going on, Mother?" Llelo said once they were on their way, riding down the track to the barn.

Gwen laughed under her breath. "You're assuming that I know. The gaping holes in our understanding of what's going on here are about to swallow us whole." She threw a glance over her shoulder.

Llelo caught the look and put out a hand to her. "Father will be fine. Really."

And then from behind them Dai added in a sour tone. "Next time Da finds himself in the thick of things, he needs to make sure we're with him!"

Gwen turned more fully in the saddle to look at Dai. "Putting yourselves in danger isn't going to help Gareth. What I'd prefer is if the three of you could keep yourselves out of trouble entirely. A faint hope, I know." She turned back to Llelo, who was looking at her gravely. She hadn't answered his question about what was going on, and as she studied her foster son, she decided that it would do no harm to tell him. He and Dai served in the king's army, and since they were accompanying her to see a body, if anyone deserved to know what she was thinking, it was they.

"I speak the truth when I say that I'm not sure what's going on. We know more about what is happening politically than the actual facts of *what happened.*"

"Are you speaking of Madog and Cadwaladr?" Llelo said.

Gwen nodded. "They were the end of our investigation last time. Now, when our only tangible evidence is Erik's body and competing accounts of events that occurred for reasons we don't know, their actions have to be our starting point." Gwen chewed on her lower lip.

"I know these people far less well than you, Mam, but since Dai and I came to Denbigh, I've learned about King Madog. He wants to get the better of King Owain. Paying either his own men or a band of ruffians, which on the whole seems likely, to sack his own monastery sounds like something he'd do. I heard about how he and Prince Cadwaladr sold Madog's own people for silver.

Sacking a monastery is a small matter in comparison—though blaming Father for the deed says to me that Prince Cadwaladr is involved."

That was a well-reasoned speech for a man as young as Llelo, and Gwen took his words as he intended—as an attempt to make sense of what she and Gareth were facing. "Our thoughts always go to Cadwaladr—and sometimes we've been wrong."

Llelo let out a puff of air. "Perhaps. Still, it could be that Cadwaladr arranged for the same band to maraud all over Powys as long as they promised to share the treasure with him and as long as he could blame the reign of terror on King Owain."

Gwen had no trouble picturing that scenario in her mind either. "So we work backwards from the ending: Madog and Cadwaladr are to blame. Who have they hired, and how have they constructed this plot—and how does that lead us to the man who killed Erik?"

"I don't know." Llelo shook his head like he had flies about his ears.

They arrived at the barn to find a handful of somber monks waiting for them, all that was left of the host of men who'd worked to put out the fire. Gwen gazed at the desolation and couldn't help but sigh. There was something particularly forlorn about the burned husk of a building, whether barn, house, or monastery. In the aftermath of the struggle to control the fire, everything was soaking wet. Burned beams stuck up at random, blackened along their full length and likely unsalvageable. The roof, which had withstood the initial onslaught of the flames, in the end was still made of thatch and was entirely gone. A half-dozen monks continued to pace around the exterior of the barn, full water buckets in hand, dousing any spark that might still be smoldering.

His robe and cloaked bunched between his knees, Mathonwy crouched by the body, which had been dragged free of the wreckage and was lying on a scrap of board some twenty paces from the burned barn. Although the dead man's hair was burned off and much of the skin was blackened or covered with ash, he wasn't completely charred. That it was a man there was no doubt since his features could still be made out. Nor could any woman be that tall or have such large feet and hands.

Even though most everyone was conveniently forgetting that Gwen was pregnant, she had not, and if she'd been inclined to ignore the child inside, her stomach wouldn't let her. It clenched uncomfortably, and she wished she hadn't eaten just now since she feared her meal was about to end up on the ground. As it was, once she dismounted, she bent over, her hands on her knees, breathing hard.

Llelo dismounted too and put out a hand to her. "Stay here." He and Dai went to where Mathonwy waited.

"Do any of you recognize him?" Gwen called from several yards away.

"No, my lady," Mathonwy said. Dai and Llelo shook their heads.

Gwen closed her eyes, struggling for composure. She didn't want to get any closer, and the men were kindly speaking loud enough so that she didn't have to, but this was too great a burden to put on her sons. She was having second thoughts about exposing them to such carnage. "Dai—"

"I'm fine, Mam," Dai said immediately. He was bent over the body, in the same posture as Gwen, though without the vomiting. Even from twenty feet away she could see that his eyes were intent.

Mathonwy ignored their side conversation and continued to speak to Llelo. "We pulled him from one of the stalls. When the roof came down, it knocked out a side wall, exposing the body. I sent two men to get him just as soon as it was safe." The monk shrugged helplessly. "I apologize that the body is badly burned, but it's better than it could be. Its location in the stall sheltered it from the worst of the fire."

Llelo frowned. "How does that make sense? Wasn't the fire set to prevent us from finding the body? Whoever did this should have started the fire around the body itself."

Mathonwy stood abruptly and walked to where one of the monks was in the process of lighting a torch. The day was waning and clouds had come in—typically, after the fire was already out— so it was growing hard to see. He waited patiently for the monk to light the torch and then took it. "Come with me." He led the boys around the side of the barn.

Gwen decided that her stomach was enough under control that she could follow, and should follow, in fact, though she averted her eyes as she passed the dead man. When she arrived on the other side of the barn, she found Llelo, Dai, and Mathonwy just inside it where one wall had stood. "What is it you're looking at?"

Llelo scraped at the ground with his boot. "Ash." He canted his head. "Pieces of straw."

Mathonwy nodded. "This is where we found the body. A beam had fallen on him, which is what lit his clothes and charred parts of his body."

"But the fire couldn't have started here," Gwen said, not as a question. "In fact, it looks to me as if the fire came here later than to other parts of the barn." She looked beyond the fallen walls to the trough in which Erik had been found. Ironically, it was untouched by the blaze.

Llelo came over to where Gwen stood and spoke in an undertone. "Da would have my head if he knew you were here without him."

"He'll have my head for bringing you too," she said. "What did you see on the body?"

"He was stabbed in the back with a dagger."

Gwen gave a tsk under her breath. "Erik was stabbed in the belly."

"It could be that the same man killed them both."

"The gash couldn't have been made by the beam falling or other damage from the fire?" she asked hopefully.

He shook his head. "I don't think so. You can look for yourself, but the body is mostly intact." He frowned. "Why would that be?"

"Bodies don't burn that easily, not unless the fire is very hot." Gwen tapped a finger to her chin as she thought. "If he was dead before the fire was set, then his death and the fire could be unrelated. Again, we're looking at two different men with two different agendas."

Llelo canted his head to one side. "Erik was murdered and left for the monks to find and then the body was stolen. If one person did all that, his actions make no sense. It could make sense if we have two different villains working separately."

Gwen noted the *we* but didn't comment on it. "And what does this have to do with the theft here or at Wrexham?" Gwen looked away, though her eyes weren't really seeing the pasture beyond the lane. As at Shrewsbury, the situation had grown very complicated—until at the end it had all become very simple. "All we have to tie Erik's murder to those crimes are the silver coins Gareth found."

Mathonwy had stayed out of earshot while Llelo and Gwen talked, but now he lifted a hand to gain their attention. "Geoff is here, and it may be that he can tell us more." Mathonwy signaled to a stocky man with a water bucket that he should come closer. "He's an old friend of the abbot's from his days in King Henry's service. He came to St. Asaph when he discovered that the abbot was here. He owns the inn in the village now. Fire was his specialty."

"What does that mean, *fire was his specialty?*" Gwen said.

"Starting them, controlling them, using them in war," Mathonwy said with the tone of a man who'd seen its use in person. "I've heard him say that every fire speaks to him in its own language."

Such knowledge could put Geoff on the top of the list of people who could have started the fire, but apparently Mathonwy didn't agree.

"Yes, brother?" Geoff halted in front of them. He was at least twenty years older than Gwen, with a thick beard shot with gray and deep brown eyes that were almost black in the torch light.

Dai had moved off to survey the area around the barn, but Mathonwy introduced Llelo and Gwen. "Tell them what you told me about the fire."

Geoff gave a sharp nod. Gwen recognized the kind of person he was from her many years of living in a royal court. Here was a man who was the backbone of any army—the common-born soldier who'd risen above his station to lead men.

"I haven't been able to get very far inside yet," Geoff said as a caveat, "but I can tell a few things already. Namely, the fire was set. If it was started by lightning, the roof would have gone up first."

Gwen nodded. "As it was, it went last. I saw that when I was here earlier."

"Right. My guess from the way the fire spread is that it started on the ground in the exact center of the building."

"What about the body?" Llelo said.

Geoff shook his head. "That's your business, not mine."

"What can you tell us about how it burned?" Gwen said.

"Oh, that," Geoff said as if a burned body was of minor interest compared to the real issue of the setting of the fire. He gestured to where the body lay, now thankfully under a piece of sacking Dai had salvaged. Leave it to him to always be thinking of how Gwen felt. "The fire was hot enough to singe off his hair and burn most of his clothes, but less so the flesh underneath. He wasn't caught in the midst of it."

"Would you say that he was dead before the beam came down?" Gwen said.

"If he was alive, why not call for help?" Mathonwy said. "You saw the state of the barn. He could have kicked his way out a side wall."

"You have a point." Gwen turned back to Geoff. "Would you say, then, that the point of the fire wasn't to cover up his death?"

"Absolutely it wasn't," Geoff said. "Or if it was, the killer did a remarkably bad job of it."

"How would you have done it if it were you?" Gwen said.

"I would have soaked the man's clothes in oil to fuel the fire. The oil soaks into a man's tissues, making the burn far worse than any other burn, even alcohol, though that works too. Then I would have piled hay all around him and lit it." Geoff spoke very straightforwardly. Fire was his business.

Everyone nodded. No household could be run without oil, which had many uses, from lanterns to cooking to the production of soaps and lotions. Its flammable nature was a given, and anyone who worked in the kitchen had to be constantly aware of oil when it was heating. In addition, pouring oil, boiling or otherwise, on a castle's attackers—and then lighting them up—was a standard tactic in sieges.

"Thank you, Geoff. If we need to speak to you more, will you be nearby?" Gwen said.

"At my inn." He bowed. "My lady."

Gwen let Mathonwy go too so he could arrange for the transport of the body to the room off the cloister where he could lie alongside Erik, and then she and Llelo walked slowly back to their horses.

"It's too bad we didn't inspect the barn fully when we were here earlier," Llelo said. "I feel like that's partly my fault. Da is tired and in pain, and—"

"It wasn't your fault," Gwen said. "Too much has been happening too quickly for any of us to devote the time needed to each aspect of the investigation. At least Conall should still have the rope that measured the shoe size of the man in the loft. When we get the dead man to the chapel, I can compare it."

"This dead man does have really big feet and hands," Llelo said.

They had reached the horses. Gwen stopped before mounting, watching the monks move the body onto a board in preparation for putting it in the back of one of their carts. "Do you see that?"

Llelo frowned, unaware of what Gwen was talking about, but she moved to the monks and stopped them.

"Look at his hand." She turned slightly to show Llelo the dead man's left arm, which had fallen off the board and out from under the sheet.

Llelo, Dai, and Mathonwy, who'd been directing his fellow monks, all converged on her, and Mathonwy raised his torch so the light would shine on the man's hand: the last finger on his left hand was missing its tip, while the rest of it was bent at a grotesque angle.

"So this is Erik's murderer," Llelo said.

Gwen shook her head in disbelief. "He may be that, but then who murdered him?"

25

Gareth

"In the middle of the investigation at Shrewsbury, Gwen and I were on the verge of telling you that we could no longer do this job," Gareth said to Hywel as they walked towards the chapter house.

"Why didn't you say anything?" Hywel hesitated on the threshold, his eyes surveying the room in a quick glance that Gareth knew had taken in the position of all the major players.

"Neither of us can turn away. We resolved to be more detached instead."

Hywel laughed out loud as if he didn't have a care in the world and clapped Gareth on his good shoulder. "I'd say this is a good day to start."

The odd thing was that Gareth didn't think Hywel's amusement was feigned. He really was in high good humor, and the only explanation that made sense was that Rhodri's public accusation of Gareth had exposed his enemy for who he was, and Hywel was looking forward to engaging Madog on his own terms. Of course, Madog had no idea that Hywel had already spoken to

Rhodri—and maybe he wouldn't have known to care if he did. According to Hywel, Rhodri believed every word he'd said, and Madog was counting on that sincerity to convince the room that King Owain was the real villain today.

The chapter house was nearly full already, with more men than earlier in the day. Likely, word had spread, not only of Rhodri's capture and accusation against King Owain, which had happened this morning, but Gareth's comedown was something men wanted to see. He had never intended to place himself above anyone else. He'd done his duty. He'd strived to be a good knight in all things. But sometimes people interpreted a man's behavior as an indictment of their own.

Evan appeared on Gareth's wounded side.

"This isn't going to come to anything," he said before Gareth could speak.

"You told me once that I could be found standing over a dead body with a bloody knife in my hand, and nobody would accuse me of the crime."

Gareth meant to keep his tone light, as a jest, but Evan didn't think it was funny. "I still believe it. We'll see what kind of evidence they bring against you, besides the word of one man who helped sack a monastery."

King Madog clearly believed it. He was holding court in the main circle. The table that had been placed in the center for the morning conclave had been removed. Rhys stood beside Madog, listening gravely and nodding at everything he said. With the arrival of the main party from Gwynedd, Rhys turned his attention to the audience and lifted a hand, asking for quiet.

The kings arranged themselves in positions similar to where they'd sat that morning, but without the table between them. Gareth sat directly behind King Owain, buttressed on one side by Hywel and by Evan on the other. Again the conclave began with a song from Meilyr and Gwalchmai and then a prayer from Rhys.

Because the seats were full, the men who ranged behind Gareth, between him and the door, had to remain standing. One glance back showed Gareth that instead of standing to prevent him from leaving, they had arranged themselves such that the path was clear from him to the door. If at all possible, they were going to ensure his free flight if it became necessary.

He turned to face front just as Madog rose to his feet. "This assembly was witness to my accusation earlier against King Owain, and I repeat it again here." He made an expansive gesture with both hands. "A fortnight ago, men paid by the King of Gwynedd did sack the monastery at Wrexham, stripping it of its wealth. I have a man in custody, who will testify not only that what I say is true, but that this man—" here he pointed a finger straight at Gareth, "—was the paymaster."

A wave of chatter swept around the room. It was one thing to have Rhodri shout across the courtyard. It was another to accuse a man in open court—for that's what the peace conference had turned into, just as Hywel had predicted.

Gareth gazed back at Madog as impassively as he could, but Hywel leaned into him and whispered, "Note how the real crime here, Madog's attempted murder of me, has been completely eclipsed by your supposed crime. Even more, because you are accused, you are silenced in this court—even though it is you who uncovered *his* crimes. It's clever, really. Cleverer than I would ever have given my uncle credit for."

"Could be it wasn't his idea." Gareth's eyes went to Queen Susanna, who was present today, the only woman in the room. But she was a queen, and as far as he could tell, nobody was questioning her right to be here.

Rhys again raised his hand to quiet the crowd, but before he could speak, Hywel rose to his feet and stepped forward into the silence. "Uncle, could you enlighten us as to when this meeting with Rhodri was supposed to have occurred?"

Rhys subsided, realizing perhaps that the conclave was out of his hands, but as it hadn't yet turned violent, it could be left to the main protagonists: Hywel and Madog. Madog looked at Rhodri and nodded, so the younger man spoke for himself. "November."

Hywel gave a sharp nod. "That would be before my brother, Rhun, was murdered by Prince Cadwaladr's men?"

"Yes, my lord. A few weeks before." Rhodri paled at the mention of Rhun, as he was meant to, and the murmuring in the crowd dissipated. Some might not have known the exact circumstances of how Rhun had died, but now everybody did, and it was a bold reminder on Hywel's part of who was really the injured party here.

"Where was this meeting?"

"He found me in Corwen, my home."

"And the sacking of Wrexham. When did that occur?"

"Just after St. Dafydd's Day. Tuesday the fourth of March, it was."

Gareth gave an internal grunt. On Tuesday the fourth, he hadn't yet left Aber, as any man here could attest. If the sacking had been any later, it would have posed more of a problem, since Gareth had then traveled to Shrewsbury with his family at Prince Hywel's behest. They'd arrived there only to become involved in another investigation. Even ten days after it happened, nobody in Shrewsbury had heard about the sacking. They'd had their own problems, of course, and an absent sheriff. Gareth assumed they knew about it by now.

"So he came to you in November, but you didn't raid Wrexham until March? Why the delay?"

"Now see here!" Madog stepped between Hywel and Rhodri. "That's enough questions."

Rhys stepped forward himself, his hand out, and spoke mildly. "We need to ascertain the facts, and Prince Hywel is within his rights to question his captain's accuser."

Madog's eyes narrowed, and Gareth sensed that it occurred to him only now that Rhys's mildness of earlier was a permanent state, not an indication that he favored Madog's position. Nevertheless, Madog subsided, and Rhys gestured to Hywel that he should continue.

Hywel raised his eyebrows at Rhodri, and for the first time, Rhodri hesitated. "I don't know the reason for the delay. It wasn't supposed to be that long. He just wanted my agreement to do it at first, and he told me that he'd be in touch as to when I was to go to Wrexham."

"What did you think when you didn't hear from him again?"

Rhodri shrugged. "His money was good, and if what I was paid to do never came about, it was no loss to me. But then I got a message that it was time."

"What do you mean *a message*? You can read?"

"No!" Rhodri scoffed. "He paid one of the village boys to tell me. I never saw him myself."

"You never saw him again?"

"Not until after the raid."

"When and where did you meet?"

"Our final payment was on the fifteenth, the Ides of March, back in Corwen."

Gareth eased out a sigh that he tried not to show. On the Ides of March, he'd been in Shrewsbury within moments of being captured by a very different band of ruffians. The next day had been Sunday, and Gwalchmai had sung at mass in the church of the Abbey of St. Peter and St. Paul. They'd left Shrewsbury on Sunday evening, the sixteenth, ridden three days to Aber, taking the path through the mountains to avoid Powys. Upon their arrival at Aber on Wednesday afternoon, King Owain had been ready to ride, and they'd left with him, reaching St. Asaph's just past midnight on Friday morning. And here it was Saturday again. No wonder Gareth was exhausted.

"And it was Gareth who met you?"

Rhodri hesitated again. "Yes."

Hywel's eyes narrowed. "You saw his face?"

Rhodri seemed to think better of his assertion. "I thought it was him. He wore a cloak and hardly spoke, but he knew all about what we'd done. He said to meet him here, at St. Asaph, and he would have another job for me."

"Just you?"

"Yes." Rhodri stuck out his chin, back to defiance.

"What about the other men he hired? Where are they?"

"I don't know!" Rhodri said, as if it was obvious. "We scattered."

"Had you known them before?"

"N-n-no. We met at an abandoned farmhouse outside Wrexham a few days before the raid. Everything we needed was there when we arrived."

"Including the surcoats with the crest of Gwynedd?"

"Yes."

"What happened to the treasure?"

Rhodri looked down at his feet, and somehow Gareth knew exactly what was coming. "I spent my share."

The man was a naïve fool and an idiot. A criminal too, with no sense of right and wrong—or of self-preservation, apparently.

Madog intervened again. "Surely, that's enough to know that Rhodri speaks the truth. Gareth paid him and other men to sack Wrexham. What more do we need to learn, and why isn't that man in chains already? Arrest him!"

Madog's men surged towards Gareth, and an equal number of men from Gwynedd were there to meet them. It was a good thing that nobody had been allowed a sword because there would have been bloodshed.

King Owain still hadn't moved or spoken, and neither had Gareth. Hywel and Evan stepped in front of him, but again, it was Rhys who raised a hand and diffused the moment. "Sir Gareth is here of his own accord, and the case has not yet been proven, not to my satisfaction, not on the statement of one man who happens to be a thief. Do you have more of these men to bring forward?"

"I call Brother Deiniol and Brother Lwc of Wrexham, whom my men found in neighboring cells next to Rhodri. Apparently, men of Gwynedd put them there!"

That sent the room into an uproar again, but Hywel threw back his head and laughed. It was such an incongruous thing to do that some of the righteousness on Madog's face disappeared, to be replaced by suspicion.

Hywel waved a hand. "By all means, let's hear them."

In due course, Deiniol and Lwc were paraded before the conclave and each told the story of the sack of Wrexham in his own words, though they made no mention of the theft from St. Asaph and their role in them, and nobody from Gwynedd interrupted. During Lwc's testimony, Hywel did take a moment to step near to Rhys and whisper a lengthy passage in his ear, after which Rhys nodded. Once both prisoners had finished their statements, Rhys made sure they stayed sitting in the front row of benches, well-guarded and with no possibility of escape.

Finally, Hywel stepped to the fore again. His expression was somber, and his hands were clasped behind his back, but Gareth knew him well enough after all these years to know what the tightness in his shoulders meant. He wasn't fearful—he was excited, and if he'd allowed himself to show it, he would have been bouncing on the balls of his feet.

Hywel looked down at the floor while the room quieted, and then he let the silence lengthen. Gareth reminded himself that Hywel had begun performing for audiences larger than this, testing the temperature of a room and his effect on the people gathered before him, from when he was nine years old when his incredible voice had manifested itself. He'd become expert at reading a crowd before he'd become a man. Gareth let out a breathless sigh, forcing his shoulders to relax and telling himself that he needed to trust his prince. If anyone knew what he was doing in such circumstances, it was Hywel.

The prince looked up. "For the moment, I am willing to put aside Gwynedd's accusation against Powys that King Madog ordered his men to kill me just over a week ago. It is an accusation that Powys hasn't even bothered to deny. But if dispensing with the current matter of the treachery of the captain of my guard, Sir Gareth, is necessary before we can discuss the true matter at hand, then so be it." He turned to Abbot Rhys. "First, I want to make clear that Gareth was in no way involved in the payment of these men, Rhodri among them. If I prove that, I believe that it will go a long way towards proving that Rhodri was paid by a third party with the intent to impugn Gareth's—and my father's—name. Are we agreed?"

Rhys lifted both hands to the conclave. "I am agreed. What say you?"

General murmurs of approval swept around the room with many nodded heads, even among the men of Powys. A waft of cool air swept across Gareth's neck, and he glanced behind him to the door to see Conall slip in late and find a place among Hywel's men. He met Gareth's eyes and made a fist, implying that all was well, or so Gareth hoped that's what the signal meant in Irish. He turned back to face the front.

Rhys looked at Madog. "What says Powys?"

Madog was looking murderous, but he nodded jerkily. "Agreed, if the logic is sound."

Hywel clenched his hands into fists down at his sides, and then relaxed them. "I call first Lord Bergam of Dyffryn Ceiriog!"

Gareth blinked as his old employer rose to his feet and made his way down to where Hywel waited. He stopped beside Hywel, clearly puzzled at being called forward. "My lord?"

"Lord Bergam, you employed Sir Gareth for a time some years ago. Is that correct?"

"Yes, my lord, for a short while."

"I understand that he left your service after an incident involving your son."

Bergam wasn't liking where this was going, but the truth was required in court, not to mention on holy ground, and he told it. "Yes."

"Did Gareth tell you why he was leaving?"

"Yes."

"Can you tell us?"

Now Bergam canted his head to one side, as it dawned on him what he was expected to say, but again, he didn't balk at saying it. "Gareth told me that honor wasn't lost in a day. It was lost over weeks and years of taking the path that was easy rather than the one that was right. He said he hadn't left Prince Cadwaladr's service only to find himself beholden to another man who didn't know the difference between right and wrong, and while he didn't claim to have God's ear, he knew enough of the difference to know that he couldn't stomach another moment in my son's presence. If he had to starve, so be it. He'd go to hell for his own deeds, not for standing by while another man paved the way."

While Bergam was speaking, Gareth kept his eyes on the floor. When he'd left Cadwaladr's service, he'd been afraid. The day he'd left Bergam's, however, he'd been angrier than he'd ever been in his life, and he'd allowed his temper to get the better of him. He'd known he was going to be on his own again, but he'd felt he'd had no choice.

Evan laughed low in Gareth's ear. "By God, I do believe he's telling the truth."

"What did you reply?" Hywel said.

"I told him he was a smarmy, self-righteous son-of-a-bitch and he could take his holier-than-thou attitude and get out of my sight." Bergam immediately put out a hand to Abbot Rhys and bowed. "My apologies, Father."

"Will you tell the conclave what your son did that Gareth wouldn't countenance?" Hywel said.

"He took a girl against her will before her wedding day."

The silence in the room was so profound, Gareth himself couldn't breathe or swallow. He hadn't told more than a handful of people what had made him leave, less not to shame Bergam and his son, but because he was ashamed to have ever stood at the son's side. God knows he wasn't a saint, but truth be told, leaving Cadwaladr and Bergam hadn't been all that hard once he saw what he had to do. Standing up to outright sin was easy. It was standing up to it when it was far subtler that was the challenge—and not a challenge that Gareth felt he always adequately met.

"Where is your son now?" Hywel said.

"He died at the retreat from Lincoln, in the service of Empress Maud."

26

Conall

Gruffydd bumped Conall's shoulder. "Good that you're here. Gareth might need you."

Conall coughed. "I'm not bored yet."

"You're never bored."

Conall smirked, since what Gruffydd said was most likely true. Conall found the poor behavior of people endlessly fascinating. His time in Wales had so far been an education. And peace conference or legal court, the conclave was something Conall recognized, because his people had a similar system of settling disputes. In his duties for Diarmait, even though he hadn't been the one to do the actual investigating, he'd testified against murderers before and expected to do so again. This was the first Welsh court he'd been in, but he understood their laws to be not far off in principle from his own.

Having gained his audience's attention with Bergam's riveting testimony, Hywel moved on to his next witness. "I call Lord Morgan and Father Alun to the floor."

Gruffydd tilted his chin to look up at the ceiling, a slight smile on his lips. "This will be good. Just watch."

"I believe you." Conall so far had had no trouble watching. He'd known from his first meeting with Gareth that here was a man who couldn't be bought. He might be tested, as all men were tested, but in the end he could be relied upon. Madog never should have chosen him as the man against whom his case should be made. But then, Madog had been shocked by Hywel's questioning of Bergam. Maybe he didn't know Gareth at all. Maybe the choice of Gareth for the man to take the fall for Wrexham had not been his decision.

Instead of watching Hywel as he began his questioning of the two men he'd brought to the front, Conall kept his eyes alternately on Madog and his wife, Susanna, who sat in the row behind him. If Gareth's foster son was right that it had been she who had met Derwena last night, then her testimony might be the key to everything. Chances were, however, that she would not testify against her husband, if the conversation ever turned to the attempted murder of Hywel—or the slave ring in Shrewsbury. Even if Conall had known her once, he knew her no longer, and she had no reason to tell him what she knew about Erik's death.

Then again, he hadn't asked either.

To the conclave's silent witness, Alun and Morgan related a tale of mistaken identity and false trails, preposterous on the surface but relentless in the telling. It left the listeners with no doubt that the man who'd met with Rhodri in November in Corwen was the imposter, not Gareth himself.

Throughout the tale, Madog's expression grew more ruddy, as if he was holding his breath, though more likely it was his temper that he was reining in. Meanwhile, Susanna's expression grew more serene. It was only as Hywel reached the end of his questioning and Morgan and Alun drew their tale to its conclusion that it dawned not only on Conall but on even the daftest listener where this was leading.

The man who'd looked like Gareth had been hired by Prince Cadwaladr, whose name Conall was already sick of hearing, as a ruse in his negotiations with the Earl of Chester. It was no leap at all to wonder if it had been Prince Cadwaladr who'd paid that same imposter to hire Rhodri and the other men to sack Wrexham—all in an attempt to bring down his brother and gather to himself a sack of silver while he was at it.

"For my next witness, I call Conall, nephew to Diarmait mac Murchada, King of Leinster."

That caused a buzz in the room. Conall pulled on his ear as he made his way to the front. "Lords." He bowed to the audience and then looked expectantly at Hywel. This was a new side to the prince, and he could only marvel that Hywel had his audience eating out of the palm of his hand like a tamed horse.

"Can you tell me where Gareth was on the fifteenth of March?"

Conall didn't hesitate to answer. "He was tied up with me in an old mill in Shrewsbury."

That was news to almost everyone. Those involved had kept their mouths closed about both their adventures and their injuries, and that discretion was paying off now.

"What were you doing in Shrewsbury?" Hywel asked.

Conall gave an involuntary rumble deep in his chest. This was not going to be what Madog, for one, wanted to hear. "I had been sent by my king to track down a band of slavers who'd been stealing women from Leinster. Instead I found a conspiracy run by men of Powys, incited by King Madog and Prince Cadwaladr, selling women from Powys as a means of generating silver quickly."

Conall's words rang around the room, and the silence couldn't have been more complete. Hywel's eyes were alight with triumph, though he had so far managed to keep the emotion out of his face as a whole. Then everyone started talking at once. Madog was on his feet, shouting, his face so red Conall was afraid he would expire on the spot. Rhys had his hands raised, trying to quiet everyone down.

Then, into the uproar rose Susanna, Queen of Powys. Chin high, she left her seat and walked to stand in front of Hywel. Her voice rang out, and if the men in the room missed the first few words, they didn't miss the conclusion.

"You need to stop this, Hywel. If the time for telling the truth is here, then here it is: this is all *my* doing. Madog didn't have a hand in any of these things of which he is accused. To allow you to think it for a moment longer would be to perpetuate a lie."

27

Hywel

Hywel looked at his aunt with what he hoped was an unreadable expression. He never had any intention of calling her as a witness, because he would never ask her to testify against her own husband—or in Hywel's favor, which might well have been worse. He would never betray her trust that way.

As it was, she was standing before him, and he made a welcoming gesture with one hand. "By all means, aunt. The floor is yours." He backed away, moving not behind her, however, but more towards the semi-circle of seats so that he could watch her face. The tension in the room was such that one misstep because he misunderstood the situation could ruin all.

Susanna gave him a piercing look before turning to face the other men in the room. Every one of them, including her own husband, was staring at her with a stricken expression.

"Susanna!" Madog had been on his feet already, and now he took a step towards his wife. But if it had been a blade, the look Susanna gave him would have sliced him in half. Hywel had not found Susanna to be an assertive wife, but in this she was unbending. Madog put up both hands and tipped his head as if to say, "All right. Do what you must." He sat down again, and with his capitulation, the entire delegation from Powys sat too.

After that, the room quieted quickly, without Rhys needing to do or say anything. When she had the full attention of her audience, Susanna lifted her chin and began to speak. "You have heard testimony today that has shocked you." She nodded. "I understand your dismay at the events of the last few months. But what you think you know—" she gestured to Hywel, "—what has been revealed here is only part of the truth. The missing piece to this puzzle is that I, and I alone, am responsible for not only the sacking of Wrexham but the slave ring as well."

An indrawn breath of shocked silence followed this announcement. Hywel might have expected a clamor, but everyone just stared at Susanna instead while she looked back with calm eyes and an easy assurance. For his part, Hywel couldn't stay silent and moved closer. "Aunt, surely you can't expect us to believe—"

She whirled on him, her finger pointing, and shook it in his face. "Be quiet, Hywel. You don't know everything."

This time in the face of her ire, when he stepped back, he held up both hands, like he might if he was showing an enemy he was unarmed. "Yes, aunt. But please don't do this."

His aunt glared at him. "Father Rhys, if Hywel interrupts again, the law dictates that he should be removed from the room, is that right?"

Rhys glided closer. "Yes, my lady."

"See to it." She bit off the last word.

Hywel backed away far enough that he was within arm's length of his father, who reached out a hand to him. "Let her be, son. You've done all that you can."

As the little drama among the family members of Gwynedd's royal house had gone on, Madog had remained in his seat, his expression blank. As Hywel looked at his uncle, he realized that Madog hadn't expected this from Susanna either. He had thought she was going to betray him, and instead she was prepared to take the blame for everything he had done.

Which she proceeded to do. "You must understand that what I did, I did for love of my husband and my brother, Cadwaladr."

At the mention of the prince's name, a murmur, louder than any before, swept around the room. Susanna was making a woman's argument, which was somewhat disappointing to Hywel, but it was one that the men in the room were predisposed to believe.

"Even though Cadwaladr is my older brother, I have felt much of the time like a mother to him. I am not in any way going to apologize for Cadwaladr's crimes, of which he has committed many. I know that my brother, Owain, has overlooked Cadwaladr's misdeeds many times, and when presented with his exile, I could do no less."

Hywel felt his father stir beside him, but he didn't speak. Susanna was right, of course, and if Owain had known that his overlarge heart would lead to this, he might have reconsidered his treatment of his brother. Hywel could be thankful that while she claimed responsibility for the slave ring and the thefts, she didn't say that it was she who'd found the man to impersonate Gareth or had anything to do with Rhun's death. Even she couldn't come up with a convincing argument as to how she'd managed that.

"I know my brother well—" and here again she was referring to Owain, not Cadwaladr, "—and he loathed the need to choose between Cadwaladr and his kingdom. He did what was necessary in exiling him. I understand that—" she shot Owain a look of apology, "—but with nobody to turn to Cadwaladr came to me. I could not refuse to help him, especially when the men he might go to for help might be so very much worse."

Hywel knew without her needing to articulate who those men might be: men like Ranulf, Earl of Chester, his wife's uncle, to whom Cadwaladr had gone so often in the past; and the earls of Lincoln, Pembroke, and Hertford, siblings or close relations of his wife, Alice, and powerful Norman magnates in their own right. Or even the son of Robert of Gloucester, the most powerful man in England aside from King Stephen. Robert's body and, more importantly, his mind, were fading. Ranulf, who was married to Robert's daughter, had wormed his way back into his good graces, which would never have happened if he were well.

"I could not put all Wales at risk because of Cadwaladr's ambition." Again, she threw a look of apology at her brother. So far, she hadn't looked at Madog once, not even with a flick of the eyes—and Hywel had been watching for it. "It is I who must do penance for these crimes that have been enumerated here. It is I who arranged for my husband's men to murder Hywel rather than allow my nephew to uncover what I was helping Cadwaladr do in Shrewsbury. It is I who am to blame for the sacking at Wrexham, which was another attempt to fund my brother's exile." She turned fully to face King Owain. "Madog would go to war rather than let me be exposed and shamed, but I cannot see the two men I love the most kill each other over something I have done. Owain, you know I am equally in a position to do all these things of which you have accused my husband. It is I who deserve your anger, not Madog. It is I who must beg forgiveness and pay *sarhad*. Please be at peace, Madog and Owain."

Complete silence greeted this statement. Even Abbot Rhys seemed struck dumb by her confession. Hywel, for once, had nothing to say. His aunt had swept all arguments from the table.

And so it was that Hywel's father was the first man to rise to his feet—as in truth he should have been, and as was his right. He moved to stand in front of Susanna, blocking the view of most of the men in the room, though still not of Hywel, who sat a few seats to one side of center.

The king looked down at his sister for a long moment, and then he reached for her and pulled her into his arms.

After that, there was no more talk of war. There couldn't be. But that didn't mean that every question had been answered. In fact, as far as Hywel was concerned, no questions had been answered. By taking the blame for her husband's actions, Susanna had brought peace to Wales and cut short the conference, but

Hywel still had a dead spy whose murderer was either lying alongside him or remained at large. And that didn't even touch upon the theft of St. Asaph's treasury, which Hywel believed now had been spawned by the sacking of Wrexham.

Several hours later, Hywel stood in the darkness of his aunt's room. The feast that had followed the afternoon's session had dragged on far too long, but Hywel had managed to escape with the unlikely excuse of desiring a private moment in the church to give thanks for the peace. He'd gone back to the guesthouse instead to wait for his aunt's return. He didn't think she'd be long, seeing as how she was prone to pleading a headache. He'd always assumed she'd done so to avoid her husband's attentions. Now he wondered what else he'd misread if she was willing to sacrifice so much for him.

Light steps came from the corridor, and the door to the room opened. His aunt Susanna stood silhouetted in the doorway, and then she closed the door and crossed to the shutters. Opening them, she looked out, took several deep breaths, and then turned to where Hywel stood in a shadowed corner. "I thought I might find you here."

Shaking his head to think that even for a moment he could have fooled the woman who'd lived a double life since her marriage, Hywel moved away from the wall. "We need to talk."

"You know everything you need to—"

"Don't lie to me," Hywel said, more sharply than maybe he intended. It had been an emotional day. "You can lie to everyone else, but you have no need to lie to me." He moved closer. "You and I are two of a kind. You can trust me with the truth. You didn't order my death, and thus, I don't believe you did any of these other things either, even for Cadwaladr." When his aunt tried to interrupt, he forestalled her with a raised hand. "I understand why you did it, as does my father."

"He knows?"

"Everything," Hywel said.

"How angry is he?"

"If not for his concern for you, he'd be amused."

"I can take care of myself," Susanna said.

"That much is clear," Hywel said. "What I need to know now is what role you or Madog had in the death of my servant, a half-Dane named Erik, and the theft of silver here at St. Kentigern's."

Susanna stared at him. The moonlight was coming in the window, lighting half of her face, but the other half was deeply shadowed. He could tell, however, that she was surprised by the question. "I-I don't understand."

Hywel had one arm folded across his chest, and he rubbed at the stubble on his chin with the other hand, watching his aunt. He recognized that his aunt was one of the few people he couldn't easily read, and he didn't know if she was lying. He decided that he needed to tell the truth himself, in hopes that it would prompt her to do the same.

"Last night, you were not in bed with a sick headache, but you dosed your maid with poppy juice and saw off Rhodri's mother, Derwena, with a nine-fingered man. Erik, my servant, was strangled by someone missing strength in the last finger on his left hand and was left submerged in a trough at the barn that was burned today. Five silver pennies were found in the vicinity of the murder scene. When Erik's body was being transported to the monastery to be examined, it was stolen by a band of men and then later that day turned up in a field nearby—cut open."

Susanna listened to Hywel's recitation with wary eyes, and she continued to look at him for a count of five before sighing. She turned to sit somewhat forlornly on the end of the bed, her hands in her lap, looking down at the floor.

"The young guard told you it was I?"

"Gareth and Conall witnessed Rhodri's arrest on the other side of the monastery, picked up Derwena and questioned her, and then, after they released her, followed her to her meeting with you. Dai, the young guard, happens to be Gareth's son."

She looked up at that. "I didn't know that Gareth had fathered a son."

"I misspoke. Dai is his foster son."

Susanna gave an unladylike grunt. "You see where lies have brought us." She sighed again. "Derwena was your cousin's wet nurse. Rhodri was just starting to walk when Llywelyn was born. Derwena and Rhodri were living in Llangollen at the time, her husband had died, and it seemed a perfect solution to the burden of having a young widow in the village to bring her into my service. I have known her these many years and, of course, this connection to our court was how Madog and Cadwaladr found Rhodri as one of the men to sack that monastery."

She looked up at him. "I didn't find any of this out until very recently, you understand? Not until after you were almost killed."

"After your husband tried to have me murdered, you mean," Hywel said—and then instantly regretted it. He put out a hand to her. "I'm sorry, aunt."

"You speak no more than the truth. Very well, after Madog tried to kill you, I confronted him with it, and he confessed the whole sordid story. He feared that you might find Cadwaladr in Shrewsbury, you see. I don't know that it occurred to him that you might uncover the slave ring too. He told me also of his agreement with the slavers and then his role in the raid on the monastery at Wrexham, all designed to line his and Cadwaladr's pockets with easy silver and malign Owain in the process."

"Did Rhodri believe all along that he'd been paid by Gareth?"

"Cadwaladr set up the raid before Rhun's death and his own exile. It was the kind of mischief Cadwaladr liked well. Once the imposter was dead, Cadwaladr and Madog knew that Rhodri's ignorance was still necessary for the deception to be complete. Rhodri had to believe he was telling the truth. Not only that, but our own men had to believe it."

"So someone else tricked Rhodri into approaching Madog's encampment, where he could be recognized and arrested."

"Yes."

"Do you know who?"

"Not for certain."

Hywel stared at his aunt, waiting for more. When it wasn't forthcoming, he said, "And Derwena?"

"She had no part in any of this other than confirming for me the details of the sacking of Wrexham, once Rhodri confessed to her that he'd been involved." Susanna was firm in that. "She followed him here because she feared for his life. I promised her that I would do what I could for him and for her."

"How could you know that we had questioned her, such that you would send her away so soon after?"

"I didn't!" Susanna said. "I'd arranged for her to meet me, in order to keep her safe until I got to the bottom of the plot. It was because she was with you that she was late to meet me."

"Who is the man you sent her away with? He was missing a finger on his left hand and that implicates him in Erik's murder."

"He is one of my long-time servants, a man of Powys. He and Derwena have favored each other for years." She looked directly at Hywel. "He could not have murdered Erik. I swear it. He was traveling with me until we arrived, which I believe was the afternoon after Erik died."

"You are absolutely sure of it?"

"Yes."

Hywel grimaced. "I hate coincidences." He rubbed his forehead, feeling a genuine headache coming on. "Are you telling me that you know nothing of Erik's death?"

"Not his death." Susanna put her folded hands to her lips as she might have in prayer and looked at him over the top of them.

It had been a throwaway question, one that Hywel genuinely hadn't expected any kind of answer to. "But you did know him?"

Her eyes didn't leave his face. "Erik used to carry messages between Cadwaladr and Madog ... and between Cadwaladr's wife, Alice, and me."

Hywel rocked back on his heels. "Could he have been doing that when he was killed?"

Now she grimaced. "He was carrying messages, of that I am certain, since he brought one from Alice to me." She laughed without humor. "If I really did all the things I confessed to doing, I would know more, but I didn't do those things, so I only know what my husband told me." She leaned forward and looked intently at Hywel. "You should know, however, that Erik was first and foremost Alice's man."

Hywel blinked. "I have been blind, deaf, and dumb."

"You have been preoccupied."

"What will happen to you now, aunt?"

She canted her head. "Madog will put me aside for a time as punishment. Owain has agreed that I may confine myself to the nunnery at Llanfaes." She paused. "I have friends on the island, you know."

She was referring, without a doubt, to Alice, Cadwaladr's wife. Clearly, Hywel had underestimated his aunt. He didn't want to think about what those two women could contrive together either—and perhaps what they'd already contrived without his knowledge. "All the way to Anglesey? Madog doesn't mind you returning to Gwynedd?"

Susanna canted her head. "He owes me."

28

Gwen

"He surely does owe her—more than any husband ever has," Gwen said the next afternoon once Hywel finally had a moment's peace to relate to her and Gareth the entire conversation with Susanna. "Unfortunately, that doesn't help us with who killed Erik, stole him, or set the barn on fire. And we still haven't been able to determine whether Deiniol was involved in these thefts or just Lwc."

"Deiniol and Rhodri claim never to have seen each other before, either on the road to St. Asaph or otherwise," Hywel said, "so it may well be that the burned body in the barn is Erik's friend—not that Deiniol recognized him either."

"The body was badly burned," Gwen pointed out.

They were talking in the common room of the guesthouse, just the three of them. Last Gwen had seen, Conall and Evan had been at the top of the gatehouse tower, keeping an eye on the comings and goings of men in and out of the monastery. With the peace conference over, Sunday mass celebrated, and the celebratory feast eaten, most of Owain's men had gone back to the camp in order to oversee to the dispersal of the army. The spring planting and lambing called to them. Nobody was sorry to be going home.

Gwen had seen King Owain in passing that morning, and he had been in high good humor, despite the fact that everything Susanna had said at the conclave was a lie, and he knew it. But he'd played his part. Susanna had saved Hywel from Madog at Dinas Bran, and she was coming to stay at Llanfaes, across the Menai Strait and within sight of Aber. In one sweeping gesture, she'd given Owain breathing room to get his barons back in order and saved her husband from having to fight a war he might not win.

In fact, the two kings had reconciled to such an extent that they'd accepted Prior Rhys's suggestion that they betrothe Madog's daughter, Marared, to Iorwerth, King Owain's son, as a means to further secure the peace. Not only had neither young person objected, but for once it looked as if an arranged marriage would be a happy event for all parties. The church wouldn't put up any barriers either, since Marared was Madog's daughter only, and thus not Iorwerth's first cousin.

Although Gwen was happy that Gwynedd wasn't going to war against Powys, she had lain awake much of the night listening to her family breathe and thinking long and hard about the way the investigation had stalled out. They still had two bodies on their hands, and it seemed time for some drastic action. "I've had an idea, but I don't think you're going to like it."

"What is it? I can tell you that there are few things I like less than having a murderer roaming free in Gwynedd," Hywel said.

"What if we let Deiniol and Lwc go?" Gwen said.

Hywel coughed a laugh. "Why would we do that?"

"Because we could follow them and see what they do—and if they do it together. We have only Lwc's word that Deiniol is involved. I, personally, am not satisfied that Lwc is telling the whole truth." She threw out a hand to point beyond the walls. "Somewhere out there still is the band of men who stole Erik's body. What if they are the men who sacked Wrexham, and they came here to do the same thing? What if they're simply waiting for the army to leave so they can sack the monastery? We shouldn't be leaving it unguarded."

"I haven't forgotten them, and you're right about the guards. At the very least, we can't leave until we bring this investigation to a conclusion." Hywel leaned back against the stones beside the fireplace.

Gareth's expression turned thoughtful. "What if we enlist Rhodri's help? Madog left him in our charge without stipulating that we keep him imprisoned."

"The boy might want a chance at redemption." Hywel canted his head towards Gareth. "Why don't you go get him and let's see?"

Gareth stood. "It would be my pleasure." He strode from the room.

Hywel looked at Gwen, and she had the sudden sense that he had wanted to speak to her alone. "When this investigation is over, I want you to ride to Dolwyddelan to be with Mari. I want you to bring Saran with you."

Gwen looked at him warily. "She had nothing to do with this, Hywel. She's an old friend."

"Whose sister was nursemaid to the royal house of Powys, and who came looking for her just as these events were taking place." He put up a hand. "But that's not why I want her at Dolwyddelan. Last week when we were there, Gruffydd had a cough I didn't like. I know you trust her healing skills, and I want her to look at him."

Gwen had known that she'd been on borrowed time in regards to staying with Gareth beyond these last weeks, and she was opening her mouth to agree to Hywel's request when the outside door opened and King Owain himself entered the room. He was alone, which was rare enough to remark upon, though neither Gwen nor Hywel did. Both got immediately to their feet.

"My lord." Gwen curtseyed.

"Father." Hywel straightened first. "What is it?"

"Your Aunt Susanna has already left for Llanfaes."

Hywel drew in a breath. "I was waiting for her, hoping to speak to her one more time."

"You can visit her at the convent," Owain said. "For now, you have something more important to attend to."

"I know. You want me to ride with you to Mold—"

King Owain was shaking his head before Hywel had finished his sentence. "She has paid the *sarhad* as her debt for the attempt on your life. It includes a patch of land a mile to the south of St. Asaph that came with her on her marriage as part of her dowry. She said you would want to inspect it." He handed Hywel a rolled up piece of parchment. "Taran has already made over the land to you."

Hywel took the deed his father offered and unrolled it. "What is this about?"

King Owain spread his hands wide. "I don't know anything more than I've told you."

"What exactly did she say?"

King Owain pursed his lips as he thought and then said, "*Tell my nephew that if he and that fine captain of his should visit the place sooner rather than later, they might find themselves well rewarded for their efforts.*" He laughed. "You know how she is when she's trying to tell you something without actually telling you, but I don't know what this means."

Hywel looked at Gwen, who shook her head and said, "I don't know either, but you ought to do as she asks, don't you think?"

"I'll keep a few men with me—Gareth, of course. Evan and Gruffydd. Conall, if he will come."

King Owain's eyes narrowed. "Are you sure about keeping Conall at your side?"

Hywel shrugged. "It's seems a little late to second guess his presence, and I don't think we'll be sorry to have someone we know well among Diarmait's court in the coming years."

"I give way to your judgment in this, son. Your brothers and I will move out at dawn tomorrow. Catch us up when you can—after you've sorted out everything here."

"Yes, Father." Hywel bowed again, looking pleased that his father had accorded him such confidence. His approval had been casual, as if this kind of trust in his son was an everyday occurrence.

King Owain left, and Gwen could hear him shouting for his horse in the courtyard. Gwen and Hywel looked at each other appraisingly. "You should go look at that farmstead," Gwen said.

"Doing what my aunt asks has always been the wise choice," Hywel said. Then Gareth's voice telling Rhodri to stand up straight resonated outside the door. "First, however, we'll talk to Rhodri."

Gareth entered the room holding Rhodri by the scruff of the neck. The young man wasn't resisting exactly, but he had a sullen look on his face that Gwen recognized. He'd been deceived, and he didn't like it. If she had to guess, never having spoken to him before, his mother had spoiled him, and he'd never taken on the responsibilities of a man, despite being one.

Gareth dumped him onto a stool in front of Hywel, deliberately making Rhodri look up to see the prince's face.

Hywel studied him for a moment, no more impressed than Gwen, and then he said abruptly, "Would you like to earn back a portion of your lost honor?"

Gwen wasn't sure that Rhodri knew what honor was, but his expression cleared slightly, and he nodded. "Yes, my lord."

"The two monks beside you in the cells—have they spoken?" Hywel said.

Rhodri scoffed. "One blubbers constantly about how he was made to steal and he never meant it. He goes on and on. The other I've heard from less, since his is the first cell and mine's the last, but all he does is pray."

Hywel kept his gaze on Rhodri, but Gwen and Gareth exchanged a glance. The two monks were staying in their respective roles. It wasn't going to be easy to catch them changing their story.

"We are going to arrange for you to escape, and then we want you to free them and go with them to wherever they go."

"How am I to escape?"

Hywel raised his eyebrows at Gareth, who answered, "When we return you to your cell, I will throw you roughly inside, Prince Hywel will haul me off of you—and then forget to lock the cell. The monks will be called away for Vespers, at which point you can free your fellow captives and escape with them. We will follow the best we can, and we're counting on you to find us and tell us where their hideout is."

Rhodri looked from Gareth to Hywel and back again. "You're asking me to risk my life for you."

"We can leave you in that cell until my father decides what to do with you. Maybe Conall wouldn't mind taking you back to Ireland with him and selling you," Gareth said.

Rhodri's eyes widened. "He wouldn't!"

"I would if the alternative was to leave you at Denbigh, which has real prison cells, and throw away the key. It's seems such a waste when you could be put to work." Hywel paused. "Do I really have to threaten you to get you to cooperate?"

Rhodri looked down at his feet. "No. I'll do it. We'll go at Vespers like you said. But you'll have to stay well back. If they really are villains and they find out I talked to you, they'll kill me."

"We will do our best." Hywel nodded at Gareth, who lifted Rhodri to his feet, and the two men hauled him back out to the courtyard.

Gwen followed to find Saran standing somberly by herself at the entrance to the church, watching them go. Gwen stopped beside her. "What will you do now? Will you return to Carreg Cennan?"

Saran shook her head. "That part of my life is over."

"Would you like to come to Dolwyddelan with me and Tangwen? Hywel's wife, Mari, is there, and Hywel specifically suggested that when I go to visit her, you come with me."

Genuine hope lit Saran's eyes. "Thank you. I would like that."

29

Gareth

"Do you see them?" Gareth ran back and forth alongside the monastery wall, looking for the three 'prisoners', who had disappeared without a trace. Though the initial escape had gone off without a hitch, and the three men had headed straight for the northeast corner where the wall was lowest, Gareth and Conall had been forced to hang back. By the time they arrived at the wall, the trio were gone. Even Deiniol, who was older and less fit than the other two, had disappeared completely. "Did they double back?"

Conall cursed fluently in Gaelic and swung himself into the same tree that overhung the wall, which Gareth had climbed the other day. "I don't see them."

Gareth managed to get himself up onto the wall too, not without some curses of his own, and gazed into the darkness.

"Puts me to shame, it does." Conall said in an undertone. "I'm not as young as I used to be." And yet, with an agility that still eluded Gareth, he dropped to the ground outside the monastery.

"None of us are." Gareth sat on the wall to minimize the distance he had to drop and pushed off, landing with a thud beside Conall. "Which way should we go?"

"East. Madog's men are gone, and going that way means they could leave the monastery grounds behind them all the more quickly. Going west takes them to the river, which has one bridge across it, and the next ford is all the way at Rhuddlan. Lwc would know that. They'll head in any direction but west, by my guess."

Gareth loped along beside Conall, who'd started across the pasture before Gareth had even agreed that east was the way they wanted to go. A faint light remained in the sky behind them, but the sun had set, and it would soon be full dark. They hurried as quickly as they could through the woods to the road that ran along the east side of the monastery grounds, coming out slightly south of where Rhodri had been arrested by Madog's men.

Knowing that once the prisoners left the monastery grounds, it would be easy to lose them, Hywel had recruited twenty men to follow them. These men included Gruffydd and Cadoc, the assassin-archer, as a first look at what an elite fighting force might look like. Hywel hadn't counted on Gareth losing his prey before they'd gone a hundred yards.

"Has Rhodri betrayed us?" Conall said.

"There was always a chance of that. He willingly sacked a monastery after all. If the bandits here are the same men, then he knows them, despite all his denials. He could even be their leader."

"I wouldn't have said he was that smart—or that good of a liar," Conall said.

"We have been fooled before."

Conall laughed mockingly. "And will be again, it seems."

Gareth and Conall came out onto the road, and a moment later Gruffydd stepped out of the woods on the other side and tilted his head to point south. "They went that way. I was waiting for you before I followed."

Gareth let out a breath. Rhodri may be double-crossing them, but Hywel had planned for that, posting men on the roads all around the monastery, as well as in the fields and pastures. That caution had paid off. "Did you have any trouble?"

"There must be a secret passage through the eastern wall, because they crossed the road a hundred feet south of where you came out. We almost missed them."

"Did you warn Hywel?" Gareth said. The prince had been posted on the other side of the monastery, guessing that Lwc and Deiniol would choose to run south, as it appeared they were doing.

"I did."

With Gruffydd at their side, Hywel and Conall went straight through the crossroads rather than turning right to reach the entrance to the monastery. A few yards farther on, Gareth spotted Hywel, who was standing on a three-foot-high stone wall to the left of the road, waving at them. Gareth had been so focused on the road before him that he hadn't seen the prince until they were almost upon him.

Hywel jumped down from the wall. "We are the last. Everyone else is following ahead." He shook his head, laughing a little under his breath. "They are moving fast. Rhodri is making no effort to slow the other two down."

"Conall and I lost them before they'd even left the monastery, so either Rhodri thinks we're better than we are, or he is really trying to lose us," Gareth said.

"Or one of them is," Hywel said. "I have horses waiting."

Gareth grunted his thanks. He could run, but he would really rather not have to. "We should stay far back and make even Rhodri think he's lost us."

"Those were the orders I gave," Hywel said.

"Do we have any idea where they're going?" Conall said.

"I don't. That's why we did this," Hywel said.

They kept to the margins of the road to hide the sound of their horses' hooves. One by one, they caught up to the rest of Hywel's men, who'd continued to follow on foot. Most were men-at-arms, used to riding. To a man, they were breathing hard and happy to be overtaken. Gareth was in no way surprised to learn that it was only his two foster sons who'd been able to keep up with the three fugitives.

After a quarter of an hour, Llelo himself appeared from a side road and put up a hand to stop them. "There's an old farmstead up ahead. I counted a dozen men in and around it. Lwc and Rhodri ran right up to them as if they were recognized."

"Lwc and Rhodri? Where's Deiniol?" Hywel said.

"I'm sorry, but I don't know. You told us to hang back, and it was hard to judge how far that needed to be. We came around a corner, and he was no longer with them."

"Where's Dai?" Gareth said.

"He's set up on a rising hill to the north of the farm. It's on the other side of a pasture with a good view of the front door and the barn. Unfortunately, fifty yards on every side of the house is pastureland and fallow fields, with nary a tree to hide behind. If they weren't on watch before, they surely will be now that Lwc and Rhodri have joined them. They'll see us coming long before we reach the house. But I can lead you at least as far as Dai without being seen."

"Lead on. Let's see what we have to work with." Hywel gestured to the men who'd gathered around him. "Spread yourselves out and keep your heads down." He indicated the eastern horizon. "The moon has risen, and I don't want to spook them."

Llelo had given a good description of the layout, and Gareth was more than pleased at how mature his son had become. He could take only a modicum of credit for it, since all he'd done was set him on a course, and the boy had done the rest for himself. They left the horses in a thicket invisible from the house with two men to guard them and crept forward until they were crouched in a stand of trees behind a stone wall at the base of the hill Llelo had mentioned.

Gareth had observed for only a moment, however, before a voice spoke from behind him. "I think these are the thieves you were looking for."

Gareth swung around. "Rhodri?"

A head popped out from behind a tree a few feet away. "Rhodri? No. It's Deiniol."

Gareth sprang on him and dragged him down behind the wall. Hywel noted the commotion and came over, along with Conall and Evan.

"What are you doing here?" Gareth said.

Deiniol's eyes were wide by the light of the moon, which was three-quarters full and waning. "What do you mean what am I doing here?" He pointed across the field. "Those men are villains!" At the last word, his voice rose, going high in his outrage. Gone was the austere, superior monk with whom they'd all been acquainted, to be replaced by a frightened man. Gareth still didn't know if Deiniol was frightened because Hywel had brought an army to stop the thieves, or because his time among them had made him finally understand the seriousness of the charges that had been brought against him.

"Why did you flee the monastery with them if you aren't one of them?" Conall said.

"I was more afraid to stay than to go, given what you accused me of! With them gone, I could have been hanged because someone had to be."

Gareth shushed him with soothing words, and Deiniol continued in a more modulated tone. "Rhodri escaped his cell and freed Lwc first. I begged to come with them, and they said that I could if I didn't slow them down."

"Why are you here now?" Hywel said.

"I started having second thoughts almost immediately. I feigned a sprained ankle and told them I'd make my own way. Since I didn't know where they were going, if you caught me, I wouldn't have anything to tell you. I hid myself while I tried to decide what to do, but then when your company passed by, I followed."

Deiniol was either blessed with a remarkable presence of mind nobody had noticed before or an incredible sense of self-preservation. In honesty, it was looking like both.

"You're saying that Rhodri and Lwc are working together?"

Deiniol nodded, but then he frowned. "Lwc seemed to know what he was doing, far more than I would have thought given his behavior up until now."

Hywel pursed his lips and looked at Gareth and Conall. "We've misread this entire situation."

"I told you he was lying about me being involved, and you didn't believe me." Deiniol's self-satisfied look was briefly back. "I tell you, he knew exactly what he was doing and where he was going."

"Did they talk about what their plan was?"

"No. Not to me. Deliberately, I think, and I was afraid to ask."

30

Hywel

Hywel had been without Gareth often enough in recent weeks both to have grown used to his absence and to long for the days when it was just the two of them. More often than not, it had been Gareth extricating Hywel from an untenable situation. But he had been the one to save Gareth a week ago in Shrewsbury, and as Hywel watched the farmhouse across the field, his stomach clenched at the similarities. He could be grateful, however, that a captive Gareth was not one of them.

"It looks like they're preparing to move out." Gareth had his hands cupped around his eyes, narrowing his focus as he turned his head, scanning from side to side. "Many men have crossed to the barn."

"I don't think we should wait." Hywel made a motion with his hand to indicate that his men should spread out. Every soldier with him, with the exception of Gareth, who didn't have the strength, and Conall, who didn't know how to use one, wore not only a sword but a bow and quiver. It had been a long time since Hywel himself had gone to war as an archer, but he still practiced several times a week. With the numbers and strength of the bandits uncertain, Hywel had tried to plan for every contingency.

A light showed through the cracks in a shuttered window by the farmhouse door. A second light shone from inside the adjacent barn, which, as at the monastery, had a paddock attached.

From the size of the house, the farmstead had once been prosperous, and Hywel wondered what had caused the owners to leave such fertile land. War, possibly. Because of its proximity to the border with England, the lands between St. Asaph and Denbigh had been fought over ever since the Normans came to Britain, changing hands half a dozen times before his father had gained control of the region a few years ago. Too late for this family, perhaps.

"I don't like this, my lord." Evan spoke low in Hywel's ear.

"There's nothing to like about it," Hywel said.

"Rhodri knows we could be coming, and yet nobody seems to be in a hurry," Evan said.

"It may be that Deiniol misread the situation, and Rhodri remains on our side." Hywel raised himself up slightly, realizing that this was the chance they'd been waiting for. The cleared space in front of the house was empty. He had seen at least four men enter the barn since they'd arrived. He raised a hand to his men and brought it down.

As one, Hywel's men rose to their feet and converged from all directions on the farmstead. In short order, all twenty men reached a spot a hundred feet from the house and stopped, crouching down and breathing hard. Nobody had yet come out of the house or the barn.

"This isn't right." This time it was Gareth who sounded the warning. He held up two fingers to indicate that two of the men should approach the entrance to the house and two the entrance to the barn. Both pairs of men raced across the clearing unmolested, and each pair set themselves up on either side of their respective doors.

Meanwhile, Gareth straightened, his hands out at his sides, showing that he held no weapon, and walked alone into the cleared space in front of the house. "This is Gareth, captain of Prince Hywel's guard. You are surrounded. Come out with your hands up. If you surrender yourselves freely, you will not be harmed."

Silence greeted this announcement. Gareth remained where he was. Hywel pursed his lips, not liking how exposed Gareth was, vulnerable to an arrow that could come from any direction. In the time they'd watched the farmhouse, they hadn't seen that kind of preparation, but it was still a risk.

For another few heartbeats, nothing moved, but then one of the men by the door to the barn screamed, the sound almost instantly cut off by a gurgling breath. He fell to his knees in the dirt an instant before the soldier on the other side of the door collapsed too. Hywel vaulted to his feet, and he and Gareth reached the fallen men at the same moment, catching them as they fell forward into their arms. The man Hywel held, the one on the left, had been stabbed through the wall of the barn with a sword, spine to sternum.

"Fall back!" Hywel waved an arm at the two men by the house, who hadn't had a direct angle to see what had happened. With Evan's help, Hywel dragged the body of his man away from the barn door. A moment later, a spurt of flame shot through the thatch roof of the house. Despite the rainy weather, the wood was dry, and the heat of the fire was already tangible on Hywel's face. In less time than it took to cross the clearing, the entire house became an inferno.

Gareth stood over the body of the soldier he'd dragged away from the barn. "They were prepared for our numbers."

Then the side wall of the barn opened outward, where no door had seemed to be before, and a host of men burst from it—somewhere in the vicinity of a dozen—mounted on horses. They galloped down the road away from the farm. Though still recovering from the shock of seeing two of his men die before his eyes, Hywel's brain started working, and he shouted and pointed at the riders, "Bring them down! Bring them down!"

Hywel's bow was still in its rest on his back, and his hands were full of the man who'd died, but his men had been ready to shoot anyone who exited the farmhouse. They simply shifted as they stood, turning their bows to follow the riders. The distance was two hundred feet and made easy shooting, especially for those with skills, like Cadoc. At least half the arrows in the first volley hit either a man or a horse, which was a far larger target than the man on its back.

Four horses went down, and then those that had escaped the first volley were stopped by the second or the third. One man did a complete somersault over his horse's head to land with a sickening thud on the ground. As Hywel's men converged on the fallen, swords replaced bows.

"Keep at least one alive!" Hywel glanced at Gareth. "It's time we got some answers."

Gareth nodded and walked beside Hywel to where the bandits had fallen. Rhodri was unconscious on the ground. One of Hywel's men was binding him at the wrists and ankles as a precaution. Lwc had taken an arrow just below his collar bone. He was fortunate in that it had lodged high in his chest, having missed his heart. It had to be intensely painful, but not so much that he hadn't been able to clear his feet from the stirrups as his horse was shot out from under him.

He hadn't been able to run more than a few steps, however, before Gruffydd stopped him by grabbing the arrow's fletching and holding on. Lwc was frozen into position, unable to move and barely able to breathe for the pain it would cause.

Hywel approached with Gareth a pace behind. "If you tell the truth, the whole truth, I will see that you don't hang. If you lie to me about even one detail, I will leave you to bleed to death beside this road. Do you understand me?"

Lwc mouthed a *yes*.

"This is the crew that sacked the monastery at Wrexham?"

A nod.

"Where's the rest of them? This can't be all."

Lwc carefully cleared his throat. "They're gone."

Gruffydd moved the arrow a hair's-breadth to the right. "Gone where?"

The flash of pain that crossed Lwc's face had Hywel's own stomach clenching.

"East to England."

By now Conall had arrived, and he observed Lwc with arms folded across his chest. "Everything you claimed back at the monastery was a lie."

Lwc managed a swallow. His wound was bleeding, and unless he wanted to make it worse, he couldn't move any part of him but his eyes, which flicked from one man to another. He would find no sympathy in any of them.

"Rhodri was part of this gang?" Hywel said.

"Yes. We agreed beforehand not to know each other if we were caught."

"What about Deiniol?" Gareth said.

"He was never one of us." For a moment, a spark appeared in Lwc's eyes, and he added, "You almost believed me! You might really have done so, and the timing of finding him in the stable couldn't have been better."

"Better for you. Worse for him," Hywel said. "What did he say when you came face to face at St. Kentigern's, and he learned you'd become the abbot's secretary?"

"He was confused as to how it had come about, but happy for me. Deiniol really is a simple soul." Lwc grimaced. "We didn't know about the peace conference when we planned this." Hywel sensed that Lwc would have spat on the ground if it didn't mean moving.

"Who paid you to steal from St. Kentigern's?" Gareth asked.

"Paid? Nobody. It was my idea." Lwc seemed very proud of this fact.

Hywel rubbed his chin. "When did you conceive the plan?"

"Our gain was considerable at Wrexham, even with what we had to give to our masters—Queen Susanna, I suppose, though I believed it was King Owain, myself," Lwc said. "Why not try it elsewhere?"

Hywel dropped his hands, genuinely puzzled. "You were raised at the Wrexham monastery from birth. Why did you destroy it?"

"I hated it there! I snuck out whenever I could. But if I was going to strike out on my own I needed money. I knew people by then. People who could help me get free from the monastery. That's when he came to me."

"Me?" Gareth said.

Lwc scoffed. "No. That was Rhodri's contact, earlier."

"Then who?" Hywel didn't know if he could believe anything Lwc had said so far. He'd lied so often, maybe Lwc himself didn't know the truth anymore.

"A man named Jerome."

"By the fingers of St. Peter, who is Jerome?" Hywel said.

Lwc made a helpless gesture with his right hand, the only one he dared move. "Jerome was our leader. He organized everything. Before Wrexham, he brought us the surcoats with Owain's crest, the weapons, and the food, but he disappeared the night Erik died. I figured from the start that he killed Erik and ran off." Lwc waggled a finger. "I know you were looking for someone with a damaged tenth finger, and that's what he had." Lwc tried to gesture again but stopped instantly at the pain that shot through him.

"Who was Erik to you?"

"He was nobody to me; he was Jerome's friend. At times it seemed as if Erik outranked him. When Erik found out that we were planning to steal from St. Kentigern's, he was very angry. I know he and Jerome argued about it more than once."

If Hywel hadn't been so angry himself, he might have admired the complexity of the plot, and Lwc's apparent ability to carry it out—if not for ending up caught and most of his men dead. "I think Erik was going to stop you from stealing from St. Kentigern's, and you killed him."

Lwc seemed momentarily dumbfounded by this conclusion. "I—we—had nothing to do with his death. Everything went wrong from the moment he died."

"Amazingly, we don't believe you now any more than we did earlier." That was Conall again, and his detached amusement reminded Hywel that he would get nowhere with anger.

"How many times do I have to deny it before you believe me! Neither I nor any of my men killed him! But—" Lwc stopped abruptly, swallowing, as if he hadn't meant to add the *but*.

Hywel had caught it, however, and knew not to let it go. "But what?"

Lwc didn't want to answer, and thus it was Gareth who said, "You didn't kill him, but you cut him open? How did you gather your men quickly enough once you found out he was dead to arrange for that?"

"I saw the body with Prior Anselm and Abbot Rhys, and then the abbot sent me to fetch you. Before I did, I ran to the village to wake Rhodri, who'd found a girl to stay with a stone's throw from the monastery."

Conall grunted. "You took your secret passage under the wall."

Even wounded, Lwc still had the capacity to smirk. "Nobody noticed I was gone, and there was plenty of time for Rhodri to ride to the farm, roust the others, and set up the ambush of the cart, which I knew the monks would need to haul Erik back to the church. I knew exactly the path it would follow."

"Why would you do all that?" Gareth said.

"We needed to have a look at him before you did. We didn't know who killed Erik, but we feared what Erik might have on him that could be traced back to us. Besides, if he had a token from the King of Gwynedd, that could have been useful."

"But why cut him open?" Gareth said, not mentioning that out of all of what Lwc knew, or thought he knew, that Erik worked for Gwynedd was the nearest he'd come to the truth.

"It was something Jerome said to us about swallowing incriminating evidence if we were caught." Lwc made a disgusted face. "Anyway, I figured it was worth a look, and it isn't as if he could be more dead than he already was."

"Did Erik have anything in his stomach?" Gareth said.

"No. Whoever killed him had already taken all his possessions."

"Why dump the body?" Gareth said.

"I was raised in a monastery. I know that monks view such things as the work of devil worshippers. It was to put you off our trail. I knew as soon as I saw you—and with the few things that Abbot Rhys said—that you would dig and dig until you found answers. I couldn't allow that to happen."

"What about the barn?" Gareth said.

"What barn?" Lwc's eyes strayed to the barn currently going up in flames as the fire had jumped from roof to roof and nobody had seen fit to try to put it out.

"Back at the monastery, you denied that you set fire to the monastery's barn as a distraction so you could rob the treasury," Hywel said. "Do you deny it still?"

"With Erik dead and Jerome gone, I decided things were falling apart. One of my men set the fire as a distraction—which would have worked out too if not for those meddling boys."

"You destroyed the monastery at Wrexham. Why not wait for the peace conference to be over to destroy St. Kentigern's?" Gareth said.

"What kind of sense would that have made?" Lwc's laugh was disbelieving at the stupidity of the question, even as he was growing paler by the heartbeat. Hywel wanted this over before Lwc passed out from pain and blood loss. "At Wrexham, we had no chance of entering the treasury. With me as the abbot's secretary, we did. The point of this was wealth, not destruction. Besides, with the peace conference over, you wouldn't be distracted anymore, and I'd heard by now that you always got your man. I didn't want that man to be me."

Hywel couldn't look at Lwc anymore. "Get that arrow out of him and bind his wounds. We may have more questions later." He turned away. Though complex in its implementation, the villainy was unremarkable. He hadn't encountered a band like this before, but the lengths to which they'd gone for greed were entirely familiar.

Gareth nudged Hywel's elbow, indicating he wanted a more private conference. "Do you believe that he didn't kill Erik?"

"I don't want to, but I can't help but believe him. Jerome must be the man we found burned in the barn."

"But who killed him and took Erik's belongings?" Gareth said. "Your ring is still at large."

"Someone we haven't yet thought of." Hywel gazed around at the wreckage of the farmstead and the carnage at his feet. "We're a mile south of St. Asaph, Gareth."

"I thought of that as soon as we saw the farmstead. It could be that if Rhodri and Lwc hadn't led us here—"

Hywel nodded. "My Aunt Susanna would have."

31

Gwen

The first thing that was obvious about the burned man was how tall he was. Even in death and slightly shrunken from being burned, his feet hung off the end of the table. His boots were larger than any man's she'd ever seen, and—his missing fingertip aside—his hands were the size of serving platters. Few men would have been strong enough and large enough to get the jump on Erik, but this man was among those who could have.

Gwen began by cutting what was left of his coat and shirt off him, and she was immediately struck by a series of cuts on his forearms. She'd noticed the slashes in his coat, but hadn't looked closely since large parts of it were burned anyway. With a lantern in one hand for light, she lifted up the arm to see it better.

"Defensive wounds." Abbot Rhys's voice spoke from behind her.

Gwen turned at the sound. "It looks that way to me too."

"I won't bother telling you that you shouldn't be here and that you promised not to, so instead I'll just ask if he was more wounded than what we see here? Particularly, did he have a wound that would have made him unable to leave the barn?"

"He was stabbed in the back." Gwen swept the light over the man's body. "I'll show you if you help me turn him over."

Rhys took the man's shoulders while Gwen pushed up on his hip and rolled the corpse onto its side. The skin was badly charred along the whole length of his back, indicating to her that he'd been face down on the ground when the fire had reached him.

The abbot sighed. "He could have killed Erik but been wounded in the fight, resulting in his death at a later hour."

"It would be convenient if our two murdered men murdered each other." Gwen settled the body back onto the table. "It might even be true, but we would still be missing the most important piece of the puzzle."

"What would that be?"

"Why he killed Erik and, once he was dead, what happened to Erik's possessions?"

Footsteps sounded outside the room, and Prior Anselm poked his head between the half-open door and the frame. "It is almost time for Compline, Father."

Anselm's warning was as much for her as for Rhys. It wouldn't be appropriate for her to be examining a body while the monks were at their prayers. From the passing sneer on Anselm's face, he didn't think her being here had ever been appropriate. It was his right to think so, and Gwen was enough used to that attitude by now that she was able to (mostly) ignore it. "I'll be off to check on Tangwen."

Gwen flipped the sheet back over the top of the dead man, and the two men moved out of the way to let her precede them into the cloister. She walked along the flagstones a few yards and then stopped near a pillar. Alone in the dark, she debated waiting for the monks to leave and then returning to finish her examination.

Then Rhys and Anselm exited the church, and she heard Rhys say, "How are you feeling Anselm? You've been ill for a few days now, haven't you? You have a strong singing voice that we've missed at the last few night vigils."

That was pure flattery, but Anselm didn't seem to know it. "I am much better, thank you, Father. These illnesses befall me every now and again."

Rhys and Anselm had turned in the opposite direction, heading towards the dormitory so they could process into the church with their fellow monks. Their voices echoed among the stones, and Gwen stayed where she was so they wouldn't know that she was eavesdropping.

"I'm glad to hear you're better. The other night after Matins, I went to the infirmary to check on you, but you were not there."

"What day was this?"

"It must have been just before King Owain's party arrived at the monastery."

"I was probably in the latrine," Anselm said. "I've been on the mend since then."

"I'm sure you're right."

Their voices echoed away down the passage, and Gwen moved out of the shadows, listening and wondering. Anselm might not realize it, but any time a man said, *I'm sure you're right*, what he was really saying was, *I don't believe it for a heartbeat, but I'm not going to argue with you about it.*

She stood alone in the covered walkway, hesitating not because she was unsure of what she needed to do but because she was struggling to find the courage to do it. It might even be that Rhys guessed she was still in the cloister and inquired of Anselm's whereabouts so she could overhear. Anselm hadn't appeared ill that first morning when Mathonwy had found Erik's body. He didn't appear ill now. Was that what Rhys was trying to tell her?

Anselm was the one man throughout everything that had happened whom nobody had questioned—and yet, he'd arrived at St. Kentigern's with Lwc only a week ago. He'd been a constant fixture at Rhys's side since they arrived, and because he was a smaller than average man with perfectly formed hands and fingers, soft and unused to manual labor as appropriate for a prior at a monastery, she hadn't seriously considered him to be a part of this.

Maybe it was time to reconsider that assumption.

The monastery bell began to toll, and then the Latin processional rose in chorus from the monks' dormitory. The sound decided her. With hasty steps, though on tiptoe so they wouldn't echo, she hurried down the passage to the west side of the monastery where Prior Anselm had his quarters adjacent to Abbot Rhys's. The brothers were still processing when she reached his door, looked both ways down the walkway, and slipped inside. In a monastery, no door but the treasury was ever locked.

As befitting a monk's sensibilities, the room was neat and clean, with few possessions: a table, stool, and bed, and three hooks on the wall, one empty. A monk's robe and a fine, soft wool cloak hung from the others. A quick look in the trunk in the corner revealed nothing more than a few spare garments. Gwen swung around to survey the room. She didn't know what she'd hoped to find, but she wasn't seeing anything out of place.

Deciding she could afford a few more moments of looking, she unfolded and refolded the blanket on his bed and then lifted up the pallet to see what was underneath. It was a basic rope bed surmounted by a mattress stuffed with sacking and cloth. Down would have been more comfortable but was inappropriate for a monk, even a prior.

However, as she moved around the bed to make sure everything was in place, she noted a lump in the mattress near the head of the bed. Lumpy mattresses were more normal than not, but she pulled the sheet away and lifted up the mattress to reveal a mostly flattened leather satchel, which couldn't have been comfortable to sleep on. It was the kind of bag that a man would wear on his lower back with the strap at a diagonal across his chest.

On her knees beside the bed, she opened the satchel. Inside lay a packet of letters bound with a ribbon, along with another that was loose. Beneath them in one corner of the bag was a gold signet ring.

Hywel's signet ring.

She clenched it in her fist, her heart pounding, and then slipped it into her purse. For the first time, she understood why a spy might choose to swallow their lord's token rather than allow it to fall into enemy hands. It didn't appear that Anselm had done anything with it yet, but he hadn't had it very long either.

She eased out a breath she hadn't realized she'd been holding and pulled off the ribbon that held the documents together. All of their seals were broken. The first one was addressed simply to 'A', which could have been *Anselm*, but a quick scan of the letter revealed that it was a detailed list of the writer's activities in England over the last month, some of which Gwen already knew about. It was signed with the words, *your devoted husband* and a flourished 'C'. She put the letter aside, and with trembling hands picked up the one that had been loose. It had been sealed with the crest of the Deheubarth and was a letter of introduction for Anselm from King Cadell to the Bishop of Bangor.

"I should have memorized the contents and burned them. More to the point, I should have left immediately after I acquired them."

Gwen had become absorbed in reading and thus negligent of her surroundings. Now she gaped at Anselm as he stood in the doorway. The door was open, so she could hear the monks' chorus from the church. She hadn't been wrong to think that Compline was ongoing, but Anselm had left early, and she was frozen on her knees on the other side of his bed. She put her hand on the hilt of her knife and then slowly eased it away again. She didn't want him to think she was going to fight him. The letters were evidence of wrongdoing but not worth her life.

She looked past him to the cloister. Nobody moved in it. "Why didn't you?" It was a stall for time, though she really did want to know the answer.

"Hubris, mainly, and the feeling that if I left, I would leave too   much   undone." Anselm gently closed the door, blocking her view of the cloister beyond and dashing whatever hope she might have had of calling for help. The monks were singing so loudly that she could hear them even through the door. If she screamed, nobody was going to hear her.

Anselm lifted the cloak from its hook, swung it around his shoulders, and then crossed to the trunk. He opened it and removed the clothing, which he rolled into a tight bundle and tucked under his arm. "There was more happening here than I supposed when I first came to the monastery. St. Asaph is the crossroads of Wales."

"You killed Erik."

"I did no such thing."

"I don't believe you," she said. "You serve King Cadell."

He glanced down to where she knelt by the bed with the letters in her lap. The one from King Cadell was on top, his seal plainly visible. "King Cadell sent me to pick up the trail of Prince Cadwaladr, who betrayed my king as he has betrayed so many others." He bowed. "I came highly recommended from my king and the Bishop of St. Dafydd."

Gwen held up the letters. "One of these is from Prince Cadwaladr to his wife, Alice. What are the others?"

"Communication between Susanna and Alice; several missives from Cadwaladr to various lords in Gwynedd, asking for their support in his quest to regain his lands; and a letter from Cadwaladr to King Cadell, discussing a return to their alliance."

"How can you say you didn't kill Erik when you have his things?"

"Because I didn't kill him. I witnessed his murder. To his credit, Erik fought back. He managed to stab his companion, but not before he himself was so weakened, he couldn't fight anymore. While they were arguing, I took the bag."

The calm way he denied the murder but confessed to thievery was disconcerting. She also didn't know that she believed him. Jerome could have been stabbed in the back in a fight with Erik, but she found it equally likely that Anselm had done it himself, either in defense of Erik or so he could take the bag without resistance. Regardless of whether or not Anselm was telling her the truth, she was determined to continue asking questions, to keep him here as long as possible and to distract him. "Why would his companion kill him?"

"Why does any man kill another?" Anselm tsked through his teeth. "Greed. They were arguing about money, or the apportionment of money that was yet to be made. Erik's friend wanted more, and Erik wanted out. He'd fallen in with a common thief and lost his life because of it. He used to be smarter."

Gwen didn't know about that, but the Erik she'd known had had a strong sense of self-preservation. Not enough of one, apparently. "Why were you there at all?"

"Erik and I had arranged to meet in the barn, so he could give me the letter to King Cadell. Before I could show myself, Erik's killer surprised him."

"Why didn't you bury the bodies, or hide them, or ... or something? You could have disappeared, and nobody would ever have been the wiser."

Anselm scoffed. "Do you know how hard it is to get rid of a body on short notice? Really get rid of it?" He shook his head. "Better to leave things as they were." He eyed her sourly. "I didn't know about your husband—or you—at the time. I left Erik in the trough where he died and piled hay on the other fellow, who'd managed to crawl back into the barn to nurse his wound, but then bled out where he lay. You'll have to find someone else to blame for the fire. Your husband neglected to leave a watch in case the culprit returned to the scene of his crime." He cocked his head at her. "I imagine he won't make that mistake again."

Then he stepped closer, true menace emanating from him for the first time. He held out his hand. "I need my letters back."

Without arguing, Gwen handed him the bundle of letters. He quickly went through them, taking out the ones he wanted and tossing the rest onto the bed. Then, he grabbed the bag from where it lay beside her and stuffed his bundle into it.

Gwen kept both hands up, knowing she couldn't keep him any longer. He knew better than to stay when Hywel and Gareth, not to mention Abbot Rhys, could return at any time.

He backed towards the door. "It was a pleasure doing business with you, Gwen. I haven't met many women quite like you. Give my regards to your lord." Anselm saluted her with a hand to his temple—and then was gone.

32

Gareth

Gareth, Hywel, and Abbot Rhys found Gwen still in Anselm's room a quarter of an hour later. She was sitting on the bed, looking forlorn, a pile of letters in her lap.

"*Cariad,* what happened?"

Gwen looked up and her eyes widened. Gareth looked down at himself and for the first time realized he was covered in blood. "It's all right, love. It isn't mine." He tugged the surcoat off over his head, exposing his mail armor, and dropped the bloody fabric to the floor. Then he knelt in front of her and took her hands in his. "What are you doing in Anselm's room? Something— something else—has gone wrong?"

Gwen let out a breath and looked down, and Gareth knew her well enough to know that she was fighting tears. "Gone wrong, yes. Though I suppose in a way it's gone right too." She raised her head, and when she looked at him, and then past him to Hywel, her eyes were clear. "You lost a man?"

Gareth nodded wearily and told her what had befallen them at the bandits' hideout. "Lwc and the other survivors are being taken to King Owain's camp. It's better that we keep no more criminals here."

"The last few days haven't been good for my flock." Rhys gestured to indicate the room. "Though I'm thinking what you've discovered won't be either. I almost hate to ask what you are doing in Anselm's room."

Gwen sighed. "It's the last piece of the puzzle." Then she related her conversation with Anselm.

As she told the men about giving up the letters that proved who Anselm was, Gareth pulled her into his arms. "You couldn't do anything else, *cariad*. He claimed not to have murdered Jerome, but I don't believe him. He could have killed you too."

"I know. I knew it at the time—" she pulled away enough to reach into her purse and pull out Hywel's ring. "You'll want this back, my lord."

Hywel took the ring and clenched it in his fist. He held the packet of letters in his other hand.

"I'm tempted to ask you to throw those in the fire," Rhys said. "The last thing we need is more disunity."

Hywel held them out to the abbot. "Do it."

Rhys put up a hand, his expression rueful. "I have kept secrets and lived lies for most of my life, but I am not that man anymore. Gwen is right that you need to keep them. Your father's rule is precarious because of Cadwaladr's actions. King Owain needs to know who his enemies are."

"They circle round him, nipping at his heels like wild dogs." Gareth moved to sit beside Gwen on Anselm's bed and kept his arm around her.

Meanwhile, Hywel weighed the packet of letters in his hand. "Cadwaladr implicates these lords simply by writing to them. Some of them were here at the peace conference, ostensibly on my father's side."

"Is our final conclusion that Erik betrayed you, my lord?" Gareth said.

"I don't think so," Hywel said. "He may have been involved with the sacking at Wrexham, but Lwc also said that he was angry about the bandits turning their sights on St. Kentigern's, and I'm convinced now more than ever that Aunt Susanna meant for me to find them at her farm. She couldn't tell me outright about her husband's misdeeds, but she could help me stop them."

"You believe Lwc that it was Jerome who was working for Madog, not Erik?" Gwen said.

"Erik was working for Susanna, and now that I think back to my conversation with her, more to the point, he was working for Alice. And perhaps it was Alice all along to whom he gave his allegiance. Just because Cadwaladr let him go does not mean that he turned his back on her."

"He shouldn't have accepted your patronage," Gareth said.

"He certainly shouldn't have," Hywel said, "but again, looking back, I can see how he thought he might serve me and her at the same time. Alice would have wanted to know Cadwaladr's whereabouts too, and who's to say she herself wasn't looking to

Ireland for support for Cadwaladr's cause, as Cadwaladr did four years ago."

"What are you going to do about the letters?" Gwen said.

"Now that war with Powys is averted for a time, I think I will go to Anglesey. I'd like to know that my aunt is settled comfortably."

"Which aunt?" Gareth said.

"Both." Hywel held up the letters. "I will personally deliver Alice's to her."

"What about Anselm and King Cadell?" Gwen said.

Prince Hywel shook his head. "I am perturbed to learn that King Cadell has been meddling in Gwynedd's affairs. I had said that I wanted you to go to Dolwyddelan, Gwen, and I do, but now I think that after Anglesey, Gareth and I will join you—and from there we will all go on to Ceredigion."

"You think there's more to Anselm's story than he told me, don't you?" Gwen said.

"Oh yes," Hywel said. "Of that I have no doubt."

The End

About the Author

With two historian parents, Sarah couldn't help but develop an interest in the past. She went on to get more than enough education herself (in anthropology) and began writing fiction when the stories in her head overflowed and demanded she let them out. While her ancestry is Welsh, she only visited Wales for the first time while in college. She has been in love with the country, language, and people ever since. She even convinced her husband to give all four of their children Welsh names.

She makes her home in Oregon.

www.sarahwoodbury.com

CPSIA information can be obtained
at www.ICGtesting.com
Printed in the USA
LVOW13s1025130717
541239LV00023B/845/P